Dear Reader,

Thank you s
Dreaming of
agreed with
woman for him.

Now it's Pierce, the playboy, the logical one, the thinker, whose turn it is to fight falling in love. We've watched him play the field in *Until There Was You*, *You and No Other*, and *Dreaming of You*. Pierce called it "storing up memories" for when his time came and he was next on his mother's infamous marriage hit list. He firmly believes no woman can tame him, but that's before he meets stunning Broadway actress Sabra Raineau. Things are about to heat up in Santa Fe.

The next and last Grayson is Sierra, the baby sister, the loyal one. Beautiful, stubborn, and reckless, Sierra might meet her match in reclusive real estate mogul Blade Navarone. I hope you enjoy the excerpt of Sierra's story, *Only You*, which will be in stores in October.

By the way, besides Blade, the other dark and dangerous men in *Dreaming of You* might show up in their own books. Time will tell.

Please visit my Web site and sign up for my mailing list. I look forward to seeing many of you during my tour.

Have a wonderful life,
Francis Ray
P.O. Box 764651
Dallas, TX 75376

E-mail: francisray@aol.com
www.Francisray.com

ALSO BY FRANCIS RAY

Dreaming of You

Any Rich Man Will Do

Like the First Time

Someone to Love Me

Somebody's Knocking at My Door

I Know Who Holds Tomorrow

Trouble Don't Last Always

You and No Other

ANTHOLOGIES

Rosie's Curl and Weave

Della's House of Style

Going to the Chapel

Welcome to Leo's

Gettin' Merry

IRRESISTIBLE YOU

FRANCIS RAY

St. Martin's Paperbacks

NOTE: If you purchased this book without a cover you should be aware that this book is stolen property. It was reported as "unsold and destroyed" to the publisher, and neither the author nor the publisher has received any payment for this "stripped book."

This is a work of fiction. All of the characters, organizations, and events portrayed in this novel are either products of the author's imagination or are used fictitiously.

IRRESISTIBLE YOU

ISBN: 0-312-93974-4
EAN: 978-0-312-93974-8

Printed in the United States of America

St. Martin's Paperbacks edition / March 2007

St. Martin's Paperbacks are published by St. Martin's Press, 175 Fifth Avenue, New York, NY 10010.

10 9 8 7 6 5 4 3 2 1

To my wonderful daughter,
Carolyn Michelle Ray,
who is never too busy to listen, to encourage me,
or to say I love you. You mean the world to me.

THE GRAYSONS OF NEW MEXICO—THE FALCONS OF TEXAS

Cousins by marriage—friends by choice
Bold men and women who risk it all for love

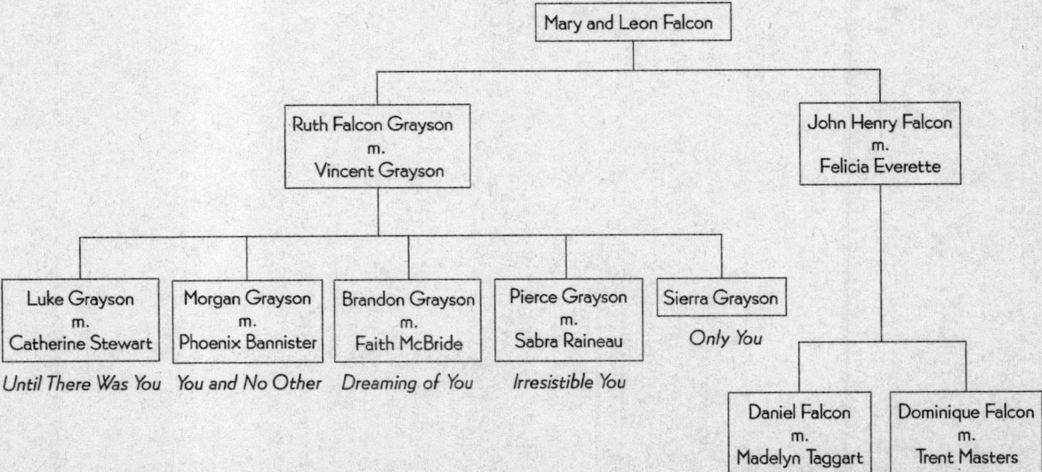

CHAPTER ONE

PIERCE GRAYSON WAS A MARKED MAN.

That chilling certainty was never far from Pierce's mind. It sat like a millstone around his neck. As hard as he tried to push the thought to the back of his mind, it always managed to pop back up, usually at the most inopportune time, as it did now as he strode down the crowded concourse of Albuquerque International Sunport, deftly dodging rolling luggage and people hurrying to catch their flights.

Pierce moved aside for a group of stewardesses and unhappily recalled the exact moment his time had run out. He'd been sound asleep after a very pleasurable evening with a beautiful young woman when he'd been awakened by the phone on his nightstand. He'd opened one eye long enough to read the red dial on the black lacquer clock. Seven thirteen. Closing his eye, he'd groped for the phone and mumbled, "Hello."

"Why aren't you up?"

Recognizing his older brother's voice, Pierce

came fully awake and sprang up in bed. Brandon was notorious for not being a morning person; if by chance he had to get up, he was a grouch. "Are you all right?"

"Faith and I are getting married," Brandon said, his voice filled with unabashed pride and a giddiness that Pierce had never heard before, not even when Brandon had fulfilled his lifelong dream and opened his restaurant, the Red Cactus.

Now, months later, those six condemning words remained startlingly clear. Pierce's reaction then and now as he moved aside for a two-seater baby carriage was a mixture of happiness for his brother and horror for himself. Pierce's carefree, happy existence was forever changed.

He was next on his mother's infamous hit list to get married.

Thus far she was three for three. His older brothers had fallen like bowling pins. As Pierce was the next son on the list, his mother would now turn her attention to her fourth child.

A delicate shudder rippled down Pierce's spine as he stopped just beyond the security point for deplaning passengers. Those waiting with him would have never guessed he wrestled with a problem. They saw a tall, strikingly handsome man with golden-bronzed skin in a tailored gray pin-striped suit. Thick black hair was secured at the base of his well-shaped skull with a two-inch band of hammered silver. Midnight black eyes were trained on the corridor from which passengers would enter the main terminal.

People around him saw what Pierce wanted them to see: a successful man without a care in the world.

As Pierce was the owner of his own multimillion-dollar investment firm, nerves of steel and a poker face were essential, particularly in the recent erratic economy. He'd weathered the fickleness of the stock market and had the faith to build one of the most lucrative investment firms in New Mexico.

Only once, early on in his career, had he made a mistake by trusting the wrong person. The incident had cost him and his investors close to a quarter of a million dollars. Just the thought made his stomach roll.

Paying his clients back every penny from his own funds had been a matter of principle and pride. There was no way he would have disgraced himself or the Grayson name. His family was respected in Santa Fe and around the country. It was unthinkable that he would bring even a hint of discredit to them. The incident had come close to wiping him out financially, but it had taught him a valuable lesson: in finances and life—it if sounded too good to be true, it probably was.

His willingness to accept the blame had earned him the respect of his duped clients and their continued loyalty. They'd stayed with him and sent him their friends and business associates. No thanks to the thief, Pierce had been able to turn a catastrophe into an asset and pull himself from the brink of disaster.

He could do so again. This time from his mother's matchmaking scheme.

He loved his mother, but he had no intention of blithely following in his three older brothers' footsteps and getting married. The way Pierce saw it, it wouldn't be fair to the woman. He enjoyed female companionship. Always had and always would. He also liked variety. He couldn't fathom being satisfied and happy with one woman for a lifetime. It just wasn't in his nature to commit to longer than a couple of months.

He liked change and tended to be bored easily. He enjoyed the challenge, the thrill, of the chase. The sweet pleasure of surrender. Although his three older brothers assured him it was possible to be happy with one woman, Pierce knew he'd go crazy looking across the breakfast table at the same woman day after day, year after year.

His mother was in for a surprise, Pierce thought as he watched deplaning passengers, some hurrying, others leisurely strolling toward the security checkpoint. He'd admit he had spent more than one sleepless night when Brandon bit the dust and fell in love. But after careful thought, and Pierce prided himself on thinking things through, he'd come to the conclusion that his carefree lifestyle would serve him well.

Giving up women as Brandon had wasn't an

option. What Pierce could and would do was continue as usual. The more women he saw, the better.

A smile lifted the corner of his sensual mouth. He'd even dated a couple of women he knew his mother had placed in his path. He'd made sure the women had enjoyed themselves, but nothing had come of it. His mother might have met her match in him.

Pierce straightened as the people surrounding him moved closer to the security checkpoint. A quick glance at his thin gold Piaget wristwatch confirmed that Sabra Raineau's flight had just landed.

His mother had shown him Sabra's bio with her picture when she asked him to pick up the Tony-winning Broadway star at the airport. The five-by-seven glossy black-and-white photo was sensually beautiful and packed a wallop. Her long black hair fell around her bare shoulders as she looked directly at the camera as if daring it to find a flaw. Pierce, who considered himself somewhat of a connoisseur of women, hadn't seen any flaws in the delicately shaped oval face, the razor-sharp cheekbones, the doe-shaped eyes, and the lips with just a hint of a pout.

How much was natural and not retouch he'd know in a bit. His mother had seen the actress the first time she'd appeared on Broadway in a small but pivotal part and had followed her career ever since. He just hoped his mother would still be happy when Sabra returned to New York four weeks from now.

Pierce wasn't a stranger to the mercurial, often

temperamental women in the entertainment industry. Unfortunately, often the more talented and popular, the more difficult they were to work with. Perhaps Sabra wasn't as self-important as many of the successful entertainers he'd met and dated. He'd have to give the actress points for not asking for a driver and all sorts of perks to come to Santa Fe and help his mother put on a play with some of her music students.

When his mother, who was on the board of the Santa Fe Council for the Arts, invited the once-renowned sculptor Andre Duval, the obnoxious man had had a list of demands a mile long. The only good thing about his visit was that it had brought Pierce's next-to-the-oldest brother, Morgan, his wife, Phoenix.

The thought made Pierce's eyebrows draw together. His mother had been instrumental in bringing Duval to Santa Fe, but her main purpose had been to bring Phoenix there to meet Morgan.

Could it be—? Pierce shook his head before the thought formed. One thing he was sure of: his mother wanted all her children close by. And although many of the top names in the theater came to Santa Fe to perform, Broadway was the Holy Grail. His mother wasn't playing matchmaker this time. He was sure of it.

He started to relax; then everything within him went still. Air stalled in his lungs. The noise around him faded to a dull hum as he stared at the most sensually beautiful woman he had ever seen. She moved toward him with an innate grace that made him think of a lazy cat. Thick curly black hair framed her heart-stopping face and flowed over her slim shoulders. Men, at least five, flanked her. One carried a designer overnight case, one a train case with the same label.

Pierce recognized her instantly as Sabra Raineau and acknowledged something else—the photograph had been a fraud. It hadn't done her justice.

At least five feet seven, she was elegantly shaped, with flawless café au lait skin. A simple white blouse that had probably cost a fortune was tucked into black jeans that encased her long, shapely legs. A crystal-encrusted western black leather belt with a silver buckle cinched her narrow waist. Large silver hoops brushed against high cheekbones with each step of her eel-skin boots. People often dressed in western attire when they visited Santa Fe, but Pierce knew instinctively that Sabra dressed for comfort and in what suited her.

When she would have walked past him, he moved into her path. "Ms. Raineau."

She stopped. He saw her delicate brows arch over the wide lenses of her Dior sunshades. The men with her sent Pierce murderous looks. Pierce almost smiled. It was his turn now.

He extended his hand. "Pierce Grayson. My mother, Mrs. Ruth Grayson, sent me to pick you up."

The warm smile started at the corners of Sabra's

sensual raspberry mouth. One slim hand lifted to settle her shades on top of a head of lustrous black hair. Pierce barely kept his jaw from dropping. He stared into her level, unflinching gaze as he looked his fill. She didn't fidget; she simply waited for his brain to clear. He realized she fully understood the effect she had on men. He absorbed the full impact and counted it as a blessing that she wasn't the one his mother had placed in his path.

He wouldn't have lasted five minutes. And then Sierra, his baby sister, would have his hide, but it might just be worth the fall.

"Hello, Pierce, and thank you." Sabra's voice was an alluring blend of warm southern grace and jasmine-scented nights. Her hand had barely settled in his before she withdrew it and turned to the men beside her to introduce them and finished by saying, "Thank you again for making my trip so enjoyable. Good-bye, and thanks again."

She reached to retrieve her luggage from the two men. Pierce was faster. "Thank you," he said to the men, who looked bereft; then he faced Sabra. He liked just looking at her. "This way to the baggage terminal."

"First, I need to make sure Isabella is all right."

"Isabella?"

"My dog. She's not a good flier," Sabra said with a half smile. "I started to catch a ride with Cline in his jet, but he and Isabella don't get along too well."

Pierce wondered what the secret smile on Sabra's

tempting lips meant. "We'll check on your dog, then get your luggage."

Sticking one piece beneath his arm and taking the other in his left hand, he curled his fingers around her elbow as she stepped on the down escalator. Warmth spread from his fingertips. For a crazy moment he wished he could keep on holding her.

"Thank you," she murmured, raising her arm to replace her sunglasses. With the overhead skylights causing the airport to be almost glaringly bright, she probably needed her sunglasses—or she might have been evading his touch.

In the baggage claim area Pierce heard a loud annoyed bark before he saw Isabella. Sabra rushed the last few steps. Dropping gracefully to her knees, she opened the cage door. Pierce stared as a large dog rushed out, toppling Sabra. He and the baggage claim attendant both rushed to her side, only to pull up when they heard Sabra's happy laughter.

"I see you missed me." Coming to her knees, she put one arm around the German shepherd. The animal had to weigh close to eighty pounds. "I hope she wasn't any trouble," Sabra said to the attendant.

With his mouth open, wearing a stunned look, the man stared at her. Pierce couldn't blame the man's reaction. It would take a eunuch not to react when the full force of all that beauty and sensuality was focused on him.

"No. No. She wasn't any trouble at all," the man finally got out.

"Thank you." Sabra palmed the dog's long face. "You have to go back inside for just a bit, and then we're going with Pierce to the house."

The dog looked over Sabra's shoulder and showed Pierce a set of sharp teeth. "Impressive," Pierce said as he hunkered down beside Sabra. "Smart dog."

Isabella sat on her hindquarters and looked at Pierce with intelligent brown eyes. Sabra looked from one to the other. "She likes you," she said, surprise in her voice.

"I'm a likable person." Pierce rubbed the dog behind her ears. "You're a beauty. I wonder what Hero would think of you."

"Hero?"

"My sister-in-law's hybrid mixture of a wolf and a dog."

"Male?"

He grinned. "Yes."

Sabra came gracefully to her feet. "We aren't likely to find out. In you go, Isabella." The dog dutifully obeyed. Sabra closed the cage. "I'll be back as soon as I can."

"If you want to stay with Isabella, I'll get the luggage and return," he offered.

"It's labeled, but it will be faster if I point it out and help."

She definitely wasn't the temperamental type. "This way." He took her arm again to be courteous but also to sec if he felt the slight punch again. He did. Only this time he had to fight the urge to lean closer.

Sabra was as tempting as he had thought on first seeing her. He couldn't decide if he wanted to get to know her better or run in the other direction as fast as he could.

Walking to the baggage carousel, he couldn't help but notice the stares that followed them. He looked at Sabra to gauge her reaction, but she had on her shades again. "Do the stares bother you?"

"This face helped me get where I am today," she said easily. A large piece of Gucci luggage came down the conveyer. As it passed, Sabra reached for it. Again, Pierce was faster. "You're supposed to point."

"How about you?" she asked, ignoring his statement as they stepped back to wait.

"Me?" He turned to her.

Folding her arms, she tilted her head to one side and openly studied him. "You really aren't aware that women are scoping you out?"

"It's pretty difficult to pay attention to anything or anyone when you're around," he said truthfully, and, for once, before he'd thought out his comment.

Sabra's laughter bubbled from her lips as she unfolded her arms. "Ruth didn't mention that her son was such a flatterer."

"I was telling the truth." It bothered him that he hadn't thought to guard his words more carefully.

The smile slowly left her face. Stepping around him, she went to the conveyer. Pierce had to almost wrestle the upright luggage from her this time. He wondered what caused her to go from playful to cool. A woman as beautiful as Sabra, and in her profession, had to be used to compliments.

"That's it. Isabella is waiting." Sabra stepped around him to obtain a Smart Cart.

Pierce put the luggage on the rolling cart, his attention on Sabra, who was becoming more fascinating by the moment. She was independent and down-to-earth. She didn't fit the usual pattern of the successful women he'd dated. He was definitely leaning toward finding out more about her.

LESS THAN TEN MINUTES LATER SABRA'S LUGgage was loaded in Pierce's Porsche SUV and they were on Interstate 25 headed for Santa Fe. Isabella was in the backseat, her tongue lolling happily. At least one of them was enjoying this trip.

"Would you like to stop and grab a bite to eat?" Pierce asked. "It's an hour drive to Santa Fe."

"I'm fine." Sabra didn't bother to look at Pierce. It wasn't likely any woman would forget his handsome face or his lean, muscular body. No wonder women stared at him. He moved with an assurance that said he knew who he was and that he was comfortable with himself.

In New York, a city where faking it was an everyday occurrence and Sabra had lived for the past nine years, it was rare to meet a man so at ease with himself. Sabra caught herself thinking about the man next to her instead of the real reason she had come to Santa Fe and firmly pulled her thoughts back.

"Must be interesting reading." Pierce nodded his head toward the laptop resting on her legs.

Reluctantly Sabra lifted her head. "Hopefully the audience will agree with you." At his puzzled look she continued. "I wrote *Silken Lies,* the fund-raiser play for the students' winter trip to New York. I'll act and direct. I'm just going over it."

Twin lines raced across Pierce's furrowed brow. "You're directing?"

Sabra's face mirrored his earlier surprise. "And I've written two songs for the play. Obviously, your mother didn't tell you." She laughed despite the sudden clench in her stomach. "I'll try not to read too much into that."

"Mama thinks you're the greatest actress she's ever seen. Clearly, your talents go far beyond just acting." He glanced at her before giving his attention back to the busy interstate. "I've never seen her this excited about meeting an artist and, believe me, that's saying a lot. She's on the arts council, and two other boards. Her fondness for her students goes beyond just being their teacher. If she didn't think you could do it, you wouldn't be here."

Sabra's stomach settled. "I'm looking forward to meeting her. When I mentioned I wanted to produce a play I'd written as well as act and direct, she sounded genuinely excited by the prospect."

"Why wouldn't she be?"

Sabra turned toward him in the seat, a smile tugging the corners of her mouth. "Perhaps because I've never written or directed before. Mrs. Grayson is taking a big chance. This will be their one and only fund-raiser. This could be a disaster."

"Do you really think that?"

She didn't have to think long for an answer. "If I say no it might sound egocentric."

"Or like a woman who has confidence in her own ability."

Her head tilted to one side again. He meant it. He wasn't just saying what he thought she wanted to hear, as others had done. "Thank you."

"Just calling it the way I see it," Pierce told her. "Mama is a good judge of character. If she thinks you can do it, you can."

Sabra thought of her father, who always had faith that she'd make it on Broadway, and fought to keep the tears at bay. She missed him so much. She'd always been closer to her dreamer of a father, perhaps because they were so much alike, than her practical mother. "You sound very close."

"We are, even when she's trying to—" Pierce broke off.

"Trying to do what?" Sabra asked, her curiosity piqued. Ruth Grayson, during their two-month-long correspondence and phone calls, had impressed

Sabra as a charming, easygoing, lovely woman. Certainly not the type to cause a man like Pierce the worry Sabra had heard in his voice.

Pierce tossed her a dimpled smile that had probably caused women of all ages to sigh in longing, then directed his attention back to the four-lane highway. "Family business. You wouldn't be interested."

Yes, she would. Perhaps too much so. Pierce was the kind of man who made a woman forget herself. Sabra had done that once. The man had been charming and too handsome for a woman to ignore, and she'd been young and stupid enough to believe every lie. She had no intention of letting herself go down that road again.

She was here to settle her father's debt, *her* debt. There was no denying Pierce was a mouthwatering specimen of manhood, but this wasn't the time or the place.

Sabra switched her attention to the screen, which proved the wrong thing to do. It was the scene where devastatingly handsome Max Chandler, the male lead in *Silken Lies,* had to face a hard truth. Max, driven to right a wrong, used his looks, money, and charm to undo a terrible injustice done to his family. But in the process he jeopardized the only woman he had ever loved.

Sabra glanced out the window at the passing scenery. What drove a man to use others to achieve his own end? Was there ever any justification? Was she any better?

"You all right?"

Surprised, she glanced back at Pierce. She was good at hiding her emotions. She only let people see what she wanted them to. To let the world see what you were feeling was asking to be used.

He nodded his dark head toward the laptop now in her arms. "You're clutching it like a lifeline."

She looked at the notebook that she had never let get far from her for the past year as she wrote Max's story, unaware that when she started writing it would almost mirror the life of the man she'd loved with her whole heart. And, like Max's story, there would be no happy ending.

"Just thinking." Turning in the seat, she reached out to Isabella. The dog immediately put her muzzle in Sabra's palm, emitting a soft whine. "You can't be hungry again."

"We'll be in Santa Fe's city limits in less than fifteen minutes," Pierce told her. "Mama said to bring you by the auditorium, but I know she wouldn't mind if we stopped to get takeout." He looked at the dog in his mirror. "Isabella won't be able to go inside, and I have a feeling she's not the patient type."

"That goes for the both of us." Sabra straightened in her seat.

"Some things are hard to wait for, but well worth it," Pierce said, his gaze a mixture of hot and hopeful.

Sabra felt the pull in his dark eyes. Her stomach tightened. Pierce was a man she definitely planned to keep away from.

CHAPTER TWO

THE BEAUTIFUL CAMPUS OF ST. JOHN'S COLLEGE was just outside Santa Fe. SJC was known nationwide for its strong academic program as well as the capacity-filled week-long summer seminars on the great works of literature, politics, art, philosophy, opera, and science. Pierce drove directly to the auditorium and escorted Sabra inside. They were barely through the heavy wooden doors before his mother rushed to them.

"Ms. Raineau, I'm Ruth Grayson. It's a pleasure and an honor to finally meet you after following your career all these years," Ruth greeted Sabra warmly, extending her hand.

Sabra liked the tall woman with striking features immediately. She was dressed in a soft blue blouse and denim skirt. "Thank you, Mrs. Grayson. The pleasure is mine. Please call me Sabra."

Ruth smiled. "If you'll call me Ruth."

"Deal." Sabra looked down at Isabella sitting

politely at her feet. "This is Isabella. I hope you and your students don't mind her coming to rehearsals."

"Not at all." Ruth laughed and patted the dog on the head. "I'm fond of animals and, truthfully, you could have brought a menagerie with you. I'm still a bit awed that you're here."

"I hope you'll still feel that way after we've worked together for a few days," Sabra said. Once again butterflies had taken flight in her stomach.

"I can guarantee that." Ruth turned toward the group of obviously awestruck students waiting patiently behind her. "Sabra, I'd like to introduce you to a group of very talented students who will bring *Silken Lies* to life."

More butterflies took flight, but Sabra's easy smile remained as she shook hands with each of the waiting students. She'd had to trust Ruth to choose the best qualified for the production. There was no time to have tryouts once Sabra arrived. Ruth had assured Sabra that the students brought with them the broad base of specialties in music, communication, fashion, and design needed to develop the stage play. "I hope my songs can do your talent justice."

"It's the other way around, Ms. Raineau," Theo, a gifted pianist, corrected. "I've been working on the music since you sent the songs to Mrs. Grayson six weeks ago."

Sabra spoke to the students. "We're going to be working closely together for the next four weeks;

please call me Sabra. And, I confess, 'Ms.' makes me feel old."

The students nodded and smiled.

Sabra turned to Theo. "Now that that's taken care of, I can't wait to hear what you've come up with."

He gulped. His Adam's apple bobbed. "Now?"

Sabra casually slipped her arm through his slim one and smiled to put the young man at ease. "If you don't mind?"

Wordlessly, Theo went to the black baby grand on the stage and sat down. Everyone followed, Pierce included. He couldn't imagine many men saying no to Sabra. The gift of her smile would induce any man to fight the devil himself.

Theo slowly sank onto the piano bench as if he were sitting on eggs. Sabra sat beside him. The poor young man's hands shook as he lifted them. He swallowed and looked at Sabra.

She smiled and gently touched his trembling arm. "The first time I had to do an audition, I was so nervous I couldn't say a word. It so happened that not only was the director there, but the producer and the two leads as well."

"W-what did you do?" Theo asked.

"Thought of all the years I'd worked to get there and how I'd kick myself later if I let the chance get away," she said. "I closed my eyes, took a deep breath, and let them have it. Close your eyes, Theo, and let me have it."

Pierce didn't have to look at his mother to know

she was pulling for Theo. She'd chosen the students who she felt needed a boost of confidence to come into their own. She took a great deal of interest in her students, always had and always would.

Theo's long-fingered hands settled on the keys and he began to play a stirring melody. The sound that joined in was pure, haunting. An eloquent, imperfect soprano that spoke of pain and heartache. Sabra's voice. It grabbed you at gut level as it told of love lost and love gained. When she finished, there was complete silence for five seconds. Then the students and Pierce's mother wildly applauded.

Pierce couldn't join them. He'd never been as moved by a song, and he had been around music all his life. He was too caught up with the emotions Sabra's voice had evoked. She wasn't just singing words; they touched her on some deep emotional level. He'd never been jealous of anyone in his life, but just for a moment he was jealous of the man who had moved her to write "Tonight Is Forever."

Pierce's mother had insisted all her children play a musical instrument. He'd chosen the drums because they could drown out his brothers' and sister's instruments. He should have chosen more wisely.

"Theo, that was absolutely perfect," Sabra said, her eyes bright. "I can't wait to hear what you came up with for the other number."

"Thank you," Theo said, grinning for all he was worth. "It will sound even better with the rest of the instruments."

Sabra swirled to face the students standing behind her. "I can't begin to tell you how much this means to me. I can tell it means as much to you. Thank you."

The students surrounded Theo and Sabra, no longer awe struck but as fellow musicians and actors. Sabra had a way of putting a person at ease. She definitely wasn't the diva Pierce had feared she'd be.

"I hate to break this up, but it's time for your next class," Ruth said, earning her protests and groans. "Sabra will be here for four weeks. In the meantime, I don't want any of your professors complaining about you not giving your best to all of the other classes."

Students scrambled for their books and backpacks. In less than thirty seconds they were waving good-bye and rushing out the door.

"They're a good group," Sabra said.

"Yes, they are," Ruth said. "You're as gracious as I knew you would be. As you suggested, I've offered the press and local media an exclusive a few days before the play. You and the students can work without being bothered. This is going to be better than I'd hoped. Isn't she great, Pierce?"

Pierce waited until Sabra looked at him before he spoke. "I've never heard anything as hauntingly beautiful."

Sabra's smile faltered. "It was Theo's music."

Pierce frowned. He hadn't gotten the impression that Sabra was the modest type.

"I can't wait until rehearsal tomorrow," Ruth said. "In the meantime, let's get you settled. You selected the new condo building downtown. On the bottom floors are offices, a coffee shop, and a hair salon. It also has a state-of-the-art fitness center and a swimming pool."

Pierce recognized the building. He'd moved in two months ago when the building was complete. He looked at his mother with suspicion.

"But if you'd like to have a look at the house or the hotel room I sent you information on, they're still available." Ruth picked up her worn leather satchel, detailed at the corner and on the buckle with sterling silver. "We want you to be happy."

Sabra shook her head and patted Isabella on the top of her head. "From the video you sent, I will be. The condo is convenient to everything, and the view of the Sangre de Cristo Mountains is breathtaking."

"Wonderful. If you like homemade fajitas, once you're settled we could have dinner at my house. I'm finished here, and we could discuss the play."

"I'd love to, but I have Isabella."

"She won't be any trouble," Ruth said. "In anticipation of your coming I picked up dog food and bowls for her."

"I accept." Sabra turned to Pierce and extended her hand. "Thanks again. Good-bye."

Her hand was soft as he'd expected. What he didn't expect was not wanting to let her go. His thumb grazed lightly over her wrist and felt her pulse jump. At least he wasn't alone in the attraction. "You and Isabella will probably see me again."

Isabella barked when Pierce said her name, but he kept his gaze on Sabra and watched with interest the pulse in her throat hammering against her soft skin. Soon he'd press his lips there.

As if reading his thoughts, Sabra pulled her hand free, but she didn't retreat. He had the impression she didn't scare easily.

Ruth spoke to Pierce. "Thank you again for picking Sabra up. You can put her luggage in my car. I'll show her where she'll be living."

Pierce couldn't decide if his mother was acting as if he didn't live at the condo because it wasn't important or to throw him off. One thing he was sure of was that he wasn't ready to see the last of Sabra. "Her luggage is heavy. Why don't I follow you and take the luggage to her place?"

"As I told you, I can handle it," Sabra said.

"There's no reason why you have to," Pierce said easily.

"Pierce is absolutely right. He can follow us." Ruth walked to Sabra. "You can ride with me and we can discuss *Silken Lies*. What motivated you to write the play?"

If he hadn't been watching Sabra so closely, he might not have seen the panic in her chocolate eyes. "I wondered what a person would sacrifice for love."

"Does the woman singing the song or the man she's singing about make the sacrifice?" Pierce asked.

"He does," Sabra answered.

"What does he sacrifice?"

"The woman he loved."

"Was it worth it?" Pierce asked.

"That's the question Max, the character, and the audience have to answer," Sabra said before turning to his mother. "Ruth, I'm ready when you are."

"We'll see you at the condo," Ruth said as she left with Sabra.

Pierce was right behind them.

"THIS IS IT." RUTH OPENED THE DOOR AND MOVED aside.

Sabra stepped over the threshold with Isabella by her side. The first thing Sabra saw through a wall of plate glass directly in front of her was the snow-capped Sangre de Cristo Mountains. They towered majestically in the distance. The second was a black baby grand to her left. A rush of happiness went through her.

Sabra turned to Ruth. "I have you to thank for this, don't I?"

"As I said, we wanted you to be happy," Ruth said. "Would you like to try it out or go to dinner?"

Smiling, Sabra went to sit at the piano, her fingers dancing across the keys. Pierce placed the luggage by the bedroom door, then just stood and listened. The haunting sounds of the music, just as her singing had done, touched him. He wondered why Sabra smiled, but her music didn't reflect that happiness.

"I thought you two were going to eat?" he asked.

"In a minute," Sabra said, continuing to play.

"That's from *Carmen*." Ruth sat down beside her. "Another troubled soul who didn't love wisely."

"Love can bring as much pain as it can bring happiness." Sabra continued to play.

Isabella, as if sensing her mistress's sadness, stuck her head beneath Pierce's hand. Absently, he scratched behind the dog's ears.

"True, but the pain is worth the pleasure," Ruth said.

"I wonder," Sabra said softly, her gaze fixed on the distant mountains.

Ruth swiveled on the piano seat. "Thanks again, Pierce. This must be boring, since you're not a fan of Broadway."

Sabra looked over her shoulder at him. Her hands paused over the keys; then she continued. "Good-bye, Pierce."

Left without a choice, Pierce give Isabella one last scratch, then quietly left, wishing the dog's owner were as easy to get to know. Outside the door, he listened to the music and the soft laughter of the women.

They had certainly hit it off. He hadn't expected any different. His mother was open and honest, and she loved people and music. He was also aware that her love of music meant that she often lost track of time. The two women could be there for ten minutes or two hours. After one last look at the door, he came to a quick decision.

Letting himself into his condo next door, he washed up, then called the sandwich shop downstairs for takeout. Hanging up the phone, he was out the door and striding toward the elevator.

If he'd had time he would have called for a to-go order at Brandon's restaurant. It would be just his luck, the way things were going, that his mother and Sabra would leave while he was going to get the food. As it was, he kept an eye on the bank of elevators while the sandwiches were prepared.

Paying for the food, Pierce hurried back upstairs. Balancing the three white paper bags, he rang the doorbell, then rang again when there was no answer. He knew they were inside. He could hear Sabra singing "I'll Always Love You." Didn't she know any happy songs?

When he was about to ring the doorbell again, the door opened. "Pierce?"

He lifted the bags to his mother's unspoken question. "I thought you and Sabra might like to stay in and talk."

His mother smiled and stepped back. "What a nice way of saying I lose track of time."

He was aware that Sabra had yet to say a word. She just watched him with those beautiful eyes of hers. He went to the kitchen and started unloading the bags. The women and Isabella followed. "I didn't know if you were a vegetarian or not, but I took a chance you weren't, since you have Isabella."

At the mention of the dog's name, she barked. Pierce chuckled and took another sandwich from the bag. "I didn't forget you." He looked at Sabra. "Meat lovers' special."

Sabra looked at Isabella, who was on her hindquarters looking up at Pierce with utter devotion and greed. "She'll be your slave forever."

"I'd settle for a friend."

"Pierce, her bowls are on the counter," Ruth said. "I'll take care of this. Sabra, there're napkins and place mats in the middle drawer."

Sabra did as his mother asked. Pierce's lips twitched. His mother might be in awe of Sabra, but that didn't mean Ruth wouldn't order her around just as she did her children, students, and just about everyone else. Since she often went out of her way to help anyone in need, no one objected.

Obtaining the bowls, Pierce filled one with water, put the sandwich in the other, and set them on the slate gray terrazzo floor. "You two go ahead and eat. I'll take care of Isabella."

"You aren't joining us?" Sabra held a third red linen place mat and napkin in her hands.

"I didn't want to intrude." He pushed to his feet.

"You wouldn't be. Perhaps we can broaden your scope on Broadway," Sabra said.

Pierce smiled and pulled out her chair and then his mother's. "You're welcome to try."

Ruth bowed her head and blessed the food. "When you were in the Broadway production of *Carmen*, my children gave me front-row tickets."

Sabra paused in taking a bite out of her turkey and ham sandwich. "Children?"

"There are five of us," Pierce happily said, taking a large bite out of his own turkey and ham sandwich.

"My daughter, Sierra, the youngest, is a realtor. It so happens she owns this condo, but leases it out. Pierce is the fourth child and fourth son." Ruth looked at him with a frown. "And at times the most difficult."

Pierce almost choked on his sandwich. The last thing he wanted his mother to talk about was her opinion that he was dragging his feet getting married. "Why Broadway?" he asked, hoping to get them back on the topic. He was having a difficult enough time as it was with Sabra.

Sabra looked from him to his mother as if aware that there was more to the story, but she was too polite to ask. "I like the challenge, the intimacy of being there with the audience. There's nothing like it for an emotional high."

Pierce could think of a couple of things. "You must have a busy schedule."

Sabra swallowed before answering. "Eight shows a week can be grueling. You have to be at the theater hours before the show, then another two and a half to three hours for the production. Many times I didn't get home until after midnight."

Pierce frowned. "I thought it was more glamorous."

"Most people do." Sabra folded her slim hands on the table. "People who come to New York for the first time are astounded by the huge billboards and all the theaters, some of which don't have glamorous façades, but it's the magic that happens on the inside that counts. You go out each night to give your best. No retakes."

"That sounds grueling and a bit lonely," Pierce said.

"It can be, but in most things you have to give up something to get what you want." Sabra sipped her iced tea from the plastic cup. "It's not the audience's fault if you're tired or had a bad day. They paid their money for you to be the best you can be."

"I hate that I've never seen you perform," he said, meaning it.

"That will be corrected in four weeks." Ruth placed her napkin on the table by her plate. "The play is wonderful, the music outstanding, and when they hear Sabra sing, they'll be moved."

"I was," Pierce said casually, watching Sabra clench and unclench her hand. "Are you writing from experience?"

She looked startled for a moment, then put her hands in her lap. "I started the play a while ago. After my father passed away four months ago I finally finished and added the songs for him."

"I'm sorry," Pierce said, instantly contrite. The pain in her eyes made him want to kick himself, then take her in his arms and comfort her.

"It was his heart." Sabra swallowed and blinked several times. "He'd never been ill a day in his life. People should cherish and enjoy every second they have because the next day, the next moment, isn't promised. It's too late for regrets once they're gone. Daddy knew I loved him, but I wish we would have had more time."

Ruth briefly closed her eyes. "Love and good memories help when nothing else can."

"Mama," Pierce said softly, gently sliding his hand down her arm.

Sabra placed her hand over Ruth's in obvious empathy. "They would have known. I've only known you for a short while, but I can tell you're a woman who loves with all her heart."

Ruth's hand covered the other woman's. Oddly, Pierce wasn't surprised that Sabra had such intuition or was that sensitive to another's pain.

Ruth glanced at Pierce, a small smile on her face. "I miss Vincent, my husband, still, but I had the children. You're right. Memories helped." Patting Sabra's hand again, Ruth came to her feet. "Thank you for letting me stay when you have to be tired from your trip."

"I enjoyed every moment," Sabra said truthfully, standing as well. Survival in the theater with all the phonies had required that she learn to read people quickly. Ruth was a warm, friendly woman who obviously had a great love for her family and music and believed in her students. "After meeting you, I'm even more excited about us working together."

"I'm glad." Ruth started to the door. "Pierce?"

He placed his hand on the back of the upholstered side chair he was standing beside. "I thought I'd stick around a bit and acquaint Sabra with the shops in the building."

"I'm sure there's a brochure," Sabra said. Being alone with Pierce wasn't a good idea.

"If there is, I wasn't aware of it, and I've been here for two months," he said with entirely too much satisfaction on his incredible face.

"You live here?"

Pierce enjoyed the shock on her face, the uneasiness that leaped into her eyes. She wasn't indifferent to him, just fighting the attraction. "Next door, as a matter of fact."

"His office is in the building as well. If you need anything, he'll be there to help you," Ruth told her.

Sabra refused to look at Pierce. That wasn't likely. "I'm sure I'll be fine." She folded her arms. "If you don't mind, could we go over the layout later? I feel tired."

"We won't keep you any longer." Ruth pulled the car keys out of her skirt pocket. "As discussed over the phone, we'll have two rehearsals each weekday at eleven and four, and one on Saturday at eleven. I left brochures on the coffee table about Santa Fe and a copy of *Santa Fean* magazine. In consideration of your travel, you don't have to come until twelve. I'll pick you up around eleven thirty."

"I'll be ready." Sabra opened the door. "Good

evening, Ruth, Pierce. And thank you again for picking me up and the food."

Pierce slowly followed his mother into the hall. "Good evening."

Sabra closed the door and leaned against it. Pierce was turning into a distraction she didn't need. Isabella sauntered into the room and sat on her haunches. "You are not to like him under any circumstances. He's too charming. Charming men are off our list. The only man we're interested in is the one who did business with Daddy."

Isabella thumped her tail. Sabra groaned, then shook her head. Isabella only listened to Sabra when she wanted to. "All right, be stubborn, but I plan to see Pierce as little as possible."

IN THE YEARS SINCE PIERCE OPENED HIS INVESTMENT firm he had gotten used to working late. What he wasn't used to was working late because he hadn't been able to get a woman off his mind.

Pierce opened a document on the computer and more data appeared on the wide monitor. He had appointments with two prospective clients the next morning. Picking up his gold pen, he made notes on the papers he had already printed out. He planned to be ready with the prospectus both men were interested in.

Pierce enjoyed his single life and the pleasure of women, but business always came first. He was thorough and cautious. His clients deserved the best he could give them. He didn't plan on it being any other way.

When the phone rang on his desk he ignored it. After five rings it stopped, only to ring again a few seconds later. On the second ring, he hit the speakerphone and continued to look at the computer screen and make notations. The callback was a signal the family had worked out when they were working late in the office. Since it was past eight, Luke and Morgan were at home with their wives and Brandon was at his restaurant. The odds were against the caller being his mother.

"Hello, Sierra?" Pierce said, calculating it was his baby sister.

"Is she as stunning as her pictures?"

Pierce had expected the call. Sierra had kept close tabs on him since Brandon's engagement. If Pierce fell—which he had no intention of doing—she was next. "Would you get on my case if I said yes?"

"If she was staying longer than four weeks I might be worried."

Suddenly four weeks didn't seem very long at all. He twirled the gold pen in his hand, recalling the golden brown hue of Sabra's skin, the silken softness, the fragrant hint of jasmine that teased the senses.

"Pierce?"

"I'm here."

"How did she like her sublease?"

Pierce frowned. "All right, I suppose. She and Mama mostly talked about the play."

"You sound disappointed."

Pierce tossed the ink pen on his neat desk. "Why would I sound disappointed?"

"I can think of a couple of reasons. Both bother me," Sierra said. "Please tell me you're not interested in her. No, that's asking too much. Just tell me you aren't thinking of asking her out."

"Why shouldn't I ask her out?" Pierce came to his feet. "She'll only be here for four weeks; then she goes back to New York."

"Where she has to make some major decisions. Since she won that Tony, she's Broadway's darling," Sierra told him. "She has offers from cutting an album to playing the lead of the play she won the Tony for on the big screen. Both are dicey."

His interest peaked. It was uncanny, the amount of information Sierra had. "Why?"

"Singing three songs onstage where the audience can see and feel the emotions is vastly different from doing ten to twelve songs for the album. She has to ask herself if her voice will translate those same intense emotions on a recording. Then, too, a number of big-time Broadway actors have bombed when they took the play to the big screen. The audience is different for both."

"How do you know all this?"

"I have my sources. Suffice it to say, Sabra might be looking at a career change. She's been quoted as saying that, in the meantime, she doesn't have time for relationships; her career has to come first. Besides, it would be bad form for you to hit on her when she's working with Mama. What will happen when you break up as you always do? Messy."

He thought of Sabra's slim body, the husky laugh, the raspberry lips, and couldn't imagine getting tired of her. "You had to remind me of that, didn't you?"

"Just keeping everything in perspective," Sierra said. "We have to watch each other's backs."

"I can handle myself."

"I've heard that before. And don't think I don't know you didn't answer my initial question. Yes or no? Is she as stunning as her pictures?"

A loaded and dangerous question, and one his baby sister could use against him. "Yes."

"Since you didn't elaborate, she must be off the chart."

Pierce frowned at the phone. Sierra was cannier than his mother when it came to reading her brothers. It was scary at times. "Sierra, I'm a bit busy here."

"Worse than I thought. So when are you taking her out?"

"I'm not." That she had turned him down still rankled.

"Come on, be for real. I know you ask—" There was silence for four full seconds. "She turned you down!"

"She was tired," Pierce said, and felt worse for making the excuse. "You should be happy."

"She's probably snotty. You're better off."

The corners of Pierce's lips hiked upward. Sierra was fiercely loyal. "Probably." He took his seat behind his desk and scrolled down on the screen.

"I think I'll drop by the college tomorrow while they're practicing."

Pierce straightened. Sierra was also unpredictable. "Mama likes her."

"I'm definitely stopping by, then. I'll meet you for breakfast at the same time."

Since Brandon had married Faith McBride, whose family owned the five-star hotel Casa de Serenidad (House of Serenity), Pierce and Sierra, the only two single Graysons left, ate at the hotel restaurant almost every morning. They both liked good food, and Brandon's restaurant didn't serve breakfast.

Knowing he wouldn't get any more out of her, Pierce said, "See you then," and hung up, wishing he could stop thinking about the woman two floors above.

CHAPTER THREE

WITH SO MUCH TRAVELING INVOLVED WITH HER career, Sabra had learned the art of sleeping in a strange bed and waking up refreshed and ready for whatever the day might hold. Mementos from home helped. On her nightstand she'd placed grapefruit-scented candles, pictures of her family, and a small porcelain music box her father had given her for her sixth birthday.

However, last night none of those things had helped.

She had tossed and turned from the moment her head hit the down pillow. Sleep had evaded her until early that morning. Subsequently, she'd awakened grumpy and grouchy. A cup of coffee, usually her panacea, hadn't helped.

Restless and out of sorts, she'd grabbed Isabella's leash and left her condo. She'd only gone a short distance down the surprisingly busy sidewalk at eight in the morning before she realized she had no idea where she was going. She'd picked up the *Santa Fean* magazine but had no idea how to get to any of the restaurants listed inside. Then she thought of the map Ruth had mentioned and started back to the condo.

And came face-to-face with the reason for her restless night walking toward her. Pierce Grayson. Sleek, elegant, six feet two of trouble coming toward her with a lazy gait.

"Good morning, Sabra. I trust you slept well."

"Yes." She winced inwardly at the lie, but her expression remained unchanged.

"I couldn't help but notice you stop and turn around. You looked lost for a moment," he commented. "Anything I can do to help?"

Stay as far away as possible for a start, so I can concentrate on what I came here for. "No, thank you. Please don't let me keep you."

He didn't move on. Pierce obviously had enough self-confidence not to take her obvious hint. Twisting his dark head, he glanced at the magazine in her hand. "I can recommend a great restaurant for breakfast. The Mesa. I checked, and they allow well-mannered pets." He glanced down at Isabella staring happily up at him. "Isabella certainly qualifies."

"What's the address?" Sabra asked.

His long-fingered hand gently circled her upper forearm. "I'll show you. I'm on my way there now."

Defeated, she fell into step beside him, felt the brush of their bodies. Her skin grew warm, heated.

"I'm sure I could find the way if you'll just point me in the right direction."

"I wouldn't dream of it. Mama would have my hide, and I couldn't blame her."

Sabra didn't like whatever it was she was feeling, and she had no intention of allowing it to continue. She balked. Unless he wanted to drag her, he had to stop as well. "The directions, please?"

His dark eyes narrowed and he studied her for a long, uncomfortable moment. "What is it about me that you don't like?"

The question was so far from the truth and so unexpectedly blunt that she was momentarily stunned.

"You can tell me. I assure you my ego isn't that fragile," he said, waiting for her answer.

She didn't doubt him for a second. One thing Pierce Grayson didn't lack was self-assurance. He was also perceptive enough to know when she was feeding him a line. "You want something from me you're not going to get, and when you don't, things could get complicated. I like your mother. We're going to be working together for four weeks. I don't want anything to jeopardize that."

His dark eyes studied her for so long she grew nervous. Men never made her nervous.

"I want to get to know you better."

Up went her brows again. "I'm sure you do."

He flashed the easy smile that probably had disarmed legions of females before her. "Haven't had many male friends, huh?"

Sabra gave him another truth. "No."

"Your fault or theirs?" he asked.

She would not be baited. "Won't you be late for your breakfast? You're probably meeting someone."

"I am. But she won't mind you eating with us."

Sabra felt a strange something she didn't want to examine too closely. "I would. Three is one too many."

He smiled and took her arm. "Not when the third party is my sister and your realtor."

She could have hit him. He'd done that on purpose. It didn't dawn on her until later that with another man she might have laughed.

"The restaurant serves an omelet that will make you sigh with pleasure," Pierce said, continuing down the street with Isabella on the other side of him. "You won't find better breakfast pastries anywhere in the city."

She started to say she wasn't hungry, but her stomach chose that inopportune moment to rumble. She enjoyed good food and thankfully had the metabolism to keep the pounds off. "I wouldn't want to intrude."

"Believe me, you won't. Besides, I have some information to give you."

Her brow lifted. "I assure you, after traveling to cities around the country and in Europe, I speak four languages and can find my way around a city."

Pierce grinned boyishly at her. "But can you find where Isabella can go with you? You don't want to be left at home all the time, do you, Isabella?"

Isabella barked and looked up at Pierce as if he had a hoagie. Pierce had certainly won Isabella's affection, not an easy task. She generally wasn't that fond of men. Sabra's agent was still watchful.

"I have a list in my pocket."

Sabra's assistant usually took care of that detail, but she had put Joy on a more pressing matter. "Why would you do that?"

Pierce glanced down at Isabella walking by his side. "If Isabella isn't happy, then you aren't going to be, and if you aren't happy, my mother isn't going to be."

"So you did this for your mother?" she asked.

"In a manner of speaking." Pierce turned into the entrance of a hotel. Lush tropical plants flanked either side of them. He greeted the valet and doorman by name, as they did him.

Men had tried to get to her before through Isabella, but this was the first time one had gone to the trouble of finding places Sabra and Isabella could go and be comfortable.

"Santa Fe is a pet-friendly town, actually. But the restaurants will be limited."

"Thank you." She didn't want him to be nice or she might waver in her resolve to steer clear of him. Her time was limited here. Every spare minute had to be spent searching for the man her father had business dealings with.

Pierce escorted her through the hotel lobby, again speaking to the passing employees. Sabra didn't miss the longing looks of the two women behind the front desk that followed them out the door leading to the open patio dining. Clay pots of colorful flowers abounded. A kiva fireplace was in the corner. "You must eat here a lot," she said.

"My brother Brandon's wife, Faith, is the executive manager of the family-owned hotel. Brandon is a great cook and owns a restaurant, but they don't serve breakfast," Pierce explained as he stopped in front of a wooden podium. An older gentleman with gray hair and a ramrod-straight back in a dark business suit greeted them with a smile.

"Good morning, Pierce, miss." The man picked up two menus. "Sierra is already here. I'll show you to your table."

"Good morning, Phillip. Thanks, but we'll find it."

The man smiled graciously. "I'll send Ben right over."

"Good, I'm starved." Taking the menu, Pierce continued on the tile floor. "If Brandon had to fall, at least we got some side benefits out of it."

"Fall?" Sabra said.

"Family joke." Pierce stopped at a black wrought-iron table where a beautiful woman sat, her gaze searching. Sabra realized she had been so intent on Pierce that she hadn't noticed the woman until now. The family resemblance was striking.

"Sabra Raineau, Sierra Grayson."

The women nodded and shook hands. Sabra realized she was being sized up and couldn't imagine why. Ruth Grayson might have taken Sabra at face value, but Sierra Grayson wasn't as easily swayed.

Pierce pulled out Sabra's chair next to Sierra and mouthed, *Be nice,* to his sister. Sierra merely picked up her orange juice and sipped. Her message was clear; she'd do as she pleased. A waiter appeared to take their orders, then withdrew quickly.

"I hear I have you to thank for my place. It's perfect and well stocked," Sabra said. "Isabella thanks you as well. There were even her favorite doggie biscuits."

"Pleasing our clients is the reason we exist," Sierra said. "Mama is very excited about you being here."

Sabra heard what wasn't said. Sierra's mother might be pleased, but Sierra wasn't so sure. "So am I," Sabra confessed, then thanked the waiter as he poured her coffee. She'd learned long ago that she wasn't going to be everyone's best buddy, but if possible, she wanted her and Sierra to at least be cordial. "She's giving me a chance to fulfill a dream."

"To write, star, and direct is very ambitious," Sierra said, sipping her juice.

Pierce wished he had sat next to Sierra so he could have nudged her to lighten up, but, on second thought, perhaps it was good that he hadn't. Sierra reacted adversely when told what to do. "From what I heard yesterday, Sabra doesn't have any worries."

"Oh." Sierra smiled as Ben served her, then Pierce and Sabra. "This looks wonderful as usual. If

I keep this up, I might have to seriously consider exercising."

"If you're going to flop, flop big, but failure is not an option," Sabra said, looking directly at Sierra over the rim of her coffee cup.

"Meaning?" Sierra asked as the waiter served their table.

Sabra folded her fingers. "Make no mistake, I want *Silken Lies* to click on all cylinders, and I feel strongly that it will, but fate and audiences can be fickle. But whatever happens, I'll learn from the experience and keep going."

"Strong words," Sierra said mildly, picking up her saltshaker.

"That I have every intention of backing up," Sabra said, not giving in an inch.

"How's the omelet, Sabra?" Pierce asked.

"Fine," she said, keeping her gaze on Sierra. "Failure is just a stepping-stone to success."

"And you would know this how?" Sierra asked

"By working my behind off, taking any part possible, for six years until I was an overnight success. By eating cold spaghetti and peanut butter." When pushed, Sabra pushed back. "I have a feeling you know what I'm talking about."

Sierra smiled. "I sold one house the first two months after I got my real estate license."

"That certainly didn't stop you from buying four pairs of designer shoes and the bags to match," Pierce said, trying to lighten the conversation.

Sierra's face grew serious. "I knew I would make it. The next month I sold five houses, each costing more than a quarter-million dollars, and I never looked back."

"Your closet can attest to that," Pierce said.

"What's success if you can't do some of the things you want? Right, Sabra?" Sierra eyed the black ostrich Chanel bag hanging on the back of the black wrought-iron chair. "Vintage?"

"Yes. I bought it to cheer me up when I was turned down for a part. For the next two months I lived off noodles and peanut butter sandwiches because it was all I could afford." Sabra laughed at the memory. "But when I went to a casting call, I was looking good."

"That was a senseless waste of money," Pierce said. Both women looked at him as if he'd just blasphemed. "Waste not, want not."

Sierra rolled her eyes. "That's the point; she didn't waste the money. The bag is now a symbol that she can succeed no matter what."

"Exactly." Sabra lifted her glass of juice. "To success in spite of the odds."

The women raised their glasses and toasted. Baffled, Pierce looked from his sister to Sabra. Money lost was seldom recouped. Sure, he enjoyed the good life as well as anyone, but he didn't believe in senseless spending.

"You have beautiful hair," Sabra said. "Mine won't stay straight no matter what I do to it."

Sierra smiled. "I was just thinking that it would be nice if mine would keep a curl like yours."

"Can you recommend a stylist?"

Sierra sat back in her chair. "I could, but I'd have to . . ."

"Kill me," Sabra finished.

Pierce's gaze ping-ponged between the two laughing women. Something had changed between them, and he wasn't sure what or why. If a man ever discovered how the minds of women worked and was willing to share the knowledge, he'd make millions—make that billions.

"Paul is fantastic." Sierra opened her brown croc handbag and pulled out a pad and gold pen. "He's fabulous. I can give you his number."

"Thank you. Since you're sharing, I guess I can tell you about a place in SoHo I found that specializes in vintage bags. She always lets me have first look."

Sierra's eyes got a gleam in them. "Thanks."

Pierce looked from his sister to Sabra. They were going to be friends after all.

"What do you plan to do when you're not rehearsing?" Sierra handed Sabra the slip of paper with the information she'd requested.

"Don't answer, Sabra," Pierce warned with a shake of his dark head. "She'll use you as a reference to influence her real estate clients."

"She is a satisfied client, but I was going to tell her all the best places to shop and show her around while she's here."

Nothing could have pleased Sabra more. "Thanks for the offer, but I'll probably be busy on the next script."

"What's this one about?" Pierce asked, and polished off his omelet.

"A love story. I haven't decided if it will end happily or not," she confessed.

"Stick around, and you'll get plenty of material. Starting now," Sierra told her.

Pierce shook his head when he spotted the couple coming toward them, holding hands. "I wonder if that silly grin on our brother's face will ever go away?"

"Going by that same expression on Luke's and Morgan's faces, I think we're in for the duration," Sierra said, then frowned at him. "Don't you even think about it."

"Believe me, I'm not," he said; then he stood to give Brandon a one-armed hug. "I still can't believe you can get up by eight thirty and smile about it."

Brandon slung a long arm around his wife and smiled down at her. "There are some things worth getting up for."

Faith stared up at her husband with complete love and devotion. "There certainly are."

"See what I mean?" Sierra whispered in an aside to Sabra, but she was smiling. Out loud she said, "Faith, you did what I thought was impossible."

Faith palmed Brandon's handsome face. Her voice soft, she admitted, "You and me both."

Brandon covered her hands with his, then gently brushed his lips against hers. "I love you."

"Brandon," Faith whispered his name on a sigh.

"Cut it out, you two," Pierce said with a chuckle. "We have company."

It took Brandon and Faith a long moment before they broke eye contact and turned to Sabra. Pierce and Sierra shared a look they had come to know well as brother after brother fell in love. They were happy for their brothers, but neither wanted to be next.

"Ms. Raineau, welcome to Casa de Serinidad, the House of Serenity," Faith greeted them, extending her hand. "Faith Grayson, and this is my husband, Brandon."

"Good morning, and welcome," Brandon said, his arm still around his wife's waist.

Sabra's eyebrow lifted in surprise. She was seldom recognized by the general public and, in fact, preferred it that way. "Thank you, and good morning. The food here is wonderful."

Brandon seated Faith, then sat beside her, his arm on the back of her chair. "Almost as good as that at the Red Cactus," Brandon said just as a mustachioed man passed.

The wiry man in a chef 's coat and hat stopped, turned, then lifted his chin. "The things I must put up with."

Brandon chuckled despite Faith's stern look. "Forgive my husband. He and my executive chef have a running feud on whose cuisine is the best."

"I already know," Brandon said, kissing Faith on the cheek. "Come over to the restaurant and you can be the judge."

"I don't imagine you allow dogs?" Sabra asked, her dark eyes twinkling.

Brandon frowned.

"Isabella," Pierce said. The dog came to her feet and placed her muzzle on the edge of the table.

Brandon whistled. Isabella barked.

"She doesn't like me leaving her," Sabra explained.

"Will takeout do?" Brandon asked with a laugh, and they all joined in.

"I suppose it will have to," Sabra conceded. "But I definitely plan to come back here for breakfast."

"Please do," Faith said. "Since you didn't check in with us, where did you decide to stay?"

"The condo," Sabra said, realizing now why Faith had recognized her.

"Sabra and Pierce are neighbors," Sierra said. "She's subleasing my condo."

All eyes converged on Pierce, then on her. Sabra, who had performed before packed houses here and abroad, before heads of state, twisted uncomfortably in her seat.

"Well, well," Brandon said. Faith elbowed him.

"I feel as if everyone has a script but me." Sabra folded her hands on the table. "Would anyone care to enlighten me?"

"Nothing you would be interested in," Pierce said easily.

"Well, I have to go." Sierra came to her feet. "Wish me luck; I'm showing the Castle estate to Mitchell Shuler."

"I don't suppose there could be two Mitchell Shulers?" Sabra said, a frown on her face.

"You mean the power-hungry, self-important, and can't-keep-his-hands-to-himself owner of Shuler Electronics in San Francisco?" Sierra asked.

"The same." Sabra's eyes narrowed. "You aren't showing him a property by yourself, are you?"

"That's one thing they didn't have to teach me in my real estate classes."

"Your brothers beat them to it?" Sabra guessed.

"You got it." Sierra looked at both brothers. "And if I see any of them at my office or at the Castle estate, I am not going to be pleased."

"Of course you won't. They know you can take care of yourself," Faith said quickly.

"If he puts one finger where it shouldn't be—" Pierce didn't finish, the deadly intent in his voice saying it all.

"He'll be singing high soprano for a month, plus explaining to our friend Dakota, the chief of police, when I press charges." Sierra picked up her attaché case. "We all know you have to work with people you don't approve of. See you later."

"Maybe I should—" Brandon began as Sierra walked away.

"You want her to think you don't trust her to take care of herself?" Faith interrupted her husband.

"I know this is none of my concern, but Shuler outweighs her by seventy pounds," Sabra said.

"She's smarter." Pierce looked at Sabra. "Did he get out of line with you?"

Sabra blinked, surprised to hear the same menacing tone in Pierce's voice. "No. With a friend of mine."

"Then he might leave Santa Fe in one piece after all. You ready to walk back?"

Sabra came automatically to her feet. Pierce might have that easy smile, but he could be dangerous in more ways than one. Perhaps if she kept remembering that, she'd stop thinking about how his touch made her tingle, how inexplicably drawn she was to him. Maybe she'd forget the warmth she didn't want to feel when she realized that he wanted to protect her even though they'd just met.

SABRA WAS ON THE PHONE TO HER ASSISTANT IN New York as soon as she reached her condo. The two-hour time difference meant Joy was up and, Sabra hoped, had the information she needed. She paced in front of the bank of windows in the living room. Any other day she might have taken time to admire the snowcapped mountains in the distance, but not today.

"Good morning," came Joy's efficient voice. Sabra could picture her personal assistant with her half-glasses perched on her nose, her short auburn hair spiked, dressed all in black because then she never had to think about what to wear.

"Good morning, Joy. Do you have anything for me yet?"

"Not yet, Sabra," Joy said. "I'm trying to cross-reference businesses of today with those eight years ago. I also think we have to take into consideration that the man you're looking for might not be in the yellow pages."

"Which means you'll have to go through the entire phone book." Sabra sank down on the camelback sofa covered in a luxurious ecru and robin blue silk stripe. "This could take months."

"Not quite that long," Joy said, the optimism that had been one of the reasons Sabra hired her three years ago clearly coming through in her voice. "If I had more computer skills to feed the data in and let the computer figure this out, it would help."

"I hired you to keep me on track, not be a sleuth." Impatiently, Sabra shoved her hand through her hair. "I don't trust anyone else with this information except you."

"I'll keep looking," Joy promised. "I sent you an e-mail with all the phone calls and messages. Dave wants you to call. He said to tell you to turn on your cell."

Sabra reached for her large black Chanel tote on the sofa beside her and dumped the contents. Moving an assortment of articles, she finally located the cell phone and turned it on. "It's on, so he'll be happy."

"He said the movie studio bosses want to lock things down. They're becoming restless," Joy told her.

Sabra stood and paced. "Both he and the studio will have to wait. I won't be pushed into anything." As if on cue, her cell rang. Sabra made a face when she saw the call was from her agent. "Perhaps I should have left it off. Dave is calling me now. Keep searching, Joy, and call me as soon as you have anything."

"I will. Good-bye."

"Good-bye." Sabra cut the portable phone off, replaced it, then answered her cell. "Hello, Dave."

"Keep your cell on. Why have the thing if I can't reach you?"

"You're talking to me now," she said reasonably.

"Smarty. Good thing I like you."

"Same goes," she parried. She and Dave Hopper had been together since the first week she hit New York. They'd met at the Italian restaurant where she'd been a waitress and he'd been a regular customer.

After one of the waiters said Dave was an agent, she'd made it a point to introduce herself. He was ten years older and had been in the business for five years. He didn't have any big-name clients, but that was all right with her. He appeared honest and, most important, hadn't tried to hit on her.

By the time he left, she'd had an agent. He'd seen her through commercials, modeling jobs, bit parts. Through it all, both of their goals had been Broadway. He believed in her almost as much as she and her father did.

"Paramount upped the price by fifty grand, but they want to start production in six weeks."

Once she would have jumped at the chance to do a movie for the top studio in the country, but that was before she lost her father and realized how fragile life was, how the wrong mistake could have far-reaching consequences. Was she ready to put her current career in jeopardy for the possibility of another?

"Dave—"

"Don't say no. Just think about it," he said quickly, cutting her off. "Sure they're pressuring you, but they can't keep the director on hold or the male lead waiting for you. As it is, it's costing them a bundle. If you can't make a decision, they'll have to move on."

She massaged her suddenly throbbing temple. "Filming in Toronto will take six months minimum. There'll be publicity I'll have to do when they release the movie. If I'm doing a play, I might not be able to break away. Broadway producers are going to be aware of this as much as I am, and might be reluctant to hire me," she said, voicing her concern. "It took me a long time to get where I am. I'm not sure I want to toss it aside to be a movie actress."

"Movie *star*."

Sabra almost smiled. Dave didn't think small. "That remains to be seen."

"Do the movie, and you'll see," he cajoled. "You'll look damn good on the red carpet."

She had to laugh. "On my way to accept my Oscar, no doubt. Of course, I would have already accepted the Screen Actors Guild and the Golden Globe awards."

"You can do it, Sabra."

"And give up my privacy, deal with the paparazzi and starstruck fans." She stared out the window. Isabella apparently sensed her distress and came to sit by her feet. There was one fear she couldn't tell her agent about.

What would happen if her father's duplicity got out? Nothing tabloids loved more than digging up past indiscretions of a famous person or their relatives, then plastering them on the front page. It would destroy her mother. It was enough that Sabra carried the guilt.

"You know as well as I do that some of that is generated by their publicists," Dave told her. "Joy knows better."

"I hired Joy and have control over what she does. I have none over the studio. We've both seen the contract. Once I do the picture, publicity is at their discretion." Sabra's hand clenched. "I won't have another incident like last year."

"Henderson was just looking for publicity with that lie about you two spending the weekend at the Ritz, but it backfired on him when you proved you were at a very public benefit in Atlanta instead of with him."

"But how many people still believe his lie that

he'd mixed up the date that we were supposedly holed up at the Ritz?" An edge entered her voice. "All because I refused to date him."

"Well, it backfired. His parts are getting smaller and smaller, while your star is rising."

"A shooting star eventually falls," she said quietly.

There was a long silence. "Thinking about your daddy?"

"Yes." She missed him, wished they'd had more time, wished he hadn't felt he had to break the law because of her. "I'll think about things."

"I guess that is the best I'll get," Dave said, disappointment clear in his voice. "Give me the number where you're staying. At least, if your cell phone is off, I can reach you there."

Sabra picked up the card Ruth or Sierra had thoughtfully left with the address and phone number and gave him the information. "Good-bye, Dave, and thanks."

"I only want what's best for you."

She believed him. She'd also believed her father when he said the same thing. The only problem was what they felt was the best for her might not be in the long run. "I know, Dave. Bye."

"Bye."

Sabra shut off the phone, then tossed it in the direction of the rest of the paraphernalia on the sofa and went to the bedroom. Like the rest of the condo, it was in shades of blue and beige. This time, sumptuous sky blue with bronze highlights, which dominated the spacious room.

The focal point was the king-sized bed draped with a luxurious woven jacquard damask duvet finished with onion ball tassels. The accent pillows had elaborate beading, tassels, and faux pearls. The sheeting in ivory was Egyptian cotton and embellished with blue and bronze embroidery. She should have slept like a baby.

The perturbing reason popped into her mind and before she could stop it she saw herself and Pierce entwined on the bed, their bodies straining to get closer, taking, giving.

Sabra made a strangled sound and turned away. In an instant Isabella was there, teeth bared, her eyes searching for the danger that had alarmed her mistress.

"It's all right, Isabella." Sabra knelt to hug the dog, briefly laying her head on the animal's shoulder. "The only danger is in my head." Or was it her body? Not wanting to search too deep for the answer, she pushed to her feet and continued to the desk to pick up her laptop.

She'd planned to work there, but now her forbidden thoughts wouldn't let her. In the living area, she took a seat in the corner of the sofa and turned on the computer.

Anything for Love came on the screen. The story of a woman trapped by obligation to a man she didn't love, who didn't love her. Would she be tempted by the chance meeting of an old love or remain in a name-only marriage? Was she selfish to want to be happy, knowing her children would suffer emotionally?

Sabra rubbed her temple. She knew what choice she would have made. The same choice her father had made when he'd committed a crime to keep his family safe and happy. But was it the best one? She couldn't fault him for his decision, but she had to wonder if she would have succeeded if her father hadn't always been there to supplement her financially. She hadn't had to worry about losing a job or getting rent or grocery money. Her father always seemed to know when she was running short of funds. She didn't even have to ask.

She'd never know. Juliette, her main character, was another story.

Sabra began typing. Sometimes in life there were no easy answers. She was learning that more and more each day.

THE DOORBELL BROUGHT HER HEAD UP. FEELING the stiffness in her neck and shoulders, Sabra stretched and glanced at her watch. Eleven thirty. Ruth was punctual. But Sabra had gotten a lot done. The story was coming together.

Sabra saved the information, turned off the computer. Standing, she went to answer the door. The welcoming smile wavered, then firmed. "Hello, Pierce."

"Hello, Sabra," he greeted her. "Mama is tied up at the college in a meeting and asked me to pick you up," he said by way of explanation as he stepped into the room.

Sabra closed the door, then went to pick up the scattered items on the sofa to put back into her tote. "I can't imagine what kind of job you have that you can just take off at the drop of a hat."

Pierce scratched Isabella behind the ears. "The kind that you and Sierra need."

Sabra glanced up, then dropped her sunshade case into her large tote and reached for her lipstick. "You're a hairstylist?"

"Hardly. Certified investment consultant."

Sabra's heart lurched. Her fingers tightened on the cylindrical jeweled tube in her hand. With Pierce's help, they might be able to cut down on the amount of research Joy had to do. But the thought of using him to get information didn't set well with Sabra. It was bad enough that she had an ulterior motive for accepting Ruth's invitation.

"Are you all right?"

Sabra glanced up and stared straight into a pair of mesmerizing black eyes that saw too much. If he had any idea what she was up to, there would be hell to pay. The Graysons were very protective and a close-knit family. "Just thinking." Casually she continued putting the spilled contents back into her purse. "I must admit I don't always understand the jargon."

"Some agents try to confuse you on purpose."

Sabra came to her feet and shoved the interwoven gold chain and leather strap over her shoulder. "How long have you worked for your company?"

He opened the front door. Isabella trotted into the hallway. "Nine years."

"You must have a very understanding boss."

"I try to be."

"What?"

"I own the business."

Her eyes widened. "You can't be over thirty."

The easy smile disappeared. "You sound like some of the prospective clients I've met with. Just because I don't have gray hair doesn't mean I don't know what I'm doing."

"No, of course not," she quickly assured him. "Believe me, I know how it feels when your qualifications are questioned. In the beginning, I had to fight for every part. Sometimes they wouldn't even let me read."

Pierce pushed the button on the elevator. "They saw the face, the color of your skin, and didn't look further."

"Exactly."

"You showed them differently. Now you have your pick of roles." The elevator opened, and they stepped into the chrome and glass enclosure. "Your hard work and determination paid off. It was worth the sacrifices and all the doors slammed in your face."

"Yes," she answered because it was what he expected. But since finding her father's papers she had begun to wonder. Perhaps the price had been too high for both of them.

CHAPTER FOUR

PIERCE HAD PLANNED TO DROP SABRA OFF AT THE college auditorium, pick up a sandwich, then return to his office for a working lunch. Instead he found himself several seats back from the stage, watching her for the past thirty minutes. She was easy to watch.

It wasn't just her stunning beauty; it was the sensual way she moved on those long, sexy legs, the glorious body. She was a woman who would capture attention wherever she went.

He now understood Sierra's questioning if Sabra's unique ability to connect with the audience would translate to the movie screen. Pierce was no expert, but he didn't think Sabra had anything to worry about. She had a face a camera would love. She'd own the wide screen just as she did the theater audience.

He wished them luck on the production of *Silken Lies*, but they'd have a tough sell in making the audience believe that the young man playing Max was cold and calculated enough to woo and win Helen,

Sabra's character, with the sole intention of using her to avenge his family. The student looked as if he was ready to bow down and worship at Sabra's feet. She acted as if she didn't notice as she read lines with Helen's "best friend," Debra, who kept looking at her feet instead of Sabra. Pierce was sure talking to her feet wasn't in the script, any more than the young woman's almost constant sneezing.

"Cut," Sabra said. "Are you all right?" she asked the young woman.

"Debra" nodded and kept her gaze trained on her tennis shoes. "Yes, thank you."

"Ginny, what's the matter?" Ruth came out of the wings offstage. "You've been sneezing for the past fifteen minutes."

Her head finally lifted. Tears crested in the brunette's dark eyes. "I'm sorry."

"It's all right," Sabra began, reaching out to comfort the young woman, who sneezed and stepped back. "Do you have allergies?"

"Yes," the young woman confessed, her voice barely above a whisper. "I took my medicine. It'll kick in in a minute. Please let me stay."

"No one is sending you away, Ginny," Ruth said. "What are you allergic to?"

Ginny's gaze flickered to Isabella sitting just offstage to their right. "Dogs."

"But you knew Sabra was bringing her dog with her. I made that clear," Ruth said with the patience she was known for.

Ginny's dark eyes filled again. She sniffed, sneezed. "But I had already gotten the part by then. I thought if I took enough medicine there wouldn't be a problem."

"How much medicine have you taken?" Pierce asked, having gotten out of his seat when Ginny confessed her allergy.

Ginny bit her lip and didn't answer.

"Twice as much as she's supposed to," answered a slim woman wearing a gray St. John's College sweatshirt not far away. "We're roommates."

"I'm sorry, Gin—," Ruth began.

"Please, Ms. Grayson, let me stay," she pleaded, cutting her off. "I can take more medicine. Maybe a shot."

"You want the part that badly?" Sabra asked slowly.

Ginny pressed her hands to the middle of her chest. "To work with you is one chance in a lifetime. One day I want to be on Broadway." She sneezed, then swayed.

Pierce bounded onto the stage and took her arm to steady her. "I think her meds are kicking in."

"Crystal, help her back to the dorm," Ruth said. "We'll break for lunch and return at four for rehearsals this afternoon."

Ginny blinked back tears. "Please don't give my part to someone else."

"We'll discuss it later." Ruth patted the young

woman gently on the shoulder. "Just get some rest. I won't do anything until I speak with you again."

Looking shattered, Ginny allowed Crystal to lead her from the stage in the opposite direction of Isabella. At the bottom of the steps, Ginny looked back one last time, then continued with Crystal out a side door.

"All right. I expect everyone to be on time and back at four," Ruth said.

Talking quietly among themselves, the students filed out of the auditorium.

"You aren't going to replace her, are you?" Sabra asked when the last student had left.

"I might not have a choice," Ruth said slowly. "She can be replaced; you can't."

"I think I have a solution," Pierce said. "Isabella can stay with me at my office."

"No," Sabra said quickly.

"May I ask why?"

A reasonable question and one she might have expected from Pierce, who liked answers. She couldn't very well tell him that he bothered her on a very elemental—all right, sexual—level, and being around him was asking for trouble. There had to be another way of finding the answers she needed. "Isabella likes space."

"I haven't noticed that," he said calmly, his dark gaze never leaving hers. "She usually stays in one area."

"You've only been around her for a day," Sabra reminded him.

"You have a better solution?" Pierce asked.

"I'll think of one," she said tightly. That bulldog tenacity of his was another reason she didn't want to be around him. Unanswered questions bothered Pierce. He wanted everything laid out for his analytical mind to chew on. One slip and he'd start looking for answers that she couldn't allow him to find.

"I advise you to think fast. You have less than four hours. Mama. Sabra." He strolled off, and Sabra wanted to throw something at him.

"Sabra, I know it's your decision to make, but Pierce might be right."

Sabra hated to admit it as well, but she wasn't going to give in that easily. "Let's think about it over lunch."

THREE HOURS LATER SABRA STOOD WITH ISABELLA outside Pierce's corner office on the second floor of their condo building. As with everything in the building, there was a sense of understated elegance in the quiet hallway painted ecru, the plush beige carpet beneath her feet, the richly textured oil paintings on the wall.

He'd done well for himself. She'd expected as much. A man that intelligent, shrewd, and perceptive wouldn't let anyone keep him from reaching the top. She had to admire his accomplishment, but she'd give anything not to be standing outside his door.

As hard as she had tried to come up with an alternate solution, she hadn't been able to. Asking Ginny to step down wasn't an option. Sabra remembered all too well her own dreams of working on Broadway. Taking a deep breath, she entered his outer office.

The room was large and airy, with recessed lighting, impressive artwork, statues and paintings, and buttery soft leather furniture. The room was masculine without being staid or stuffy, and it quietly stated that money invested on Pierce's advice would be in good hands.

"May I help you?" asked the pretty dark-haired woman behind a sleek swirl of glass that somehow didn't overpower her petite status. Perhaps it was because of the warmth in her brown eyes.

"Yes. I'd like to see Pierce Grayson."

"Sabra Raineau?"

"Yes," Sabra answered, wondering how the woman knew she was coming.

The secretary picked up the phone and dialed. "Mr. Grayson, Ms. Raineau is here. Yes, sir." She hung up the phone and sent Sabra another warm smile. "You and Isabella can go on in."

He'd known. It didn't sit well that Pierce was always a step ahead. Usually she was the one a step ahead. Trying to remember that she needed him more than he needed her, she entered the office.

Self-assured as usual, Pierce sat behind the massive cherry desk, the surface in front of him bare except for a folder. To his right was a computer and phone. He wasn't paying attention to any of that. His hot gaze was trained on her. She didn't fidget, but she wanted to. She was used to being looked at, sized up, but with Pierce it was different.

"You were expecting me." It was a statement, not a question.

He folded his elegant long-fingered hands atop the folder. "Isabella isn't a show pet; you care about her. You wouldn't leave her with anyone you weren't sure would take care of her."

It was the truth. She wasn't sure how she felt about a man she'd known only for a short time being able to read her so easily. "Isabella can be difficult as well. She'll let you know if she's not happy."

"That's a good thing." Standing, he came around his desk until he stood in front of Sabra. "Keeps a person from wondering what's on her mind."

The way he was looking warned Sabra he was not talking about her dog but her. He was too close, too overpowering. Time to leave. She unclipped the leash from Isabella's collar. "I appreciate you looking after her. I've already contacted my assistant, and she's looking for a place or a dog sitter. You certainly won't be able to keep her every day."

His gaze never leaving Sabra's, he reached down with one hand and scratched behind Isabella's ears. "We'll cross that bridge when we come to it."

Sabra didn't want to wonder what his hands would feel like on her, but she wasn't able to stop the thought. Would they be gentle, rough, demanding?

Irritated with herself, she held out the leash. "I'll pick her up as soon as I leave rehearsals."

He took the leash. His hand brushed against her, causing her skin to tingle, her body to shiver. "I plan to work late tonight, so we'll be here."

She might have known Pierce worked as hard as he played. "I'll be on my way. A cab is waiting downstairs."

He caught her wrist as she turned away. There was strength in the fingers curled loosely around her forearm, but there was also tenderness. Another zip of awareness went through her. "Why do you smile at everyone except me?"

She lifted a regal brow and fought to keep her breathing even, her pulse from skittering. "I didn't know your ego was so fragile, Pierce."

Tossing the leash on his desk without taking his eyes from her, he took her other arm. The man didn't back down. "My next appointment is an hour away."

"You'll be in the emergency room by then if I sic Isabella on you."

The grin was slow and infuriating. "That desperate, are you?"

She was, and it only increased her irritation and need to leave. "Ruth isn't going to be happy if I'm late."

"So tell me what I want to know."

Sabra realized she'd handled Pierce all wrong. A man who looked as mouthwatering as he did probably hadn't been turned down for a date in years.

Refusing to go out with him would just make him more determined. "We've already had this conversation."

He stepped closer. She smelled the tangy aftershave, felt the heat from his muscled body. It was all she could do not to move closer, to whimper in surrender. "Refresh my memory."

She took a shallow breath and hoped her voice sounded bored rather than hot and getting hotter when she spoke. "Casual dating can be fun if both parties understand that's all there ever will be. Otherwise things get complicated and nasty."

"Point taken under advisement. How about a movie tonight?"

She should have suspected he'd keep pushing. "Dogs aren't allowed in movie theaters."

"We won't have to worry about that pesky detail, since we'll be at my place," he said easily. "We'll have dinner first. Prime rib, rare. Seven all right?"

"Make it seven fifteen."

They both knew changing the time was her way of taking control, but there was something in Pierce's eyes that made her think perhaps she should have kept running. "Seven fifteen, then. You can leave Isabella with me until then." He rounded the desk and took a seat. "Have a good rehearsal."

"Thank you." His easy dismissal annoyed her, and her pulse had yet to settle. Sabra went downstairs to catch the taxi, very much aware that she might have made a strategical error. Pierce was a man who took opportunity wherever he found it. Tonight at his place it could be two people becoming better acquainted or two people getting hot and heavy.

She chastised herself as her breath hitched on thinking about them locked in a heated embrace, his tempting mouth taking hers. She'd just have to chance it. Pierce she could handle; it was her own emotions that might trip her up.

PIERCE HAD ALWAYS COUNTED HIMSELF FORTUNATE that he had a brother who loved to cook and cooked well. But opening his door that evening and seeing Faith behind Brandon, he wasn't so sure.

"Hello, Pierce," Faith greeted him. "I hope you don't mind my coming. I was at the restaurant when you called."

"Of course he doesn't." Brandon entered carrying two large-handled take-out bags high above Isabella's head. The dog matched him step for step to the kitchen. "I guess I don't have to ask who your dinner guest is."

"Don't tease, Brandon," Faith said, and smiled. "I think it's sweet."

Brandon chuckled and Pierce wanted to deck him. "It's just dinner."

"Of course." Faith lifted the handled bag. "I wasn't sure what you had on hand to set the table, so I brought a few things."

Pierce almost blurted he hadn't thought that far

and frowned instead. He didn't do impulsive. He always thought things through. At least he had until Sabra. "We could eat on the stoneware."

"You could use your everyday dishes, but the lovely china your mother gave all of her children when they moved into their first homes would look nicer," Faith said. "If you don't mind, it won't take but a second."

Faith enjoyed taking care of people as much as Brandon enjoyed cooking for them. They made an unbeatable pair. "I'd appreciate it, and I'm sure she would, too." Pierce took the bag and went to the round oak dining table.

"The meal I prepared deserves the best presentation," Brandon called from the kitchen. Isabella's excited barks followed.

Pierce winked at Faith and straightened the red hand-stitched table runner. "How do you stand his ego?"

"Because she loves me and knows it's not brag, just facts." The refrigerator door closed and Brandon joined them. "Pierce has decent stemware, but it's a good thing you brought serving dishes."

"Brandon, you were no better before Faith did you the honor of taking you and the disaster you called an apartment in hand." Pierce placed the white dinnerware edged with red on the scalloped wooden charger.

"And I thank her for it every day." Brandon kissed Faith on the lips. She gazed up at him as if he'd hung the moon.

Pierce just stared at them. Like his two older brothers and their wives, Brandon and Faith couldn't seem to keep their hands or lips off each other. They made it a point, no matter what was going on, to always start the day together and eat lunch or dinner together. They were determined to keep the magic.

Faith, her pretty face shining with love, leaned easily into Brandon. "Loving Brandon is what I do best."

"Honey." Brandon's voice trembled as his arm tightened.

Pierce might not want to take the fall, but it was nice knowing his older brothers had found amazing women who loved them back with the same unconditional love that Pierce had no doubt would last a lifetime.

Pierce felt something brush his leg and looked down at Isabella. The dog grinned up at him with a satisfied smirk. "So Brandon fed you, huh?"

The dog barked and licked her muzzle. Everyone laughed.

Pierce placed his hand on the dog's head. "Thanks for everything, both of you."

"You're welcome," Faith and Brandon said. Their arms still around each other, they went to the door.

Pierce opened the door. "I'll return everything tomorrow."

"No hurry. There might be an occasion to use them again," Faith said with an impish grin.

"If so, you better not let Sierra find out."

"And exactly what am I not supposed to find out?"

All three turned to see Sierra, her arms folded, her onyx eyes narrowed. "I'm waiting."

"You're on your own, Bro. Bye, Sierra." With Faith in tow, Brandon walked toward the elevator.

"Bye, Pierce. Bye, Sierra," Faith called as her husband hurried her down the corridor.

Sierra stepped inside the apartment and closed the door. Her gaze stopped on the beautifully set table. She arched a brow at Pierce and went to the table. "I guess she finally said yes."

"It's just dinner."

"Uh-huh." Sierra nodded toward the dog. "And keeping her pet would be what?"

Pierce didn't like explaining himself, but neither did he want Sierra to get the wrong impression. His little sister had a way of making her displeasure known in a way that truly ticked a person off. "One of the students in the play is allergic to dogs, so I'm keeping Isabella."

"Of course there were no other options?"

"Not on such short notice. Isabella can be temperamental. Sabra's assistant is looking into something for tomorrow."

"But of course you told her there was no hurry."

He frowned. "You're getting spookier day by day."

"Men are just becoming easier to read." Sierra turned toward the kitchen.

Pierce knew it was disloyal, but he almost wished

there was a man out there whom his little sister couldn't figure out so easily, but with that thought came another. If any man messed with her, he was dead meat.

With her nose for food, Sierra found the dinner in the refrigerator. It hadn't been difficult. His refrigerator was bare except for milk and juice. "I was going to ask you if you wanted to eat dinner to celebrate."

"The Castle estate?"

She smiled over her shoulder. "At the inflated asking price. I knew if I held on to the property long enough, it would quadruple in value. Before the end of the year, I'll be ready to open my own brokerage firm in a showcase of an office."

Pierce playfully tugged her bone-straight unbound hair that reached to her tiny waist. "My sister, the real estate tycoon."

"You better believe it."

"We'll celebrate at lunch tomorrow. The whole family," he promised; then, knowing his sister's love of sweets and feeling a bit guilty, he reached inside the refrigerator and picked up the container marked "Dessert." "In the meantime. Triple fudge cake."

"What will you have for dessert?" she asked.

"Take it," he said, pushing the box closer.

"No. It was enough that you offered." Taking the box, she returned it to the refrigerator. "What time is she coming?"

"Seven fifteen."

Sierra glanced at her watch faced with diamonds.

"Thirty minutes. You do remember how to warm things up, right?"

He smiled down at her teasing face. "You know we can nuke with the best of them."

"That we can." She went to the front door. "This is the first time you've invited a woman to dinner at your place."

"Because of Isabella," he answered quickly. Too quickly.

"People tell themselves what they want to hear," Sierra told him, and opened the door.

"This time it's the truth." He certainly hoped it was.

"Just remember, we're the only two left."

"That thought is never far from my mind," he confessed. "There'll be two standing when she leaves."

Sierra nodded. "I certainly hope so. Night, Pierce."

"Night, Sierra, and congratulations again." Pierce stood in the doorway until she got on the elevator. Sierra didn't have anything to worry about. He wanted to get to know Sabra better, and as with the women before her, when it was over he'd walk away and not look back.

THE DOORBELL RANG AT SEVEN FIFTEEN JUST AS Pierce placed their plates of food on the chargers. In the middle of the table was a floral arrangement of poppies. Compliments of Faith. The flowers had arrived only minutes earlier.

"You think she'll like the table?"

Isabella barked. "Well, we're about to see if you're right. Your mistress is a hard woman to get to know." Pierce went to the front door and opened it.

Sabra, in a flared floral sundress with spaghetti straps, had him clenching the doorknob. He wondered if there would ever be a time that she didn't move him. Probably not. "Hello. You're right on time."

"Hello, Pierce." Sabra knelt gracefully to hug Isabella, who barked happily. "I missed you, too." Still smiling, Sabra looked up with her slim arm still around the animal's neck. "I hope she wasn't too much trouble."

"She wasn't." Pierce closed the door, then extended his hand. After a moment, Sabra placed her hand in his and he pulled her to her feet. Her hand was soft and delicate. He knew she would be that way all over. His mouth dried. "How were rehearsals?"

"Ginny didn't sneeze anymore," Sabra told him.

Still holding her hand, he tugged her with him to the kitchen. "What's the rest of it?"

"The cast does great in their scenes or when I'm directing them, but when I come onstage they freeze," she told him, wondering why she found it so easy to talk to him at times. She decided it was because he listened well and appeared genuinely interested.

"Understandable." After washing his hands over the kitchen sink, he pulled the loaf of yeast bread out of the oven. "It will wear off soon enough."

Sabra washed her hands and accepted the paper towels Pierce handed her. "That's what Ruth and I think. To help things along, she's having a get-together at her house Friday night."

"Mama knows her students." Pierce seated Sabra at the dining table across from his place setting, then returned to the kitchen for the bread, vegetables, and salads. "You're going to have a hit on your hands; don't worry."

She picked up her napkin and placed it in her lap. "How do you know? You've only heard one song and a few lines of dialogue."

Pierce took the food from the serving tray. "My mother believes in you, and from what I've heard, you have a knack for picking scripts that are winners." Taking his seat, he bowed his head, blessed their food, then served her wine.

"Picking out a script is much different from writing one," she said softly, silently admitting the fear that, no matter how hard she tried, she couldn't push away for long.

"True. But what does your gut tell you?" He put ground pepper on his salad, then hers.

"I'm not sure," she confessed, aimlessly moving her salad greens around on her plate.

"You might not want to hear this, but it's too late to turn back now. All you can do is forge ahead and have faith in yourself, the students, and Mama." He picked up his fork. "Don't let a few bumps make you doubt yourself."

She straightened. "I'm not afraid. I'm just . . ." She searched for the right word. "Concerned. Surely, in your business, you've felt the same way."

"Sometimes on a daily basis," he told her with a smile. "But it's a family tradition that giving up is not an option. You go down fighting for what you believe."

Sabra thought of her father. He would have gone to any lengths to ensure the welfare of his family, no matter the cost. No matter what, she couldn't condemn him for doing what he believed. "My father was of the same sentiment."

"You're lucky. I was very young when my father died. I don't remember much about him, except the laughter and being held high in the air."

She didn't have to think long to know that, despite everything, her father had given her so much. He'd believed in her and loved her. "One of my oldest memories is of us having tea together in the garden, and my father delicately balancing the tiny cup in his large hands."

"What do you think he'd have to say about your play?"

" 'You can do it, Sabra. Don't let anyone tell you differently,' " she murmured softly. "He told me that when I left for New York, and every time things weren't going well and I'd call."

"And for the first time, he's not here to cheer you on," Pierce said gently.

Sabra realized why this time was so difficult for

her. Her father had understood her better than anyone. Things weren't clear-cut with him gone. "My mother loves me, and I believe she is proud of me, but she's more practical. She has never been one to live in the moment." Sabra's hands flexed. "Daddy believed in going all out for what you wanted. The payoff was worth the risk. He was my biggest fan."

Pierce reached across the table and placed his hand on hers. "If you'll let us, you'll have a new cheering squad."

Warmth she had told herself she wouldn't feel coursed through her. Pierce easily slipped through her plans to keep him at a distance. She even understood that as well. Like her father, she was by nature outgoing and friendly. It took more effort to keep people at a distance than to accept and enjoy them. That "flaw" had once caused her more pain and heartache than she thought she could stand.

"Sabra?"

Pierce's deep, compelling voice drew her out of the past. She stared into his dark eyes. What could getting to know each other better hurt? Obviously, they were going to see a lot of each other. Any discord or tension would make it difficult for his mother and for them. It would make more sense if they were amicable to each other. She knew how to handle men. "I'd like that."

"Good." He squeezed her hand.

She drew her hand back, determined not to worry about the tingling sensation that radiated up her arm, and began to eat instead of playing with her palm salad. She discovered she was hungry and the food wonderful. "Delicious."

"Glad you like it."

"How did the day go?"

"Fine. I gained two new clients, and three more who came in for their annual review were very pleased with their investment growth."

"They didn't mind Isabella?"

Pierce smiled. "They probably didn't notice her. She likes to sleep in the corner by the bookcase and sofa."

Finished with her salad, Sabra cut into her prime rib and took a bite. "Your brother's or your sister-in-law's restaurant?"

Pierce's lip twitched. "I guess no pots or pans on the stove gave me away."

She ate another bite of her rare prime rib before answering. "With food that tastes this good, why cook?"

"Exactly what I've always thought." Pierce cut into his meat. "Why Broadway?"

"My dad again. He loved the movies and every Saturday off he and I would go. I dreamed of being onstage, and actually did my first neighborhood production of *Snow White and the Seven Dwarfs* when I was seven." She smiled at the memory and sipped her wine. "I used to perform for the family. I always said that one day I'd be onstage."

"And you are."

"Easy, pizzy. As I said before, It took six years, countless casting calls, and trying to run down every lead my agent sent me on before I was declared an overnight sensation. That was three years ago." There was no bitterness in her voice. "I was one of the lucky ones."

"Sounds as if you know a lot about hard work and not giving up." He topped off her wine. "I understand better why you purchased the bag, although it was still an unwise buy."

"Haven't you ever done anything because it felt good?" she asked, staring at him over her steepled fingertips, her wine forgotten.

"Yes. Having dinner with you."

Sabra sat up in her seat. She believed him. Honest to a fault, Pierce was a man of many talents. She'd arrived full of self-doubts, and he'd helped her banish them. If she wasn't careful, she might find herself wondering where the attraction both were dancing around would lead, but she didn't have affairs. "Good friends, remember."

"I certainly hope so," Pierce said.

"Why investment?" she asked, finding she really was interested in the answer, and not just to help her learn the identity of the man her father had business dealings with eight years ago.

"I majored in math in college. One of my assignments was to prepare a stock portfolio with actual stocks." He polished off his beef. "The assignment challenged my mind. The stocks I picked did well.

By the time I graduated with a master's in math, I knew what I wanted."

"How long ago was that?" she asked.

"Almost ten years." He sipped his tea. "How about you?"

"I only obtained an associate degree in liberal arts to satisfy my mother, I'm afraid, then I was off to New York," she told him, feeling better that she could scratch Pierce off the list. It would be next to impossible for him to have amassed clients with disposable income of over two hundred thousand dollars in that short period of time. "I talked her into letting me have two years to prove myself and if I didn't succeed, I'd come home."

"Savannah."

"Yes, but in two years I had begun to get small parts. Together, my dad and I were able to talk her into letting me stay. You know the rest."

"Your father's faith in you and you in yourself was vindicated," he said.

"Yes." She might have known he'd understand it was more than seeing her name in lights, the big contracts. "Just like your family's faith in you."

"We succeeded." Pierce lifted his glass in a toast.

"That we did." Sabra touched her glass to his.

Pierce kept his eyes on Sabra as he sipped, and wondered if he would be successful with her. "If you're finished, we can go look at the movies I rented."

Sabra came to her feet and picked up her plate and his. "I'll help you clean this up first."

"Bless you." Pierce picked up the serving dishes. "I detest washing dishes."

She lifted a brow. "I was planning on letting the dishwasher do that."

He grinned. "You read my mind." Working together, they cleared the table and loaded the dishwasher.

Finished, they went to the living area. Sabra stopped abruptly. In front of the black-lacquered entertainment center was a stack of movies at least ten inches high and as wide.

"I couldn't decide." He picked up *Mr. & Mrs. Smith*, *Hitch*, *Deliver Us from Eva,* and *Die Another Day*. "Some movies can get a bit racy. I didn't want you to get the wrong impression."

An unsure Pierce was endearing and one she probably wouldn't see too often. "How about *Chicago*?"

"Works for me." Taking the case, he inserted the DVD into the player. "Make yourself comfortable. Take off your shoes if you'd like."

Pierce sat beside her and toed off his Italian loafers; Sabra slipped off her sling-back pumps and tucked her feet under her. Isabella plopped down at their feet. Pierce casually placed his arm on the back of the sofa. *Harmless,* she told herself, but as the movie played she wasn't so sure. She couldn't concentrate.

She kept expecting Pierce's fingers to touch her bare skin, trail through her unbound hair, curve around her shoulders. Nothing happened, but that didn't stop her body from wanting to feel his touch, his lips. When the movie ended, she was up like a shot.

"Thank you, Pierce; I should be getting home. It's late."

"I'll get Isabella's leash and walk you." He picked up her heels by the back straps.

She opened her mouth to refuse, then closed it. Pierce was old-fashioned enough to want to see his date home. It wouldn't matter if "home" was twenty feet away.

"All right."

"Let me help you with these." He crouched before her, a shoe in one hand, his other waiting, palm up.

It seemed innocent enough until she extended her foot and his hand curved around her ankle. She began to tremble. She pressed her hand against his shoulder for support, felt the flex of his muscles as he slipped her shoes on, the gentle strength of his hands.

He looked up at her, and she experienced the slow curl of desire and clenched her hands. Letting Pierce touch her was a bad, bad idea. She almost sagged in relief when he finished. But then he pushed to his feet. Their bodies were inches apart, the sexual pull almost irresistible.

He stared at her a long time, then turned away to retrieve the leash and came back to take her arm. "Ready?"

She was more than ready, but that wasn't what he

meant. Or was it? Unable to speak, she nodded. After opening his door, he walked her to her apartment. "Thanks for sharing dinner with me."

"Thank you and the chef," she managed. She unlocked the door and turned, nervous, unsure if he might try to kiss her, and even more unsure of her response.

"I have a breakfast and dinner appointment, but my secretary has already said Isabella could stay with her," Pierce said.

"I'd appreciate your help. My assistant is working on an alternative."

"Don't worry about Isabella or the play." The backs of his knuckles lightly stroked her cheek. "Night."

"Good night." Sabra went inside her apartment. As the door closed, her fingertips gently touched her cheek. Pierce had taken her at her word and was keeping their relationship on a friendly basis. It was what she'd asked for, what she thought she wanted.

Wasn't it?

CHAPTER FIVE

PIERCE STEPPED INTO THE SHOWER AND TURNED IT on full blast. He sucked in his breath as the cold water hit him square in his chest, but it did nothing to ease the ache in his groin. He shouldn't have touched her. He almost laughed.

Who would have thought Pierce Grayson would be turned on by touching a woman's ankle? So small, delicate, he'd wanted to slide his hand upward to . . .

Pierce hissed out a breath, then pressed his hands against the black tiled wall. Thoughts like that were what got him into his current predicament. With another woman, he might have given in to the need pulsating through him. He'd changed no to yes in the past. He knew that was the way many women played the game at which he considered himself somewhat of a master.

The look in Sabra's eyes had stopped him.

She'd stared down at him with uncertainty in her

chocolate brown eyes. There was desire there as well. He'd known that when he'd felt her tremble at his touch, heard the hiss of her breath when his hand circled her ankle. He could have built on that.

He couldn't, hadn't wanted to. When they finally made love, and they would, she would be with him all the way.

The ringing of the telephone finally penetrated through the fog of desire and the rushing water. Shutting the faucet off, he opened the door, snagging two towels from the warming rack. Wrapping one around his lean hips, he rubbed the other through his hair as he picked up the wall phone in the oversized bathroom. "Hello."

"That's a relief."

"Sierra." Pierce's hand paused.

"You sound as grumpy as Brandon used to in the morning."

"Your call could have come at a most inopportune moment," he said with a hint of annoyance.

"Not your style on first dates."

Pierce felt his face heat. "Sierra—"

"Before you go all big brother on me, I wanted to let you know that I won't be able to break away for lunch until around one."

"You couldn't have called in the morning?"

"Yes, but I'll sleep better now. Mama knows all of us. You've dated so many women that it will take one very special, even unique, woman to get you."

Sabra instantly leaped into Pierce's mind. Beautiful, exotic, the stuff of man's most secret fantasies. "I think you're stretching it a bit."

"Women come and go in your life like a revolving door. If possible, you've dated more since Mama started on her quest to marry us all off. Storing up memories, you said." Sierra snorted. "You should have enough for two lifetimes."

"I like women," he said by way of explaining himself.

"I think we've already established that fact. Did Mama happen to mention when she invited Sabra?" Sierra asked.

"No."

"I could be way off here. Sabra has a lot of demands without the complications of adding a man to the mix."

"Some complications are worth it," Pierce said, recalling the softness of Sabra's skin, the jasmine scent that teased and beckoned.

"Is marriage one of them?"

Pierce muttered beneath his breath.

"Sorry. I guess this is making me a bit tense."

"I must have water in my ears. You're fearless. That's why we all hated to babysit you."

"After Brandon fell in love, I finally realized something: you can't control how your heart feels, and that makes this dicey."

Sierra had always been able to see the big picture. None of them, least of all Brandon, had thought he'd fall in love with his best friend's little sister, a woman he'd teased and bantered with most of his life. "I'm attracted to her, but I'm not falling in love," Pierce said.

"For some reason, I'd feel better if you'd said her name," Sierra said. "I can't believe I'm saying this, but if it happens—"

"It won't." He shot the towel he'd been drying his hair with into the open stainless-steel hamper.

"If it does," she continued as if he hadn't interrupted her. "As long as you're as happy as the rest, I guess I can live with it."

"Don't reserve the church yet. We haven't even kissed." Pierce meant the words as teasing, but as the silence grew he knew some of the pent-up sexual frustration must have slipped into his tone.

"I'm not sure if that's good or bad. Night, Pierce. See you at the Red Cactus at one sharp."

"Night, Sierra." Pierce hung up the phone, pulled the towel from his waist, and noticed he remained semiaroused. Sabra definitely could be a problem if he let her. He wouldn't allow that to happen. He wasn't a one-woman man. She was just different, a challenge. Once she was in his arms and in his bed, he'd stop thinking about her all the time.

In the meantime, he walked back into the shower stall and turned the cold water on full blast.

SIERRA AWOKE A LITTLE AFTER SEVEN THE NEXT morning after a good night's sleep. As she'd told Pierce, she'd come to the very logical conclusion that she couldn't control what happened with him and Sabra or any other woman. However, she could and would make double damn sure that no man complicated her life. And despite what Pierce said, for her it would be a complication.

Dressed in one of her favorite power suits, a Dior black houndstooth that she accessorized with the lustrous double strand of pearls with a diamond clasp her mother had given her when she graduated from high school, she opened her stainless-steel refrigerator to find it as bare as it had been yesterday morning.

She'd been on the run most of yesterday and forgotten to pick up juice and milk, which proved her point. She only had to satisfy herself. Not some man who wanted to run her life.

She was doing a fabulous job of taking care of herself, all by herself, thank you very much. Closing the door, she reached for her calfskin handbag that was free of a designer label on the outside, but aficionados would instantly recognize it as a Manolo Blahnik. The black double-strap shoulder bag with pocket and belt details had set her back two thousand dollars on sale, but it had been worth every penny. A man wouldn't understand the purchase.

Even Pierce and Morgan, who spent thousands on a suit, thought it wasteful on a handbag. They didn't understand how wonderful it was to be impractical at times, giving her the little *umph* in her step when she knew she looked great. Plus, she could afford it.

In minutes she was out the door and in her

Mercedes ATV, heading for Casa de Serenidad and breakfast. Perhaps she'd see Faith and Brandon, the two turtledoves. Their feet hadn't touched the ground since they announced their engagement. Sierra doubted they ever would.

Sierra's manicured fingers tapped impatiently on the steering wheel at the slow-moving traffic. She'd only had a bag of popcorn to eat the night before. She put on her signal to change lanes, then checked in her rearview mirror and caught a glimpse of a woman with long curly black hair and a big dog coming out of a storefront.

Sabra, and she didn't look happy.

Instead of moving into the next lane, Sierra cut across two lanes, receiving rude finger gestures and hooked horns. She waved her hand in apology. Sabra was her mother's guest. It would be rude not to see if there was anything she could do to help. Then, too, she could get a better feel for what was going on between Sabra and Pierce.

Not seeing a parking space with a meter, Sierra swung into a no-parking zone. She personally knew the police chief, but Dakota didn't bend the law for anyone. He'd chew her out, then write her a ticket, if he caught her illegally parked. She didn't plan on letting him catch her.

Her stiletto sandals clicked loudly on the sidewalk as she ran the forty feet or so to where Sabra still stood. "Good morning. Problems?"

Startled, Sabra swung around, her eyes wide, her

curly black hair tumbling around her shoulders. Sierra could see how a man, even a practical one like Pierce, might find it difficult to resist such a woman. She wore a sleeveless coral sweater that complemented her skin tone and coffee-colored ankle-length pants. On her feet were a darling pair of Bruno Magli coffee and coral heeled sandals.

"Sierra. Good morning." Sabra shoved her wind-tossed hair out of her face. "Isabella is being obstinate this morning."

Sierra glanced at the storefront they had just come out of, Maxine's Dog Grooming. "Hero doesn't like baths, either."

"The hybrid wolf. Your sister-in-law's pet?"

"Pierce tell you about him?" Sierra asked. Hybrid wolves' lives were tenuous at best. They could be euthanized if they bit a human. They weren't considered easily domesticated. Because of this, the family didn't talk about Hero. Not even their closest friends knew Catherine kept Hero at her and Luke's mountain cabin.

"Only that the pet would like to meet Isabella," Sabra answered.

The way Sabra's chin lifted, Sierra didn't think it would happen in this or any other lifetime. Out of the corner of her eye, she saw a patrol car. "Can I give you a lift? But it has to be in a hurry; I'm in a no-parking zone."

Sabra glanced at Isabella. "I might as well. Today has been a washout."

"Come on." Sierra took off at a brisk pace with Sabra and Isabella right with her.

"There's another grooming store on my list, but after three I don't think a fourth will help."

Sierra was half-listening. The police car, red lights flashing, had stopped beside her Mercedes. Sierra rounded the hood just as the patrolman got out of his car. Sierra breathed a little easier at seeing Jimmy, a longtime friend and easygoing deputy. "Morning, Jimmy. Moving it now. I stopped to pick up a guest of Mama's, Sabra Raineau."

"Hello, Jimmy." Sabra waved, flashed a big smile, then opened the back door for Isabella. "Sorry. Sierra saved my life."

Jimmy's jaw came unhinged and he just stared. Sierra didn't wait. She started the engine, saw a small opening, and took it, earning her more displeasure from motorists. "Thanks for the assist." Smiling, she glanced in her window as she turned the corner. "Hopefully, Jimmy has snapped out of it by now."

"You're as unique as your brother, and as warm as your mother."

Sierra whipped her head back around to see Sabra staring at her. Sierra wanted to do some staring herself. She'd never heard any woman call Pierce unique.

"I hope you don't get the wrong impression, but it's liberating to be around a woman with as much self-confidence as you, your mother, and Faith have."

The pieces clicked together. "If I can't trust a man, I don't want him. And no offense, but if all he's looking for is a face to stop traffic, so to speak, he's not worth my time."

Sabra held her hand out, palm up. Sierra slapped it with her open palm and both women laughed. "People here are used to you. In another city, you'd do your fair share of traffic stopping."

"Only if they'd want to buy real estate." Sierra pulled up to the curb in front of the condo and kept the motor running. Sabra wasn't just a pretty face. "If you haven't eaten, care to join me for breakfast?"

"Thanks. I'd love to." Sabra turned in the seat as Sierra pulled off. "And you won't get any after the way you acted," she told the dog.

Isabella put her muzzle on the seat, her expression one of contrition.

"What did she do?" Sierra pulled under the portico of the hotel. Valets rushed to open the doors.

"Kept growling at the attendants." Sabra picked up the leash as Isabella hopped to the ground.

Sierra studied the dog's benign expression. "She looks harmless."

"Ha." The women fell into step together, unaware of open stares as they passed through the lobby. "Her pedigree goes back a hundred years. She was the runt of the litter and thought unfit, but I wanted her for that reason."

"You didn't fit in, either, I take it," Sierra guessed.

"Hardly. I didn't always look like this. Five years of braces, ballet classes, piano lessons. I was the geek who didn't fit until I turned sixteen and the body started to change." Sabra's voice lowered as they stopped a few feet behind a couple waiting in line for breakfast. "As I told Pierce, it took six years to get the role that started my career."

"Last night during dinner?"

"Yes," Sabra said, leaning down to pet Isabella.

Sierra caught the hint of color that bloomed in Sierra's cheeks. Pierce was dating a woman who blushed. Interesting.

Sabra straightened. "No one in your family seems to have any trouble around Isabella."

"We have a special affinity with animals," Sierra told her. "It's a gift and part of our heritage as Muscogee Creek Native Americans."

"You were also gifted with striking looks."

"Should I tell Pierce?" Sierra asked to find out if she'd see the hint of color again. She did, but Sabra's chin lifted. Pierce might have accepted the attraction, but Sabra was of a different mind.

"I'd rather you didn't. Too many women have probably told him that already."

Sierra's eyebrow lifted. Was there a twinge of jealously in that terse statement?

"Good morning, Sierra, miss," Phillip greeted them. "Will Pierce be joining you ladies?"

Sierra smiled at the elderly man. "Good morning, Phillip. Not this time."

"Your favorite table is available." He plucked two oversized menus from the podium. "Follow me please." He stopped at a table for four near a spewing fountain and pulled out first Sierra's, then Sabra's chairs and handed them the menus. "Enjoy your breakfast."

Sierra knew the menu by heart. She placed her handbag in one of the empty seats. What she didn't know was Sabra's true feelings for Pierce. Women, rightly so, were more complicated than men. "I dropped by Pierce's apartment last night just before he was expecting you for dinner."

"The food was delicious. Brandon is a fabulous cook." Sabra lifted the menu.

There was one way of getting her to stop hiding. "How is the play coming?"

As expected, the menu lowered. Twin lines furrowed Sabra's brow. "We're getting there."

A waiter appeared with a glass of orange juice, water, and a steaming coffeepot. "Good morning, Sierra. I took the liberty of bringing you your usual." He turned to Sabra. "Would you like coffee?"

"Please?"

"And for breakfast? The crepes are delicious this morning."

"You talked me into it, with French toast, pan sausages, fried potatoes, strawberry jam, and orange juice."

"I'll have the same," Sierra told him.

The waiter's olive-colored face broke into a wide

grin as he took their menus and tucked them under his arm. "It's good to see women with robust appetites. I'll have your food out shortly."

When the waiter moved away, Sierra asked, "What do you plan to do about Isabella?"

"I'm not sure." Sabra glanced down at the dog, who grinned up at her. Sabra's frown quickly turned into a fond smile. "I can't board her because she hasn't had her Bordetella shots, and I must admit I wouldn't want her caged every day. I'll have to take her into the shower and bathe her myself."

"Luke and Catherine are dripping wet when they finish bathing Hero." Sierra sipped her juice.

"Isabella hates taking a bath as well. All I can say is that I'm glad the bathroom is spacious and tiled." Sabra folded her arms on the table. "While Pierce is out with appointments, his secretary will keep Isabella. They're both lifesavers."

Sierra mulled over the new information. Pierce seldom talked business with women he dated, and he'd never kept anyone's pet before. "He's never too busy for friends."

Something flickered across the other woman's face; then it was quickly gone. "So I'm finding out."

The waiter returned with their food and served them. "Ladies, is there anything else?"

Both women shook their heads. "Enjoy." He withdrew and stopped at the table next to them.

Sierra blessed their food, then picked up her fork.

"I take it you found he likes order and everything spelled out."

Sabra picked up her fork. "Has he always been that way?"

"Always. But in his business, it's been an asset." Sierra cut into her French toast.

The frown that came on Sabra's face stayed this time. "I never would have guessed he owns his own investment firm at such a young age."

"All of my brothers own their own business. Luke is a private investigator, Morgan a lawyer." There was pride in Sierra's voice that she didn't even try to hide.

"He said giving up wasn't in his family. What an understatement." Sabra sipped her coffee. "Any other woman besides Ruth would have been broadcasting the fact."

A frown darted across Sierra's brow. "She usually does."

Sabra bit into her crepe. "I didn't even know she had children until Pierce picked me up."

Sierra's attention peaked. If you were around her mother longer than ten minutes, you knew about her children, especially the married ones.

"How is the prettiest realtor in the country?" boomed a loud voice.

Sierra went still, then glanced up to see a jarring reminder of why she didn't want a man in her life.

CHAPTER SIX

"I DIDN'T EXPECT TO SEE YOU UNTIL AFTER LUNCH to sign the papers," Sierra said, hoping against hope that Mitchell Shuler would take the hint and leave.

He grinned instead. "I called your office, and one of the realtors said I might find you having breakfast." He pulled out a chair next to Sierra and scooted it closer. "Guess my luck is still holding." His grin was just short of a leer when he looked at Sabra. "Sitting with two beautiful women."

Sierra reluctantly introduced Sabra, remembering all too well her comment about not having to like people to work with them. Famous last words.

"Sabra Raineau, the Broadway actress." His large hand closed around Sabra's and held on. "Thought I recognized you. I'm not much for plays, but some of my business associates like that kind of thing."

"I'm sure," Sabra said blandly. "I'd like my hand back."

He laughed as if she'd said the funniest thing in the world. "I like sassy women." He turned so his body edged closer to Sierra's. "I thought we could go someplace and get better acquainted without that other realtor guy being in the way."

Subtlety was not his forte. So she'd be just as blunt. "I'm busy, as you can see."

The jovial smile disappeared. "You're not very friendly after the sale."

Sierra's temper spiked. "You purchased a piece of property. Not me."

His dark eyes narrowed. "Maybe I've changed my mind about that as well."

Sierra didn't even have to think. "Your deposit will be returned by registered mail as soon as I can get back to my office."

His head snapped back. "You can't brush me off like I'm a nobody."

"I just did."

"You—"

"If the property is available, I'd like to see it," Sabra said.

"It is." Sierra caught on quickly. Sabra was smart and had hit where Shuler would feel it the most. His ego. "Will one this afternoon be all right?"

"Perfect."

Shuler bristled. "Wait a minute. I didn't say I didn't want the property, just that I don't want it from you."

"That might be difficult, since I'm the exclusive realtor and own the property. Good-bye." Sierra turned away.

"No one flips me off." His large hand clamped around her upper forearm.

Sierra slowly looked at him, her eyes simmering with anger. "Take your hand off me."

His laugh was nasty and loud. "Like I'm scare—" His words ended on a yelp of pain as Sierra twisted his thumb back. He fell out of the chair, landing on one knee yelling in pain.

Growling, Isabella came to her feet and started for Shuler. Sabra grabbed her leash, but from the rage on Sabra's face she was clearly considering letting the dog go.

"Hold her," Sierra ordered.

"Sierr—"

"No," Sierra interrupted. "I know what I'm doing." Releasing Shuler's hand, she stood, her legs braced, her voice and eyes as sharp as icicles and as cold. "Don't ever touch me again."

Staring at her with fury in his eyes, he came slowly to his feet. "You just made the biggest mistake of your life."

"Not me, you," Sierra told him. Her hands came up, flexed at the wrists.

"Why don't we just see."

"Stop!"

Sierra recognized Faith's frantic voice but kept her gaze on Shuler. She didn't have a doubt he'd attack if she turned her back on him. She stepped out of her heels and stayed ready. Faith didn't know a thing about self-defense.

"I'm Faith Grayson, executive manager. My family owns this hotel." Faith insinuated herself between Sierra and the angry man. "You're causing a disturbance. Please leave."

"I could give a rat's behind about who you are or what anyone wants. I'm not going anyplace until she pays."

Sierra nudged her sister-in-law aside. "Stay out of it, Faith. I can handle this."

"I'm well aware of that. I just don't want the hassle of doing the paperwork when he ends up in the hospital. My lawyers hate that sort of thing."

"Sierra's hotshot attorney brother won't mind." Gripping Isabella's leash, Sabra rounded the table. "He'd probably be thrilled. After he took you apart, Shuler. That is, if Sierra's other three brothers left anything."

Shuler's eyes narrowed. "You threatening me?"

"Just giving you a friendly piece of advice. You probably didn't pay any attention to Faith's last name when she introduced herself, but she's married to Sierra's brother." Sabra stopped beside Sierra. "The two brothers I've seen are six feet plus and have hard muscles and bad attitudes when upset. And they love their little sister. You know how protective older brothers can be."

Uneasiness flickered in the man's eyes. "I haven't done anything to her."

"When you mess with one Grayson, you mess with them all," Sierra said.

"I'm married to one," Faith said.

"I'm dating one," Sabra added.

"Leave," Sierra told him. "My breakfast is getting cold."

"You—"

"Say it." Sierra stepped closer. "Make my day."

Faith took her cell phone out of her jacket pocket. "I guess I better call for an ambulance."

"We tried to warn him," Sabra said, shaking her head. "I hope you don't have any plans that can't be postponed while you're recovering."

"You're all crazy." He turned and stopped abruptly.

Two security guards pushed their way through several male employees who stood a few feet behind the women. The men didn't stop until they had insinuated themselves in front of the women. Neither smiled. Neither had an ounce of fat on his six-foot frame.

"Emmit and Conrad, please escort this gentleman out of the hotel, and make sure the staff is made aware that he is not to return," Faith instructed.

The men in plainclothes stepped forward. "Easy or hard. Your choice," Emmit said. From the look in his eyes, he didn't mind hard.

Shuler moistened his lips and glanced around as if expecting help or looking for a way to escape. A short man with a mustache and a chef's hat and jacket was behind him. Shuler swallowed when he saw that the man had a stainless-steel rolling pin in his hand and anger in his eyes.

"In three seconds, we're going to make the choice for you," Conrad said, his eyes narrowed.

Shuler needed no further urging. He hurried away with the two men following closely behind.

Nodding her appreciation to the male staff and a fond smile to her executive chef with the rolling pin, Faith spoke to the watchful guests. "Please forgive the interruption of your breakfast. It is a source of pride that at Casa de Serenidad the safety of our guests is our number-one priority. Breakfast is on the hotel."

Faith took a seat at the table and spoke to the waiter who hurried over. "Please bring me a cup of coffee and fresh plates for our guests."

"Right away, Mrs. Grayson."

"How much time do you think we have?" Faith asked when the man hurried away.

"Not enough." Sierra made a face.

Faith nodded slowly. "I don't want to add to your worries, but Pierce called this morning while Brandon and I were having breakfast to invite us to your celebration lunch at one P.M."

Sierra groaned, then let her forehead rest heavily in her open palms. "Why couldn't I have waited until after the deal was signed to celebrate?"

"You don't have to worry. Shuler is too much of a coward to come at you again." Sabra gave Isabella an affectionate pat and picked up her coffee. "He tried that heavy-handed crap on a friend of mine until her boyfriend set him straight. He left so fast the bottoms of his shoes were probably smoking."

Sierra lifted her head. "I would have already forgotten about him if it wasn't that the loss of the sale will interrupt my plans."

"Then what is it?" Sabra replaced her cup without drinking.

"You weren't that far off when you told Shuler about my brothers. If they find out what happened, one or all of them will pay him a visit, then they'll come looking for me."

"I'll have Brandon and my brothers to deal with." Faith wrinkled her pretty nose. "I'll probably get a call from Daddy as well."

Sabra frowned. "This wasn't either of your fault."

"They won't see it that way, especially since Brandon and Pierce knew Shuler was a lech. I . . ." Sierra paused as the waiter served them, then left. "I should have passed on the deal."

Sabra looked thoughtful. "Sometimes we don't have a choice."

Sierra wrinkled her nose. "In this case I did."

"I'll speak to Brandon," Faith offered.

Sierra almost smiled. "He's usually putty in your hands, but I'm not sure about this time."

"Is there anything I can do to help?" Sabra offered.

"No, I don . . ." Sierra's voice trailed off as she lifted her head and stared long and hard at Sabra. Sierra slowly smiled. "Since you're dating a Grayson, there just might be."

Sabra spluttered. Sierra smiled, then picked up her glass of orange juice and toasted her.

• • •

SABRA DIDN'T KNOW HOW SHE'D LET SIERRA TALK her into attending the luncheon. Ever since she had achieved a fair amount of success, she'd received numerous calls for assistance in one way or another. No one rolled over her, that is, until Sierra. Faith, whom Sabra had thought quiet until she'd faced down an angry man, had teamed up with Sierra. Perhaps if Sabra hadn't liked them and wanted them to like her as well, she might have had a better chance.

On the cab ride to the college, Sabra rehearsed what she planned to say to Ruth, but when the time came she stammered worse than one of the college students. "Sierra, er, invited me . . . to the . . . em . . . luncheon this afternoon."

"I wasn't aware that you knew my daughter." The affable, sweet woman Sabra had known for the past few days was gone. In her place stood a no-nonsense woman with shrewd, all-knowing eyes.

Sabra moistened her lips. "Pierce introduced us. This morning we happened to meet and had breakfast together," she explained. She clamped her teeth together to keep them from nervously chattering. The less said, the better.

"We'll leave immediately after rehearsals."

"Wonderful." Sabra thought that was the end of it until she kept having the feeling that Ruth was watching her. Yet when she looked, Ruth would be speaking with one of the students or doing some other task. After rehearsals, they went directly to the restaurant.

"Good afternoon, Mrs. Grayson," greeted the smiling hostess in an off-the-shoulder white blouse and black slacks. "This way please."

Tense, not knowing what to expect, Sabra followed. She wasn't looking forward to sitting with Pierce. Then, too, she wasn't sure how he'd react to her being there. From what she'd learned from Sierra and Faith, only family was coming.

Sabra stopped in her tracks on seeing the Grayson brothers. The resemblance was too strong for any other explanation. Any one of them would cause a stir. Dangerously seductive, they would be impossible to ignore. She'd been right. It would take a strong woman to raise such commanding and self-assured men. Not to mention a fearless woman like Sierra.

Ruth glanced over her shoulder. "Did you say something, Sabra?"

"Your family is striking."

"Thank you. I think so." Ruth continued to the booth.

Sabra smiled as Ruth introduced her. On one side of the booth were Luke and his wife, Catherine, sitting beside Morgan and his wife, Phoenix. Facing them were Sierra, Pierce, Faith, and Brandon. As if they'd done so hundreds of times, Brandon, Faith, and Pierce scooted out of the booth. Ruth slid in beside Sierra.

"Please sit down, Sabra," Ruth instructed.

Left without a choice, Sabra did as directed. She

thought she was prepared for Pierce to sit next to her. She wasn't. She felt the heat and hardness of his muscled body from her shoulder to her thigh. Why did this man make her body yearn?

"Do you want to tell Mama or should I?" Luke asked.

Sierra casually dunked a chip in salsa. "The sale fell through, but there's no reason we can't have a wonderful lunch. Glad you could come, Sabra."

"Thanks for the invitation," Sabra said dutifully, but from the looks on the faces of Sierra's brothers, they weren't going to let it drop.

"What caused the sale to fall through is what I'm talking about," Luke said easily.

"Boring." Sierra reached for her cola.

"What happened at the hotel, Sabra?" Pierce asked.

Sabra had an answer ready. "Sierra and I had breakfast; then later Faith joined us."

"So we heard. Faith and I are going to have a talk about her part in this when we get home," Brandon said, his easy smile gone.

"Brandon, you know I love you, but I have no intention of shirking my duty to my guests," his wife told him.

"You will if anything like today happens again."

"Back off, Brandon," Sierra ordered. "I don't want your first argument to be because Faith helped me."

"It won't be," Catherine soothed from across the table. "Brandon understands that Faith feels the same way about her hotel guests that he does about his at the restaurant."

Brandon's brows knit. "Of course I do. I just want her to be safe."

"She was," Sabra said, ready to defend Faith for her bravery.

"I understand you had a part in this as well," Pierce said.

The words were spoken quietly, but the look in Pierce's black eyes was anything but. "A minor part actually. The credit goes to Faith and Sierra."

"I'm not sure I'd call it credit," Pierce said.

"I would," Phoenix said. "Faith alerted security as soon as she learned there was a problem."

"But they weren't close enough to protect them." Pierce's worried tone clearly said he didn't think any of them had acted wisely.

Sabra could understand his concern but not his condemnation. "If Shuler would have tried anything again, Sierra would have put him down just like she did the first time."

"Chips, anyone?" Sierra jerked up the basket so fast a few chips fell over the side.

Sabra became aware of the silence that seemed to stretch on forever, the tenseness of Pierce beside her, the hint of danger in the air. "What did you say?" Luke asked.

"She was just speaking figuratively." Sierra put the basket on the table. "Brandon, where are the appetizers?"

Brandon didn't move. Ruth twisted in the seat toward her youngest child. "I want to hear everything, and leave nothing out."

"Mama, I—"

"Now." Her mother's tone and face said she didn't want an argument.

Sierra didn't even think of refusing. Her mother was the best mother in the world, she'd sacrifice anything for her children, but when she had that look, no one pushed her. Sierra told everything. "His check is in the mail, and the property is back on the Web site."

Ruth stroked her daughter's unbound hair. "You were always fearless."

"I had good role models in you and my brothers," Sierra said. One more hurdle and she'd be home free.

"There's a difference between being foolish and fearless," Pierce commented.

"I had good role models for that as well." Sierra leaned over so she could see Pierce. She had a very good idea why he was more upset than her other brothers. "I promise to yell if I need help again."

"That's probably as good as we're going to get, but I don't want to have this conversation again."

Sierra was over the last hurdle. Luke was the leader. They all deferred to him. The crisis had passed. "Brandon. Chop-chop. I'm hungry."

"When aren't you hungry?" There was affection in Brandon's voice.

"Who wouldn't be when they can eat food prepared by the best chef in the country?" Sierra dunked a chip.

"Laying it on pretty thick, aren't you, Sierra?" Morgan asked, the corner of his mouth kicked up.

"She's just telling the truth." Faith gazed adoringly at her husband.

Brandon kissed the inside of her wrist. "How did I get so blessed to have a beautiful and smart wife?"

"It takes a wise man or woman to know when they've found their soul mate." Ruth smiled serenely at her two youngest children. "Soon you'll know."

Sierra's hand stopped inches from her mouth. "You want to make me lose my appetite?"

"You were never at a loss for words," Ruth said to her youngest and most unpredictable child.

"She likes giving orders too much," Brandon said. "We were right to call her the Little General."

"Then it isn't just me she can talk into anything?" Sabra asked.

"Unfortunately not," Pierce said.

Unoffended, Sierra chomped down on the chip and chewed with gusto. "One of my many talents. Brandon?"

Brandon held up his hands. "I'm going."

Faith watched him walk away. "Isn't he the most beautiful thing you've ever seen?"

Phoenix looked at Morgan, Catherine at Luke, and both women said, "Yes."

Sabra felt the pull of Pierce's gaze and refused to

look at him. He might get her body to click on all cylinders, but nothing was going to happen between them. Nothing but an intense attraction that she was finding more and more difficult to resist each time they were together.

SABRA HAD BEEN AT THE TABLE LESS THAN FIFTEEN minutes before she came to the conclusion that the Graysons had what every family should have, love in abundance and a deep, abiding loyalty. They might tease one another, but they gave as good as they got. And heaven help the person who did one of them wrong.

"Sabra, I might have to have the plate you're eating out of bronzed and put in a glass frame to commemorate your eating here," Brandon said as he sat at the end of the booth.

"Just as long as I can keep it until I finish eating." Sabra piled sizzling strips of beef on her soft flour tortilla.

"Be careful of the salsa," Pierce warned. "It can burn the roof of your mouth."

Her hand paused. "How hot on a scale of one to ten?"

"Try twenty," Pierce said.

Sabra put two generous scoops of the salsa with red and green peppers on top of her meat, then took a hearty bite, watching Pierce as she did so. Then she smiled. "In college, there were a lot of students from all over. You can get pretty hungry at night, so you learn to eat a lot of different foods." She looked at Brandon. "Although I've eaten in some of the best restaurants in the world, not many have food this good."

Brandon nodded briskly. "I'm definitely having the plate bronzed."

"I'd be happy to send it to the foundry with my next shipment," Phoenix joked.

Sabra straightened. "Phoenix. The sculptress?"

"And all mine," Morgan said.

"I went to one of your openings," Sabra mused. "By the time I arrived, everything was sold."

"I'm pleased my work is so well accepted." She placed her head on Morgan's shoulder. "It helped bring us together."

"It also put Casa de Serenidad in several national art magazines because her work is displayed in the lobby." Faith picked up her glass of diet cola. "I still can't thank you enough."

"Art should be appreciated by as many people as possible." Phoenix turned to Sabra. "I imagine you feel the same way."

"I do. That's why I started the mentoring program." Sabra picked up her cola. "The theater is hard work, but it's worth it."

"Rumor has it that you're thinking of leaving the theater for the big screen or a record deal," Pierce said.

"There're always rumors." Sabra leaned forward to prop her arms on the table and admitted what she had to few people. "But, in this case, there is a nugget of truth. There have been offers, but I haven't made up my mind."

"The theater would lose a great actress," Ruth said. "But a movie would certainly widen your audience."

"And put me in the spotlight." Sabra sighed. "Eating a normal meal like this would be impossible. I went to LA to talk with the producers, and everywhere I turned there was a photographer or a reporter. I'm not sure I want to live under a microscope."

"When do you have to give them an answer?"

The others at the table might want to know, but Pierce was the only one bold enough to ask. "Sooner than later. My agent said the studio is getting anxious."

"Surely neither your agent nor the studio can expect you to leave in the middle of rehearsals of a play you've written," Pierce said.

"That's the thing," Sabra said.

"What are you talking about?" Pierce asked.

"The people at this table and my assistant are the only ones who know I wrote the play," Sabra confessed. "The students, like my agent, think I wrote only the two songs."

"You told me," Pierce reminded her.

"I'm not sure why. Maybe it was because Isabelle liked you and you're Ruth's son. Besides, you looked like you could keep a secret." She glanced around the table. "All of you do."

"You'll be able to stay and perform, won't you?"

Sierra asked. "Mama and the students are counting on you."

Sabra turned to Ruth. "I've never missed a performance or broken a promise. We're going to blow the audience away."

"I have never thought differently." Ruth glanced at the eighteen-carat gold watch on her wrist, a present from her children. "I have class in twenty minutes. Sabra, I'll see you at four. Sierra, well, just be careful. Faith, perhaps it would be wise the next time to wait on security, but I'm extremely proud of you."

"Yes, ma'am," Sabra, Sierra, and Faith chorused.

Faith, Pierce, and Sabra slid out. Ruth followed and stood. "I'll see you all Friday night around seven."

"She's wonderful." Sabra stared after Ruth as she walked away.

"We think so," Sierra said, sipping the last of her diet cola. "Apparently she feels the same way about you."

"I'm flattered." Sabra's lips twitched. "The students admire her, but they have a healthy fear of her as well."

"Don't we all," Luke said, and everyone laughed.

"This has been wonderful, but I should be on my way to pick up Isabella," Sabra said. "It was nice meeting all of you."

"I have to get back as well," Pierce said. "I'll drive you."

Sabra tilted her head to one side to study him. "Only if we leave what happened this morning in the past."

"All of you took a needless risk." The thought of what might have happened still made his gut clench.

"That's a matter of opinion." Sabra folded her arms. "I'm waiting."

"Pierce, I'd think real hard before you pushed this," Luke advised.

"Perhaps that's the problem," Catherine said. "He's been thinking about it too much."

"That's Pierce, the thinker," Sierra said.

"Take it from a man who's been there, sometimes you win by giving in," Morgan said.

Pierce looked at Brandon, Faith, and Phoenix. "Don't be shy. Everyone else has given me their opinion."

Smiling, Brandon slapped his baby brother on the back. "Since you don't take advice, I thought I'd save my breath."

"I don't like taking advice, so I seldom give it," Faith reasoned.

"A smart man like you can find the answer for himself," Phoenix said diplomatically.

"Nice going, honey." Morgan hugged Phoenix.

Pierce looked at Sabra. Her lips were pressed together, but her shoulders were shaking. "You find this amusing."

"And endearing," Sabra answered. "You have a wonderful family."

"They have their moments. I'm just not sure this is one of them. Good-bye." As he took her arm, they started from the restaurant.

"Does this mean you accept my terms?"

He speared her with his gaze. "Maybe."

CHAPTER SEVEN

LATER THAT AFTERNOON PIERCE SAT AT HIS DESK, HIS mind filled with thoughts of Sabra Raineau. She fascinated him as much as she annoyed him. She could be reserved, as she was when she'd entered the restaurant with his mother, or bristling with indignation, as she had been when defending Faith and Sierra or standing up to him.

Thoughts of what might have happened to the women still made his stomach clench. Cowards were unpredictable. Any man who used his strength to harm or intimidate a woman was just that. Pierce and Luke's visit to Shuler's hotel room just as he was leaving had confirmed the fact.

The man had broken out in a sweat. Morgan had been in court, and Brandon would have hit first and talked later. No one threatened their women.

Pierce shifted in his plush leather executive chair. Technically, Sabra wasn't one of "their" women, but since she had been with two women who were, she qualified. It hadn't taken much to figure out why

Sierra had invited her. Family business stayed family business. But as Sabra had been with Sierra at the hotel, none of them had thought of letting the matter slide as she had expected.

At least he hoped that was her reason. It wasn't like Sierra to miss details. A frown puckered his brow. His little sister could be crafty, almost devious at times. He almost grinned. A brother shouldn't call his sister devious even when it was flattering.

That brought him back to Sabra. He was generally a patient man. Sabra was going to test that patience to the limits. After they'd arrived back at his office, she'd taken Isabella and left. Sabra hadn't returned until twenty minutes before four. Even then she'd left Isabella with his secretary.

"Your mistress is certainly good at keeping her distance." Curled up in her favorite spot on the rug that he'd moved from under the coffee table to a sunny spot by the bookcase under the window, Isabella continued to sleep. The phone rang and he picked it up. "Yes."

"Pierce, Sabra is on the other line," his secretary said. "The students want to practice late tonight. She wants to know if we can keep Isabella, but tonight is parent conference night at my daughter's school."

Thoughtful, Pierce leaned back in his chair. Sabra was still trying to keep him at a distance. She was going to learn that he wasn't going to let her do that. "How late?"

"Just a moment," she said, then came back moments later. "Eight at the latest."

Perfect. "Please tell her I have plans for tonight, so I'd appreciate it if she would be there no later than eight."

There was a slight pause. "All right." A short time later his secretary came back on the line. "She said to thank you, and said she'll be there."

"Excellent." Pierce hung up the phone and began to plan. Perhaps it was a good idea for Faith to leave the things for the table after all.

SABRA HAD NO RIGHT TO CARE THAT PIERCE HAD A date, but she did. Only her years of acting allowed her to go on as usual. The students worked hard. They were becoming more used to her, less tense. Theo, the pianist who had written the music for her songs, volunteered to drive her back to her place.

She arrived a little before eight. Exiting the elevator, she went straight to Pierce's door and rang the doorbell. She heard Isabella's excited bark seconds before the door opened. Pierce looked as mouthwatering as ever in a white polo shirt and black jeans that delineated his lean muscles.

"Hello, Pierce." She reached down to pet an excited Isabella. "Thank you again. I'll get out of your way so you won't be late picking up your date."

"That would be impossible since she's already here."

She blinked. "What?"

"If you aren't tired, I thought we could go to an open-air theater." He glanced down at Isabella. "Pets aren't allowed inside, but I know a spot where we can park and enjoy the music."

The idea appealed to her. "You used to neck there?"

He smiled. "A gentleman never tells." He went to the kitchen and returned with a wicker hamper. "Our dinner."

She smiled, feeling lighthearted and refusing to worry about the reason. What could one night hurt? "No dishes tonight."

"That's the plan." He lifted the basket. "Brandon prepared it just for you. How about it?"

"If you'll tell me why you wanted me to think you had a date."

He stepped closer. "To see if it mattered."

She was on shaky ground, had been since she met him. "A friend wouldn't care."

His sexy mouth hovered inches from hers. "Depends on how close of a friend."

Heat zipped through her. "Pierce, I don't want to have an affair with you."

"That's not what your face, your eyes, the hitch in your breath, are telling me."

"We said we'd just be friends."

His hand tenderly brushed the tumbling mass of her hair from her face. "You said."

She opened her mouth to disagree, then closed

it. He was right. Like now, this afternoon at the restaurant he hadn't agreed; he'd changed the subject. "Is that the way you get around people? By being devious?"

He frowned. "I'm not sure I like your choice of words."

"If the shoe fits." She held out her hand. "Isabella's leash."

"You don't want to go to the outdoor concert?" The tips of his fingers stroked her cheek. It was all she could do not to shiver.

"Not if you're going to try and seduce me," she said, trying to keep her voice calm when what she really wanted to do was lean into him and let her tongue glide over his seductive mouth.

"Even though?"

Her hand remained steady. Emotions were her stock-in-trade. She could do this. "Even though."

He studied her for a long time, then closed his hand over hers. "I'll try it your way, but I'm not promising anything."

Sabra's breath trembled out over her lips. "I can't be the first woman who's said no."

He opened his door and pulled her through. Isabella trailed after them. "No, but I don't think I've ever wanted a woman as much as I want you."

Sabra couldn't think of anything to say. She certainly couldn't tell him she felt the same way about him.

• • •

THE NIGHT WAS BEAUTIFUL, THE AIR CRISP AND clean, bringing with it a hint of pine and sage. Pierce's SUV easily maneuvered the winding road up the mountain.

"It certainly is dark up here," Sabra said, glancing around.

"I know these roads. Luke and Catherine's cabin is further up the mountain. Don't worry."

"I'm not. Just making an observation." Sabra pulled her leg under her. "There's always light and people milling on and around Broadway."

"You miss it?" Pierce turned off the road.

"The convenience, I guess." She chuckled. "There's always a restaurant or a little club open into the wee hours in the morning."

"You won't find that here, but Santa Fe has other appeals," he said, his voice carrying a hint of seduction.

Sabra glanced at him. "Pierce, remember you said you'd try."

"I am. I'll let you know when I'm not." He pulled into a paved semicircle. A security light was stationed at the end of each arc to light the area, but not glaring enough to reach the interiors of the cars parked at the steel guardrail.

"Looks like others had the same idea you did." Sabra drew her leg from beneath her and sat up.

"Not exactly." Pierce swung the vehicle around and backed in between a truck and a late-model sedan.

Sabra looked at Pierce, then back at the cars; a frown puckered her brow, then cleared. The couples inside both vehicles were embracing. "I don't guess they came for the music."

"That would be my opinion. Grab Isabella. I'm going to let the back down." He opened his door.

"Maybe we should go." Sabra reached for Isabella's collar. "I don't want to disturb them."

"Outside of an atomic bomb, I don't think anything will." Outside, Pierce let the tailgate down and pulled the blanket from over the basket. "Come on."

Sabra joined Pierce. Her lips twitched. Beside the extra blanket there was an emergency kit, a first-aid kit, and a gas can. "I still can't believe all the stuff you keep in the back of your car or how neat it is."

Pierce brushed a finger down her nose. "Sudden snowstorms and rain showers happen. So do flat tires and other emergencies. I plan to be ready." He spread the basket out over the tailgate and held out his hand. "After you."

Sabra didn't hesitate. She sat and her legs hung over the end of the tailgate. Pierce sat beside her. Isabella sniffed at the basket, then barked. "You've already eaten, but if you're good I might have an extra sandwich."

Isabella barked, then sat back on her haunches. Sabra glanced from the dog to Pierce. "If you ever want a second profession, you certainly qualify."

"This one is enough." Opening the basket, he

placed a cup carrier, chips, and a container of fresh-baked chocolate-chip cookies between them. "Turkey and ham or roast beef?"

"Turkey and ham."

He handed her the three-inch sandwich filled with meat and vegetables. "Here you go. The musicians are warming up. The concert should start soon."

Sabra stopped unwrapping her sandwich and turned her head in the direction of the theater below. "I don't hear anything."

"You will." Pierce opened their bottles of water. "How did rehearsals go today?"

"Better," Sabra answered, her head tilted.

"You won't be able to hear it," Pierce said easily, and bit into his sandwich.

She straightened. "I have excellent hearing. If you can, then I should be able to."

"Part of the gene pool I was telling you about." Pierce guzzled his water.

She stared at him thoughtfully. "You're not joking."

He grinned. "Would I lie to you?"

"Not directly," she said.

"I guess I'll take that as a compliment and a no." He nodded toward her sandwich. "I'd advise you to eat up. Isabella is staring at your sandwich."

Sabra glanced up and almost bumped noses with the dog. She held the sandwich away and took a bite. "What other things can you do?"

Pierce looked at her mouth; then his heated gaze lifted to hers. "I'll show you one day."

Unleashed desire zipped through her. Her body burned. Her imagination, always active, went wild. His hot mouth on her, the curve of her neck, the slope of her breasts. "Pierce."

"You asked." He drained his bottle of water. "Finish up. If we can't neck, we can at least sit close. Friends certainly do that."

Sabra automatically ate, not tasting the food, wondering how Pierce would taste. After a few minutes, she gave up pretending and offered over half the sandwich to Isabella. She didn't give Sabra a chance to change her mind. It was gone in one gulp.

Pierce handed her a wet nap. Thanking him, she cleansed her hands and tried to concentrate on keeping her mind off Pierce. With him so close, it was impossible. She almost sagged in relief when she heard the stirring strands of Mozart.

The haunting music soothed and soared. They sat side by side, their bodies touching, listening. When he linked his fingers with hers, it felt right and natural. It was as if she could see the star-crossed lovers, their desperation, their hopelessness. She wasn't aware of the tears on her cheeks.

"Sabra."

"Love shouldn't hurt."

His thumb gently brushed the tears from her cheeks. "I'm sorry he hurt you."

Sabra jerked up and scooted off the tailgate. "I'd like to go back now."

"Is he the reason you won't let yourself trust me?"

"You don't have a right to ask that question." Sabra went to the passenger side of the car and got in.

Pierce put things away, then climbed back into the driver's seat. She could feel his gaze on her. She refused to meet it. "Please. I have some calls to make."

The motor started and he pulled off. Silence reigned on the drive back and continued during the short ride on the elevator and the walk to her door. Thankfully, for once she found her key. The lock clicked. She shoved the door open and turned, her gaze centering on his chest. "Thank—"

"Don't," he cut her off.

Her head snapped up. She stared into Pierce's angry eyes. "Don't brush me off. Don't compare me with the man you can't forget. Don't make his sins mine. You're smarter than that."

Her chin lifted. "You have no right to talk to me that way."

"This gives me the right." He pulled her into his arms, his mouth crushing down on hers. There was no time to react, to evade. As his lips warmed and seduced, she didn't want to. Her arms went around his neck, clinging. He ravaged her mouth and she whimpered in pleasure. Need became a throbbing ache that made her press closer.

Then his mouth was gone. She almost cried out at the loss. The tip of her tongue traced across her upper lip in search of his taste. "Open your eyes."

The brusque command snapped her out of her

sensual haze. Anger and desire shimmered in his piercing gaze. "I don't do stand-ins."

Anger came hot and heavy. No man had ever made her body want his like this or emptied her mind with a simple kiss. "Take your hand off me."

His hand on her arm flexed. "I can make you want me."

That he could angered her more. If he kissed her again she'd be lost. "Shuler thinks the same way about women."

Shock and revulsion swept across Pierce's face. His hand dropped.

The instant the words were out, she wanted to recall them. It wasn't worth the look of self-loathing on Pierce's face. Her hand lifted. He stepped back. "I'm sorry. You won't be bothered with me again."

Sabra closed her eyes when he entered his apartment. Isabella whined, looking from her to Pierce's door. "I hurt him." Turning, she went inside. She dropped into the first chair she reached. No matter how she tried to rationalize her behavior, she couldn't. Sure, Pierce was pushing, but moments before she had been curled around him like wet noodles.

She had what she wanted. Pierce was out of her life. She just wished the price hadn't been so high.

SABRA SLEPT POORLY. SINCE SHE WAS UP AT SIX, SHE called Joy. "Please tell me you have a place for Isabella."

"Finding a place isn't the problem. It's Isabella."

Sabra shoved her hand through her hair. "She might not have a choice."

"What happened to the man next door?" her assistant asked.

"Nothing."

"Then why can't—"

"He's not an option," Sabra cut her assistant off, then got up to pace.

"I see."

She probably did. "Fax me a list and I'll get a cab. Surely there is one place she'll like."

"She's stubborn—like another person I know."

"I love you, too," Sabra said. "Any more on the financial consultant?"

"I'll fax you that list as well. How do you plan to handle it?"

Sabra sat on the bed. "I guess as a potential client. That would give me reason to ask about their background."

"Do you really think he's going to admit to having lost that kind of money?"

"Not without prodding. I'll ask for references that go back nine years. Maybe I'll get lucky."

"We certainly could use a break. One more thing, the charity auction in LA is the day after you finish there. I have you flying out of Albuquerque on that Sunday at ten in the morning. The auction is that night. Your clothes and I will meet you at the

Wilshire. Isabella and I will stuff ourselves on room service while you're gone."

And she wouldn't see Pierce again. Loneliness hit her.

"Sabra?"

She shook her head. It was for the best. "Good job as usual. I guess I'll go wrestle Isabella into the shower so she'll be presentable."

"You might want to pull out all the stops as well, in case Isabella acts up. You look wicked in the white Yves Saint Laurent."

Sabra tsked. "So that's why you packed the outfit. It takes me fifteen minutes to get the jeans on."

"Think of it as being for the greater good of the project." Joy chuckled.

"All I can think about is taking my next breath and step." She glanced at Isabella, who was looking up at her. "The things I do for you."

Isabella barked.

"Bye, Joy. Time to go into battle." Standing, Sabra hung up the phone and reached for Isabella's collar.

PIERCE SLEPT IN FITS AND SPURTS. HE COULDN'T remember a more miserable night. And he had himself to blame. He jerked his silk tie straight and reached for his pants. Sabra had warned him up front that all she wanted was friendship. He and his ego had thought they could change her mind.

Big mistake.

He snatched his suit jacket from the wooden hanger and shoved his arms into the sleeves. Probably the second biggest mistake of his life. The look in her eyes would haunt him for a long time, if not a lifetime.

Shuler thinks the same way about women.

Pierce had crossed the line, and he'd paid for it in the aching of his body and the knowledge of what might have been. Grabbing his keys, he shoved them into his pocket and strode to the front door and almost ran into the woman who had kept him awake.

Her eyes widened. Her mouth opened, closed.

He was having the same problem. She looked like a wicked angel. All in crisp white that fit her lush body snugly and made a man's mind wonder about the smooth skin beneath.

Isabella barked excitedly. Pierce thought nothing could make him feel worse, but when Sabra stepped back, pulling Isabella with her, he discovered he'd been wrong. The apology that he had thought of giving wouldn't come.

"Good morning. Excuse me." She walked away, pulling on Isabella's leash as the dog looked back at Pierce.

He stayed where he was and tried to get his brain working. White denim cupped Sabra's hips and caressed long, shapely legs as she sauntered down the hallway on killer heels. He crazily thought that she should wear a sign that read: "Dangerous."

Her jasmine scent trailed in her wake and gave

him another punch to his gut. There was no way he was going to get in the elevator with her. A grown man shouldn't beg.

Taking one breath, then another, he went to the bank of elevators, making sure he didn't get in the one Sabra had entered. He could have slapped himself when he thought back and realized he hadn't spoken. Sabra probably thought he was still upset and that she was right with her prediction that if things went sour it would end nastily.

He was going to prove her wrong. The next time he saw her, he'd be cool no matter how much it galled him that she was punishing him for what another man did. Pierce wasn't sure what he wanted more: to get his hands on Sabra or the man who had hurt her.

SABRA TOOK A BREATH, THEN ANOTHER AS THE ELEvator descended. She had been thinking about Pierce so much that for a moment she thought he wasn't real—until their bodies brushed against each other. The spark that shimmered through her was real, the longing intense. She'd almost apologized until she'd seen his calm, cool eyes. He hadn't even spoken. That hurt. She'd hoped that they might stay friends.

The elevator door opened and she stepped out. Requesting a cab from the concierge, she waited at the curb. Isabella pulled on the leash and began to bark. Looking around, Sabra saw Pierce. Sunlight glinted off his midnight black hair, framed his angelically beautiful face. Her knees actually shook.

"Cab, miss?"

Her head whipped back around. A thin-faced man stood with the back door open. Saved. "Thank you." She scrambled to get in with Isabella and gave the man the list when he asked for an address. "We'll work our way down. I'd like for you to wait and bring me back here."

He looked at the ten addresses on the list and whistled. "You got it."

The cab pulled off. Sabra told herself not to look back. She held out until the cab turned the corner. Pierce remained at the condo building entrance, staring at the cab.

CHAPTER EIGHT

"WHAT HAPPENED?"

Instead of answering Sierra, Pierce pulled out a chair at their favorite table. He'd debated about coming to the restaurant, then decided putting it off would give more merit to the situation than it deserved.

"Coffee, Pierce?" asked the olive-skinned waiter, a stainless coffeepot poised in his right hand.

Pierce needed a gallon, but a cup was a good start. "Yes, please, Carlos, and the usual."

"Right away." The lean young man straightened. "Your breakfast is almost ready, Sierra."

"Thanks, Carlos." Sierra glanced at the waiter, then at her brother as he picked up his cup.

"Talk."

Pierce continued to drink his coffee. "You know you don't always have to be the Little General."

"What did she do to you?"

That brought Pierce's head up. The cup clattered in the saucer. "You're putting too much importance on this."

"Then why do you look like the stock market took a nosedive?"

Pierce winced. "Bite your tongue."

Sierra braced her arms on the table. "You two have a fight about what happened yesterday morning?"

The reminder made Pierce's lips tighten.

"Pierce, we told you to leave it alone," Sierra said, exasperation in her tone.

Pierce picked up his cup instead of clenching his fist. "I thought you'd be happy that she and I are not seeing each other."

"Your breakfast." The waiter served them both, then withdrew.

Sierra didn't even look at her eggs ranchero. "If you weren't wearing that hangdog expression, I would be. Talk."

Pierce said grace and picked up his fork. "I'd rather not."

She studied him a long time, then leaned closer. "Was it about se—"

"Sierra." Pierce snapped out her name. "We aren't discussing it."

"That bad, huh?" She picked up her fork. "Just when I was starting to like her."

"Just because we aren't seeing each other is no reason why you can't be friends." Pierce bit into a fluffy ham and cheese omelet loaded with chili peppers. It tasted like cardboard. Faith's executive chef would skin him alive. He took another bite. "She stood up for you and Faith yesterday."

"That's when she was dating a Grayson." Sierra savored her crepe. "Her words. Not mine."

"Excuse me?"

Sierra wrinkled her nose and related what had happened. "I thought it wise to leave the part out about us challenging Shuler."

"No wonder she despises me."

"What?" Sierra jerked up in her seat. "I'll tell Paul to do a number on her hair."

Pierce watched Sierra work up a good head of steam, and it made him smile. "I'm glad you're on my side."

She forked in more food. "Leave it to me."

Pierce laid his hand over hers. "No. This is my fault, not hers. I'd tell you, but it's between Sabra and me."

"You said her name."

Pierce withdrew his hand. "Don't read too much into that. It's over before it really began. The only thing important is that *Silken Lies* be successful, that all the hard work that Mama, the students, and Sabra are doing pays off."

"You make me proud."

He thought of last night in the hall with Sabra. "I always tried, but I made a misstep last night."

"Maybe if—"

"It's over." He picked up his coffee cup. "I guess the happy couple is not coming."

Sierra accepted the change of topics. "They spent the night at Brandon's old place over the restaurant.

They're probably eating breakfast in bed as we speak."

"Brandon cooking breakfast." Pierce shook his head. "Love sure changes a person."

"But for better or worse?"

Pierce looked at Sierra. "Let's hope we never find out for a long, long time."

SABRA WAS RUNNING OUT OF TIME AND OUT OF choices. They'd been to six of the places listed and the story was always the same. She'd wait patiently to be seen; then they'd be delighted to have Isabella until it was time to leave and Isabella would start acting up, barking, snapping at the attendants.

A muzzle would be produced and Sabra would use all her charm and clout to get them to put the muzzle away. They'd be so accommodating as to offer to isolate Isabella so she didn't need her Bordetella shot. They'd give her another chance and there would be a repeat of Isabella's bad performance.

On the sidewalk ready to check the seventh listing, Sabra was tired, her legs had gone numb from wearing the skin-tight jeans, her patience was strained to the limits. Bending, and she hoped she didn't have to do it many more times, she palmed Isabella's face.

"This is it. No more being temperamental. I have to work, and you can't go." She straightened, then started up the short steps. Isabella balked. Sabra glanced over her shoulder. "Now is not the time to push me."

After a few seconds, Isabella went up the steps. Inside, Sabra put on her brightest smile. And although she detested playing the Broadway diva in distress, she had no choice. "I'm Sabra Raineau from New York. Perhaps you've heard of me. I won two Tony awards. I desperately need your help with Isabella."

The young attendant's eyes widened, his mouth gaped, and his gaze lowered to her breasts in the snug top. Sabra kept the smile on her face. In less than twenty minutes she had to be at the auditorium. But before that happened, she had to shower and change clothes or Ginny would be sneezing all through rehearsals. "I need Isabella to be boarded."

He swallowed, moistened his lips, and handed Sabra a clipboard.

Sabra quickly filled out the information and explained her schedule. "Of course, I'll pay extra since she has to be isolated." She handed the man the leash. Isabella strained against it and barked. Sabra knelt. "I have no choice. I'll come back as soon as I can." Standing, she rushed out the door and got into the taxi.

"It went all right this time?" Joe asked, looking at her reflection in the mirror.

"I hope."

She and the talkative driver had gotten to know each other as they'd gone from place to place. She wrapped her arms around her stomach and looked back at the door. "Back to the condo. Can you wait for me while I change? I need to go to St. John's."

"Sure thing. I might call it a day after I drop you off." Whistling, he pulled away.

SABRA WAS FIVE MINUTES LATE AND CONSIDERED she'd done well. Dressed comfortably in black trousers and a pin-striped gray shirt, she greeted the students and Ruth. "Good morning."

"Good morning, Sabra." Lines raced across Ruth's forehead. "Is everything all right?"

Seemed Pierce wasn't the only Grayson who could read her. "I boarded Isabella this morning."

The crease in Ruth's forehead deepened. "Pierce couldn't keep her?"

Sabra had never been more thankful for her skill as an actress. "I couldn't keep imposing on him." When Ruth continued to stare, Sabra spoke to the students. "Let's take it from the scene we left off at last night."

The students scrambled to their marks. Max's need for revenge had brought him face-to-face with his end or his salvation. Sabra, as Helen, stood a few feet away from him, trembling in pain, tears glistening in her eyes.

"Tell me it isn't true," Sabra, as Helen, pleaded. "I—"

From the auditorium seating came the distinct ring of her cell. They'd all agreed that phones were to be turned off during rehearsals. "Sorry. I forgot. It won't take but a moment." Ruth met her halfway with her Chanel bag. "Thanks." Sabra reached inside for the phone, grateful that last night she'd put it in the holder in her bag. "Walker Animal Clinic" on the readout caused her to tense.

"What is it?" Ruth asked.

"It's the clinic where I left Isabella," Sabra quickly answered. "Is Isabella all right?"

"You have to come get her," said the voice she recognized as that of the male attendant.

"Is she all right?"

"You just better come now." The line went dead.

"I've got to go."

"I'll drive." Ruth reached for her attaché case. "Theo, turn on your cell and take over."

"If anything happened to her . . ." Frightened, Sabra couldn't finish.

"Let's not borrow trouble." They hurried out the double doors and down the steps to Ruth's 4×4 parked near the entrance. "Where is she?"

"Walker Animal Clinic. I can't remember the street address." Getting inside, Sabra buckled her seat belt.

"I have a navigation system. We'll find it." As soon as they pulled away, Ruth put on her headset and dialed. "Pierce, Sabra boarded Isabella at the Walker Animal Clinic. They just called and wanted her to come immediately. . . . Yes, we're on our way. Call Richard, and see if he's available. We'll see you at the clinic."

"Who's Richard?"

"A good friend and the top veterinarian in the state."

"Hurry," Sabra said, fear causing her to tremble.

PIERCE RUSHED TO THE CLINIC, NOT KNOWING WHAT to expect. He heard Isabella's high-pitched bark when he was on the sidewalk. Bounding up the steps, he opened the door. The waiting room was empty except for a young man and woman. Both looked to be in their late teens.

"Where's Isabella?"

"Where's the owner?" asked the young man, his eyes wide with anxiety.

"On her way." The irate barking grew louder. "I'd like her to be happy when she gets here."

The two traded worried looks. "She didn't say the dog was vicious."

"She bite you?"

When he didn't answer, the young woman did. "She nipped at him when he tried to take her back. Trying to muzzle her was a big mistake."

"She didn't say the dog was vicious," the boy whined. "Dr. Walker will be here in thirty minutes, and I want the dog gone."

"Where is she?"

The girl cracked the door leading to the back. Immediately Isabella's muzzle was there.

Pierce hunkered down and held out his hand. "After Sabra gets over her fear, you're in for it."

"Just get the leash and take her."

Sticking his hand through the opening, Pierce grabbed Isabella's collar and stood. "I've got her."

The two attendants scrambled around the four-foot check-in counter. "You're definitely in trouble." Pierce stopped at the desk with a well-mannered Isabella. "How much do I owe you?"

"No charge," said the girl. She handed him the leash. "Just hurry and leave."

"Thanks." Pierce and Isabella had just stepped outside when his mother pulled up. Sabra jumped out of the car and rushed over. "Is she all right?"

"You should be asking about the young attendants."

Fear leaped into Sabra's eyes. "Are they hurt?"

"No," Pierce quickly assured her. "They just wanted her gone before the owner of the clinic arrived. She seems fine."

After one last look at Isabella and a reassuring hug, Sabra rose to her feet. "Thank you for coming over."

"I knew you'd worry."

So simple and so much like Pierce.

"Is she all right?" Ruth asked as she joined them after finding a scarce parking meter.

"Yes," Sabra said, relief in her voice.

"I'm glad, but we still need a sitter. I've been thinking," Ruth said. "We might find a student who'll sit with her in the back of the auditorium."

"But finding that student will take time. There're a couple of places I didn't try," Sabra said.

"Do you think the results will be any different?" Pierce asked reasonably.

"No, but I have to try." She turned to Ruth. "I'll work this out, and see you at four."

"I'll post a notice at the student rec and ask around," Ruth said. "See you this afternoon."

Sabra was too aware of Pierce silently standing there. She had no choice but to face him. "Thanks for not holding what happened against Isabella."

He reached for Sabra, then put his hand in his pocket. "I was out of line. You have a right to say no."

She could be just as forgiving. "But not nasty. You're nothing like Shuler. It was cruel of me to say that."

"Why did you?"

"You have to ask?"

"With you, yes."

"Let's just say I had my reasons." She extended her hand. "Friends?"

He slowly shook his head. "It wouldn't stop there and there's no sense pretending otherwise."

Her hand dropped to her side. He was right. No matter how much she fought the attraction, it continued to grow stronger. "Then what do we do?"

He took her arm. "Find Isabella a sitter."

"I didn't mean about her."

"I know," Pierce said, and kept walking to his SUV.

THE NEXT TWO PLACES WERE A WASHOUT. ISABELLA had caught on and started acting up as soon as they entered the waiting area. Of course, her barking set off the other dogs and frightened the various other pets. Apologizing, Sabra hurried back outside, Isabella's leash clenched in her hand.

"She's never acted this badly."

"What usually happens when you have to go to rehearsals or go out?" Pierce asked as they stood on the street.

Sabra sighed in frustration. "Depends on how long I'll be gone. For longer rehearsals, I leave her at my apartment because I can't break when I want. If I go out at night it's usually not more than a few hours and she stays in the apartment."

"No one keeps her?" Pierce asked.

"Occasionally, Joy, my assistant, or a friend." Sabra stared down at an agitated Isabella. "She has a tendency not to like men, but not all of them. Perhaps I should have sent her to obedience school as everyone suggested, but I didn't want her mistreated."

Pierce hunkered down in front of the dog and swept his hand over her head and down her back. "Easy, Isabella. She's not angry with you."

"Don't be so su—"

Pierce held up his hand, cutting Sabra off; then he came to his feet and took the animal's leash. "Come on."

"We haven't found a sitter yet," Sabra said, but she followed anyway.

"I think I know what the problem might be." Before Sabra could ask what he meant, he said, "We'll talk at my office."

Sabra didn't ask again. Pierce wouldn't tell her until he was ready, and if he had a solution she was ready to hear it. In less than ten minutes they were in his office. Pierce unclipped the leash from Isabella's collar. Instead of going to her favorite spot, she looked up at Sabra.

"She thinks you're upset with her."

"She'd be right." Sabra blew out a breath. "Maybe I should have Joy fly down and take her back."

Pierce swept his hand down Sabra's arm. "I think you'd have a difficult time getting her in the carrier."

"What do you suggest?" Sabra folded one arm around her stomach, then propped her elbow on her arm and bowed her head to rub her temple.

"That you look at the deeper reason why you're so upset," he answered. "Sure she's acting up. You've taken her to nine strange places and tried to leave her. Each time you did you were more frustrated with her and the situation."

Sabra's arms came to her sides, her eyes widening. "I told her I was coming back."

"Does she look like she believed you?" Pierce asked.

Sabra looked down. Isabella was still looking up at her. Sabra knelt and hugged the dog's neck, felt her tremble, and tightened her hold. "I'd never give you away." She glanced up at Pierce. "How did you know?"

He came down beside her. "When the attendant

opened the door, I stuck my hand in to pet her. She was shaking. Her bark was different."

And Sabra hadn't noticed. She was too busy trying not to think about Pierce. "You're right. I did have something else on my mind."

He cupped her cheek. "I'm sorry."

She wanted to lean into his hand, burrow into his arms. "I don't want to have an affair. I'm leaving when the play is over."

"New York is four hours away by plane," he told her, somehow knowing this wouldn't be quick or easy, and not wanting it to be.

"It isn't just the distance; it's the mind-set. People in my business don't have a good track record with that sort of thing." She wanted him to understand.

"I've never lumped myself with other people."

The corner of her mouth tilted. "Another Graysonism?"

"You got it." Crossing his legs, he sat in front of her with their knees bumping. "From what I know about you, you don't, either."

Perhaps if she told him, he'd understand. Her arm tightened around Isabella's neck. "I trusted the wrong man. A charming, handsome man who promised forever but only meant until the next easy mark came along."

Pierce muttered under his breath, "You think I'd do the same."

Her hand closed over his balled fist. "No. You're

nothing like him. But it wouldn't last. When I leave here, my calendar is full for the next two months—that is, if I don't accept the movie role, in which case I'll be in Toronto for up to six months. It wouldn't work."

"I thought you didn't give up."

Her smile was sad. "I don't if I'm the only one I have to depend on."

His hand caught hers. "It all comes back to you not trusting me."

"If I didn't trust you, I wouldn't be here. I wouldn't have told you how I feel."

"I'm not going to stop trying," he told her.

"In a way, I'm not sure I want you to." She sat back. "What about Isabella? And no, she can't stay with you."

She trusted him to figure out what to do with Isabella and her fears. He could and would build on that. "Call Brandon."

Sabra started to get up as he pulled out his cell phone. "I didn't mean to keep you from lunch."

Pierce pulled her back down with one hand and activated the phone with the other. "Hey, Brandon. . . . Could you check with your staff to see if any of them know of someone who could sit with Isabella at Sabra's place from ten thirty to one thirty, then back at three thirty to six thirty? . . . Thanks. Call me back."

"Ruth was going to post a notice on the rec bulletin board."

"A good idea, but this might be quicker. Brandon has a lot of college students working for him." The phone rang. "Hello. . . . Great. Send her over." Pierce came to his feet, pulling Sabra with him. "One of the waiters' sister's college schedule fits. She hadn't been able to find a job because of it. Brandon knows the family and vouches for her."

Sabra stared at him. "I should have asked you in the first place."

"You asked me now."

She smiled and he smiled back.

CHAPTER NINE

SABRA LIKED THE YOUNG, VIBRANT COLLEGE STUDENT immediately. Maria, in jeans and a plaid shirt, was a senior computer science student. The moment she saw Isabella, she dropped to her knees and hugged the dog, laughing when Isabella gave her a tongue bath.

"I thought she'd be a poodle or something."

"Not my style. She likes you, so the main problem is out of the way. Now, for your fee." Sabra named an amount that made Maria's pretty face break into a wide smile.

"I can start now if you'd like."

"Good. That will give all of us a chance to find out if this is going to work." Sabra faced Pierce. "How about we pay Brandon a visit? I'm starved. My treat."

Paperwork on Pierce's desk was piled five inches high. "You've got yourself a deal." They were out the door moments later. Before long they were in line at the Red Cactus.

"Busy as usual," Sabra said as they moved up in line.

"That's the way Brandon and his financial adviser like it," Pierce said easily. A frown touched Sabra's brow. "You worried about Isabella?"

"No." She smiled. "I guess I'm still having a hard time seeing you as a number cruncher."

Pierce frowned. "I'm not sure I like that term."

"So noted." Sabra moved up and greeted the smiling hostess. "A table for two please."

"Hello, Pierce, miss," Janice, the hostess, greeted them, and picked up two menus. "Table or booth?"

"Booth," Sabra told her.

Janice's uncertain gaze flicked to Pierce. "The first available," he quickly said.

"Of course. This way please."

Close call, Pierce thought as they followed. Until Janice asked about the seating arrangements, he hadn't thought of the significance or the potential problem. The family table was for family. Their friends and associates understood that. Sierra had invited Sabra to keep herself out of hot water with her family. They didn't bring dates to the family table. The three brothers who had, had married the women.

"You all right?" Sabra slid into the booth and placed her vintage handbag on the seat beside her.

"Never better." Pierce took the menu Janice patiently held and took his seat across from Sabra. It was difficult to believe that a woman he'd only kissed once was causing him such problems.

Sabra placed the menu on the table. "What's the matter?"

"Nothing." He laid his menu aside, a twinkle in his eyes. "Can I ask you a question?"

"I'd say it depends, but what the heck." She braced her arms on the table. "Go for it."

He leaned closer. "You think I'll get a chance to see you in the white outfit again before you leave?"

She laughed, a rich, dark sound. "Not if I can help it. It took a good fifteen minutes to pull on those jeans."

Pierce thought of taking them off, sliding the denim fabric down her long legs, revealing inch by incredible inch, his mouth following. The smile on her face faded. Her breathing accelerated.

"Welcome back, Sabra."

Sabra jumped, blushed, then lowered her gaze. Pierce muttered under his breath. Brandon looked from one to the other. "Sorry. I'll come back later."

"His timing is usually better," Pierce said.

Sabra lifted her head, a rueful smile on her tempting lips he desperately wanted to kiss again. "I should have handled that better myself."

"I like knowing I get to you as much you get to me," Pierce said. "Would it sound egocentric if I admitted I'm glad you didn't?"

"No."

"Good." Perhaps if she'd stop running from him, he'd have a chance. He picked up the menu he didn't need. "What do you feel like today?"

"For starters, the triple platter for the appetizer, chicken fajitas, and double-chocolate cake for dessert." She placed the menu aside. "I didn't eat breakfast."

Marlive, the waitress, came to their table and took their orders, returning quickly with their iced raspberry teas. "Pierce, the food will be out in a jiffy."

Sabra placed her straw in her tea, a smile on her lips. "Having a brother who owns a restaurant has its advantages."

"True, but they began even before he opened the Red Cactus," Pierce told her. "We all had chores growing up. Brandon didn't mind cooking or cleaning up afterwards. He didn't want us ruining one of his precious pans. How about you and your sister?"

"We're complete opposites." Sabra dunked her straw in the glass. "She's quiet, reserved, until she picks up a violin and magic happens. She's on a solo tour in Europe. Since Daddy's gone, Mother is with her."

"What about you?" Pierce asked, seeing the sadness in her eyes.

"Me?"

He reached across the table and tenderly covered her hand with his. "Who is there for you?"

"I'm the oldest. Laurel needed her more," she said simply.

Pierce's hand tightened. Inexplicably, he wished he could have been there for her. "Age doesn't matter.

Losing a person you love hurts to the core. Mama still gets a look in her eye sometimes that makes me wish I could have known the man able to inspire such devotion years after he was gone."

"Daddy called us his ladies," Sabra said slowly. "He would have done anything to keep us safe and happy. Anything."

"That's what family is all about," Pierce said. "You do what you have to. Nothing comes ahead of that."

"Like you and your family?"

"Yes." To Pierce, it was just that straightforward and that complex. Long ago he'd learned that he and his family were the lucky, blessed ones. "Here's our food."

The plates and platters filled the table. "The plates are hot. Anything else?"

"You must be kidding." Sabra smiled up at the man. His mouth agape, he stared back.

"This is fine. Thanks again, Juan," Pierce said, feeling sympathy for the young man who was unable to take his eyes off Sabra.

"What? Er, yes." He finally tore his gaze away from Sabra. "Call if you need anything."

"You have another conquest." Pierce had intended his voice to be light and teasing. When Sabra's hands paused briefly in reaching for her napkin, he knew he had failed.

"That bothers you?"

"It would be hypocritical to say yes when looking at you takes my breath away," he told her. She so easily aroused him.

Her own breath caught. "Since this is a family restaurant, perhaps you shouldn't look at me that way." Her voice trembled, as her body had in his arms the night before.

"I'm not sure I can, but I'll try." He put his napkin in his lap and said grace, adding a prayer that he could keep it together. "Eat up. Brandon gets offended if his food isn't eaten."

"We can't have that, especially when it's so good." She picked up a stuffed potato skin. "I'm going to miss all this good food when I leave."

It was a subtle reminder that she wasn't staying, that whatever there was between them wouldn't go any further. Pierce had never been a man to give up. He had no intention of doing so now. "He has takeout."

"I'll keep that in mind, especially since I plan to hunker down and work on my next play. I'd like to be nearly finished when I leave, since I won't have much time once I'm gone." The taco shell crackled as she bit into it. "But first I have to read the scripts my agent sent me."

"I don't guess you have time for dinner tonight," Pierce said casually.

"Thanks, but afraid not," she said. "You know how it is."

"I know you're running in the opposite direction as fast as you can," he said, his voice tightly controlled. "But it won't do you any good."

"Careful, Pierce, your ego is showing."

He leaned across the table until barely a foot separated them. He saw the pulse hammer in her throat and wished he could put his lips there. Soon. "It won't be my ego that gets you into my arms."

Her mind searched for the answer. "What will?"

"I'll let you figure it out."

HANDLING MEN WAS WHAT SABRA DID BEST. SHE'D learned after the first hard knock. She'd had to to survive.

Certain men looked no further than the face and the body. They speculated how soon they could get her into bed or use her for their own benefit. Of course, there were men like her agent who looked deeper and cared about her. But, sadly, the former far outweighed the latter.

Then there was Pierce. An enigma.

Sabra, the forgotten script in her hand, leaned against the six-foot headboard on the wide bed and stared out the window to the dark night beyond. Pierce saw the body, but he also cared about the woman beneath. He pushed her to feel the desire that blazed in his beautiful eyes, but he wouldn't push her into bed.

He'd leave that to her. He wanted her willing and as hot as he would be. That was what he had meant.

Pages crumpled as her hands clenched. He'd planted the seed, and her imagination was doing the rest. The slow kisses, the pleasuring hands, falling into bed to kiss and tease until they were on the brink of exploding, and only then would he take her. Her body clenched, ached.

She groaned and shut her eyes. When she opened them, Isabella's paws were on the ecru down comforter, her head tilted to one side as if trying to figure out if her mistress was all right.

"Don't ever fall in love," Sabra said, then gasped and backpedaled. She was attracted to him, but love? No way. He was just different, unique. This wasn't love, just an intense attraction. Then the answer came to her, why the word had leaped into her mind. Throwing the "L" word into the mix would make her feel less guilty if they made love.

She had known from the first that Pierce would be trouble. She just hadn't known how much.

PIERCE HAD LET SABRA HAVE THE SPACE SHE WANTED only because he knew his chance was coming Friday night. And not a moment too soon. He wasn't sure how much longer he could have stayed away. He missed her—which, for him, was unusual.

He'd had a couple of long-distance romances, but he'd never been this anxious to see a woman, nor had one intruded on his work. Sabra did both. More anxious than he'd ever recalled being, he rang her doorbell.

The door swung open. His breath snagged. He was infinitely grateful that he had a strong heart.

Sabra wore a white snug-fitting dress that nipped at her small waist and hugged her hips. Her long, wavy black hair flowed with wild abandon around her slim shoulders. He immediately envisioned it spread on his pillow, her body flush with desire. Despite the frown on her unforgettable face, he hungered for her.

"Would it be all right to say you look stunning?"

The frown didn't clear. "Pierce. I didn't expect you."

"I know. I told Mama I'd pick you up." He glanced at his watch, an excuse to suck air into his starved lungs. "You ready?"

"I don't mind taking a cab."

"Why bother when I'm here?" She didn't give an inch. But he was a patient man. Walking into the living area, he bent down when Isabella bounded to him. "You going or staying?" The dog barked with excitement.

"Staying. I shouldn't be long." Sabra folded her arms, pushing her high, firm breasts up over the décolletage. Pierce almost whimpered. "She's used to the place now."

"I'll bring you back a snack." He came upright and prayed she didn't look below his waist. He knew the perfect way to get her moving and him some needed air. "I hate to rush you, but I thought, if we got there early, we might help Mama out if she needed anything."

"Of course. I won't be but a second." Crossing the room, she slipped a DVD into the player. Road Runner raced across the screen. "Ready."

Isabella glanced over her shoulder at the TV set, then trotted over.

Pierce chuckled. "I used to watch that crazy cartoon myself."

"My assistant still does. That's who got Isabella hooked." Sabra picked up a purse no wider than her palm from the end of the sofa. "Behave. I'll be back before the DVD runs out."

In the hallway, Pierce asked, "How long is that?"

"Two and a half hours," she answered.

"I promise to have you back by then." He pressed the call button of the elevator. But there was also another promise he'd made himself. Before the night was over Sabra was going to be in his arms.

RUTH'S KITCHEN WAS FILLED WITH HER FIVE CHILDren, her three daughters-in-law, and the guest of honor. She couldn't stop beaming. They all got along, teasing and playing, just as she'd known they would. Brandon, at his own choosing, was the only one preparing food. The rest were content to enjoy one another. Ruth was content to enjoy them until the doorbell rang.

"Shall I get it, Mama?" Sierra asked, one eye on

the coconut-fried shrimp Brandon had just arranged on a large red platter.

"I'll go." Ruth sent Pierce and Sabra a casual glance, then pushed open the swinging doors and left the kitchen. Things were working out nicely.

"Brandon, can I help?" Sabra asked.

He looked at her over his shoulder. "At least someone is considerate."

"I'm helping." Sierra popped a battered fried shrimp into her mouth.

Brandon rolled his eyes, then picked up a wicked-looking knife and expertly sliced rolled tortilla sandwiches into pinwheels.

"I can cut those." Sabra moved closer. She needed to do something. Standing so close to Pierce was making her nervous. "Or stir whatever is cooking."

Sliding the pinwheel sandwiches onto the platter, Brandon picked up sprigs of parsley to garnish the tray. "Nacho dip. Thanks, I got it."

"I don't mind," Sabra began.

Pierce's long-fingered hand circled her bare upper forearm. Her skin tingled, warmed. "Brandon is very proprietary about his kitchen and his food."

Not daring to look at Pierce, Sabra looked at the others for confirmation. They nodded.

"He gets testy," Sierra admitted.

"Culinary geniuses do not get testy," he said, and picked up the tray. "Touch anything while I'm gone at your own risk."

"He was serious, wasn't he?" Sabra stared after him.

"Afraid so." Sierra studied the dessert tray. "I wonder if—"

"I would." Brandon came back through the swinging door. "Everyone out, and don't you dare touch anything until the guests have started."

"Come on." Luke, who had been leaning against the granite countertop with his wife beside him, slung his arm around her shoulder. "Let's leave him alone."

"He'll mellow after Faith gets here," Morgan said, holding Phoenix's hand.

"Then I can eat to my heart's content, because he won't be paying any attention."

Sierra eyed Sabra's dress. "Carolina Herrera?"

"Yes." Sabra did the same to Sierra's paisley quilted Nehru-collar jacket, matching knit top, and taupe pants, then to the heeled beaded bronze rope thongs. "Donna Karan. They didn't have the Manolos in my size."

Sierra grinned. "I'm so sorry to hear that."

"They're talking clothes." Brandon gave a delicate shudder. "Please take them away."

"I'm on it." Pierce took Sierra and Sabra by the arm. "Ladies, let's leave him in peace and go circulate."

"I'm for it, since he didn't say I couldn't eat," Sabra said. "Didn't I see smoked salmon?"

"Sabra, that's about as low as you can go," Sierra said.

Sabra picked up a sliver of salmon and placed it on a cracker. Munched. "I figure you'll forgive me if I show you the pictures of the vintage handbags that arrived in the mail this morning." Sabra delicately flicked a crumb from the corner of her mouth. "I do believe there was a Birkin."

Sierra's sharp intake of breath cut across the room at the mention of the Hermes bag with a five-year waiting list. She picked up the tray and handed it to Sabra. "Talk."

Sabra chuckled. She liked Sierra and was glad they were becoming friends. "I'll bring the photo to breakfast at nine in the morning. I already called and asked her to hold everything until noon tomorrow."

"I'll be there. I feel so good I think I'll go pester Brandon some more." Sierra went back into the kitchen.

"That was nice of you."

"I thought it might appeal to her. She's beautiful and exotic enough to carry off the oversized bag. She won't let the bag wear her. Now, let's circulate."

Pierce's hands reached for the tray. "I'll take that."

She moved it aside. "Why don't I hold on to it a while longer?"

"Sure." Besides clothes, she and Sierra shared a fondness for Brandon's cooking.

With a winsome smile, Sabra moved to two

nearby students by the fireplace, serving them, chatting easily about the play, their studies, life. Pierce stayed by her side as more people arrived. She greeted each warmly, putting them at ease with her warm smile and genuine interest in them. She was down-to-earth and approachable. There wasn't a diva bone in her beautiful body.

When the president and two members of the board of regents unrepentantly dropped by to thank Sabra for honoring St. John's with her talent and time, Pierce dropped back to let his mother and Sabra do their thing. She was quick to point out that it was she who was honored. She praised his mother for her astute selection of the talented students.

"Except me," a voice said softly.

Pierce turned to see the man who played Max, the male lead in the play. The student, Charles White, noticed Pierce and tucked his head, his hand clenched around a canned soft drink. Embarrassed, Pierce thought, then glanced back at Sabra. Vibrant and stunning, she was charming the men and women from the university. It would take a very self-assured man to handle a woman like that. Pierce was still learning. Casually, he went to the student.

"Hi. How's it going?"

Charles brought his head up and looked around as if unsure he had been spoken to. "All right."

"Breathtaking, isn't she?" Pierce casually slipped his hands into his jacket pockets. "A man doesn't know if he should worship her or beg for mercy."

Charles's eyes rounded. "But . . . but you're a legend at the college. They still talk about the three dates you had in one day."

And when his mother had found out, she'd given it to him with both barrels. It hadn't mattered that all of the women had known about the others or that he was trying to decide which one he wanted to take to the frat party. Ruth had rightly known that he was just being cocky. Nothing like an irate mother and a disapproving big brother he looked up to to correct the errors of his ways . . . at least in that.

"I bet you wouldn't get nervous doing the scenes," Charles went on to say.

"You're wrong." Pierce didn't even have to think. "When I first saw her, my brain fogged. I'm not sure it has cleared yet."

Charles faced Pierce, studied his face. "You're joking, right?"

"I never joke about money or women." Pierce thought that was a nice touch and absolutely the truth.

"Wow." Charles turned to stare at Sabra, who was standing with the power players of the college. "Their eyes are bugged."

"I'd say that's a common reaction."

"Yeah," Charles said slowly. "And Max is the one man she loves. That makes him a very lucky man."

Pierce didn't expect to feel the sudden stab of

something. His hand lifted to swipe over his face. *Get a grip,* he ordered.

The student held out his hand. "Thanks. It's nice knowing the legend isn't invincible."

"Far from it." Pierce shook the student's hand, then turned to stare at Sabra as Charles went to the buffet table. She and his mother were saying goodbye to the president and the others. Sabra's hand lifted to shove her hair out of her face, causing the material to hug her breasts. Pierce's gut clenched. No, he definitely wasn't invincible.

As soon as the door closed, music, slow and dreamy, filled the room. Catherine loved to dance, and she pulled Luke to an area between the dining room and living room. Morgan and Phoenix followed. They were joined by others.

Pierce skirted the dancers and went to Sabra. "You game?"

She tossed her hair back in a reckless gesture. Her eyes sparkled as she placed her hand in his. "Another talent."

He pulled her into his arms, their bodies flush. He swayed, dipped. "With you, it just comes naturally."

She felt him, the heat, the hardness of conditioned muscles. His body, like his arms, seemed to wrap around her. "You do have talent."

"Glad you think so," he murmured in her ear, his breath brushing across her skin, causing a ripple of pleasure to sweep through her.

This could get her into trouble, but she stayed

where she was, enjoying the way they moved together, the ease with which her body instinctively followed his, as if each already knew the other. Her hand was at the base of his neck, touched his silky hair, the wide band of silver holding it in place.

She almost sighed. What would he look like if his hair were free? His chest bare? She couldn't control the shiver that raced through her.

"You're cold?"

Her laughter was part wicked, part torture. "Hardly."

His head lifted, he looked into her eyes again. His narrowed.

Her heart thudded in her chest. "I'm thirsty."

"Coward," he said, but he led her off the dance floor and into the deserted kitchen. He pulled her into his arms again. "What would you like?"

She licked her lips.

"Works for me."

His mouth touched hers, soft, gentle, and so very seductive. Between one breath and the next, her mouth opened, her tongue swept out to meeet his. She relished the hot taste. Her arms moved around his neck, her hands cupping his head.

"You taste better than my fantasy."

No kiss had ever taken her so high, made her body ache with such need.

His arms circled her, holding her tightly. "I wasn't sure how much longer I could have gone without that. I missed kissing you."

It had been only one time, but she knew exactly what he meant. "You do have talent."

His head lifted, his hands palmed her face. The teasing smile she expected wasn't there. "You think this is the norm."

"No, and that makes whatever this is uncharted territory." She pulled her arms from around his neck. "Thus filled with potential land mines."

His dark brow lifted. "I thought you liked dangerous."

"That was before I met you." Before his reaching hands touched her again she moved around the table to the cooler of drinks and picked up the first thing her nervous fingers touched. "You want one?"

"I don't think it will satisfy the craving I have." Arms folded, Pierce leaned against the edge of the countertop.

Sabra plucked another Pepsi from the ice, dried both off with a paper towel, and handed it to him. "You might be surprised."

He popped the top, then exchanged cans with her and popped hers. "I could have done that," she said.

"Home training."

Sabra leaned beside him and sipped her drink, hoping it would help her body cool down. So far it wasn't working.

Sierra pushed the swinging door open and paused on seeing Sabra and Pierce side by side. "More unexpected big shots from the college just arrived. Mama sent me to find you."

"Duty calls." Sabra placed the can on the counter and left.

Sierra let the door close as Sabra passed, then went to stand in front of Pierce. He took a swig of his drink. "Get it off your chest."

"Since you know what I'm thinking, it sort of loses its punch." Going to the cooler, she pulled out a diet cola and popped the top.

"You like her, like sparring with her," Pierce said.

"Sort of surprised me, too, given the circumstances." She leaned back against the cabinet. "But that doesn't mean I want forever for you and her."

"She plans on leaving the day after the play. Her schedule is booked for weeks afterwards," he said.

Sierra tossed him a look. "I seem to remember you flying to New York to see the owner of the art gallery that held Phoenix's first opening. Then there were those before her who lived out of town."

He rolled his shoulders. "That's different." He answered her next question before she voiced it. "We were just having fun, nothing serious."

"Meaning with Sabra, it would be different?"

"I'm not sure what it means with Sabra." Draining the can, he crushed it in with a clenched fist. "I can't get a handle on her."

"Or your hands?" Sierra said.

Pierce blinked, then laughed, throwing his arms around his sister's shoulder. "Why did we teach you how to talk?"

"Because you had no choice, but mostly because I'm irresistible."

His mouth quirked. "It's going to take some kind of man to catch you."

Sierra turned up her nose. "I've already told you. I don't need or want a man cluttering up my life. Just look at you."

His expression sobered. "There's nothing different about me."

Sierra rolled her eyes. "Why is it so hard for men to admit the truth?"

Panic gripped him. The last time Sierra had made such a statement, a Grayson became engaged less than a week later.

"I don't think Sabra is the kind of woman who just has fun, which presents a problem to a fun-loving, no-strings man like you who obviously has a thing for her."

Pierce thought it wasn't fair that women, at least in Sierra's case, knew men so well while men didn't understand women. At least he didn't understand complicated ones like Sabra. "I'm glad you're not a business rival."

"I miss the mark sometimes."

He realized she was thinking about the altercation with Shuler. "But you handled it. Shuler won't underestimate the next woman he has to deal with."

"Let's hope not." She hooked her arm through

Pierce's. "Let's go join the party. Sabra is probably looking for you."

"She's too busy."

"Why don't we go see?"

They went into the living area and easily located Sabra standing with his mother and three well-dressed men in suits. Sabra looked up, and their gaze caught. A familiar warmth coursed through him.

"It's great being right," Sierra said with undisguised satisfaction. "She's definitely interested. You still have it, Pierce, but you just might have to think up a new game plan to snag this one."

CHAPTER TEN

A NEW GAME PLAN.

Pierce hadn't been able to get Sierra's words out of his head. As he walked Sabra to her door the words seemed to boom louder and louder in his brain.

"Thanks, Pierce. I had a wonderful time."

Taking the key from her, he unlocked the door and handed the key back to her. "I'm glad."

"You've been quiet since we left the party." She slipped the key into her small clutch. "Problems at work?"

His hand played with a lock of curly black hair. "A few."

"Any way I could help?"

He wound more strands around his fingers. "Yes. Turn yourself into an ugly toad so I'll stop thinking about you."

"You first." She'd surprised herself by that admission. "This isn't just going to disappear, is it?"

His arms circled her waist, drawing her closer. "Not from where I'm standing."

She stared into his intense gaze. She had two choices: keep running or do what she'd wanted to do from almost the moment they met. Her hand splayed across his chest as he tugged her closer.

"You really are incredible. I can see why Charles is intimidated."

She made a face. "Hopefully tonight will give him confidence and help him look at me as just a woman."

"But a woman like no other." Pierce's mouth brushed against hers, once, twice, then settled. His tongue slipped into the warm interior of her mouth, tasted her sweetness, fed on both of their needs. The kiss deepened. Helplessly, she clung to him, giving back all that he asked for and more.

His head lifted, his mouth hovered bare inches over hers. "Have dinner with me tomorrow night?"

"I—"

His mouth took hers again. His hand swept the elegant length of her back, then settled over her hip. "I'll pick you up at eight."

The tip of her tongue grazed her upper lip. He made her hot all over. "You do know that you're making it very difficult to decide. As long as I keep saying no, you'll keep kissing me." Her voice trembled. "You have a real talent for kissing."

His breath shuddered out. "Say yes, and we'll continue kissing."

"Yes."

His mouth covered hers again for a long, deep kiss that emptied her brain and made her body yearn for his. He nipped her earlobe. She whimpered. "You make me weak."

"Sabra." Her name was a ragged thread of sound. He leaned her against the door. It swung open. Isabella barked excitedly, then reared up to place her paws on Pierce. "Just when I was beginning to like you."

Sabra's laugh was unsteady. "Another woman you've charmed."

"I'll see you at eight. I'll make reservations at Antoine's."

"Sounds elegant."

"It is."

"Then I'll be sure to wear something appropriate."

"I just hope my heart can take it." He kissed her on the cheek and pulled the plastic-wrapped sandwich from the pocket of his jacket and handed it to Sabra. "Night. Night, Isabella, and enjoy."

He was at the door when Sabra asked, "I won't see you for breakfast?"

Disappointment crossed his face. "Afraid not. I have appointments all day tomorrow. The first one is on the golf course at seven."

"Ouch. Good night."

"Sleep well. Night, Beautiful." He closed the door, thinking that tonight he just might be able to do the same.

SABRA LOVED CLOTHES AND DRESSING UP. AFTER her success, she indulged herself with whatever suited her rather than what was in style. For her four-week stay, she'd brought enough clothes for a week. The Louis Vuitton steamer trunk had arrived yesterday afternoon. Most of the clothes and shoes were new. She'd acquired them in an invitation-only charity auction for domestic violence in New York the week before she came to Santa Fe.

When Sabra mentioned the trunk's arrival to Sierra at breakfast she'd gotten a distinct gleam in her eyes. Moments later they left the restaurant and hurried back to the condo. As instructed, the condo's maid service had already steamed and hung up the clothes. Like two teenagers, Sabra and Sierra had oohed and ahhed over the clothes, gotten giddy over the shoes, handbag, and jewelry to match.

Seeing Sierra reverently pick up a mocha belt with smoky topaz hues and Colorado-crystal and nickel buckle, Sabra had insisted she have it and the floral-beaded jeans that went with it. Sierra had gotten the strangest look on her face and said something even stranger. "Are you the one?"

"One what?" she'd asked.

Putting the belt on the dresser, Sierra had said she had to run or she'd be late for an appointment. Sabra had stared at the closed door in confusion, then set the belt and jeans aside. She'd just be sneaky and mail them to Sierra with no return address and ask Ruth not to give it to her, either. It was nice having someone who knew and enjoyed clothes as much as she did. Laurel, her sister, unless she was onstage, rarely thought about clothes.

Now, hours later, Sabra looked at her reflection in the full-lenth mirror, a slow siren's smile blossoming on her red lips. The red-hot Vera Wang dress hugged her hips and stopped five inches above her knees.

Pierce would definitely approve. In the next second, the smile faded. What was she doing? She'd dressed for Pierce. She wanted to see approval in his face, the hot lick of desire and then what? She was still leaving. Throwing temptation at a man, then walking away wasn't her style. She was up-front. It saved aggravation in the end.

The doorbell rang. She swallowed. It was too late to change.

"Shall I get it, Sabra?"

Sweeping her hands over the dress, she went into the living room where Maria sat with her back against the edge of the sofa, a textbook resting against her propped legs. Isabella lay in front of the television with the sound turned down.

"Wow!" Maria said. "You're going to stop traffic."

Compliments were an everyday thing, yet this time Sabra couldn't smile. The doorbell came again. She made herself answer it.

Pierce didn't say anything; his sudden intake of breath said it all. Before Isabella could bound up, Sabra stepped into the hallway and closed the door. Isabella barked her disappointment. Sabra ignored her. She was dealing with her own problems. Pierce hadn't backed up.

She moistened her lips. His burning gaze followed. "I'm sorry."

"Am I supposed to guess about what?"

Only Pierce would be so levelheaded when he was eating her up with his eyes. Her hands ran down the front of the dress. "This dress is for you."

His hands settled on her hips. "Thank you."

Her hands pressed against the hard wall of his muscled chest, felt the erratic beat that matched hers. "I'm sending mixed signals."

A hard frown crossed his face. "I hope you're not going to suggest we shake hands when the night is over?"

"I don't think I have that much willpower," she blurted, then gasped aloud, her eyes widening in alarm.

Pierce chuckled. "Ah, Sabra."

Lines of confusion ran across her forehead. "I didn't mean to say that."

"Sabra." He tenderly said her name again, his hands palming her flushed cheeks. "I'm not going to lie and say I wish tonight wouldn't end up in bed. I do. But I also enjoy being with you, and respect your right to say no." He stepped back and let his gaze travel up her body. "You could wear a sack and you'd still turn me on."

She said what was in her heart. "Promise me that when this is over, we'll still be friends."

He kissed her palm. "You have my word."

"Then let's go to dinner. I'm starved."

Antoine's, the upscale restaurant located near the city limits of Santa Fe, opened only for dinner, had a month-long waiting list and two thousand bottles of wine in the specially made wine cellar. Young, handsome, and buff valets in white dinner jackets warmly greeted guests, then drove their cars to a covered and enclosed parking area in back. In the event of bad weather, the guests could leave through a special back door. No guests would ever have to worry about the elements.

The table Pierce and Sabra were shown to was quiet and intimate and on the first floor of the two-story restaurant. The other fourteen tables on the same level were spaced to give the dining guests privacy and the waiters room to prepare specialty dishes at the table without fear of bumping into guests or employees. The second floor was for parties over four and had a noise level to match.

"Mr. Grayson, miss. A pleasure to have you back, sir," greeted the wine captain in a black tux shortly after they were seated. "Do you require the wine list?"

"Sabra?"

"No. Just white wine, please."

The slender man nodded to her, then turned to Pierce. "Your usual?"

"Yes."

Nodding again, he withdrew and returned shortly

with sparkling cider for Pierce and wine for Sabra. The man waited until she tasted and nodded her approval. "If you require my services further, just tell your waiter."

On cue the waiter appeared and spread their napkins in their laps. "Would you like to hear tonight's specialty or are you ready to order?"

Again Pierce deferred to Sabra. "Sabra?"

Sabra handed the man her menu. "The blue cheese iceberg salad and the Pacific halibut al fresco."

"Very good." He turned to Pierce. "And you, sir?"

"Antoine's magnum salad, and rare prime porterhouse."

"Excellent choices." The waiter collected Pierce's leather-bound menu. "Your salads will be here shortly." True to his words, a server soon brought them their salads and a fresh-baked loaf of brown bread.

Sabra picked up her wine and held it up. "To the beginning of a wonderful evening." Their glasses clinked. Taking a sip, they set their glasses on the linen-draped table. She picked up her salad fork, then eyed the honey-glazed pecans in his salad. "I knew I should have ordered that. I love pecans."

Pierce held up his hand and the waiter appeared. "Please bring the lady a small salad like mine with extra pecans."

"My pleasure."

Sabra just stared at him. "I would have settled for a bite."

"No offense, but I've heard that before from Sierra."

She laughed. She didn't doubt for a moment that he wasn't kidding.

"Here you are."

Sabra looked at the salad in a plate stretching nine inches across, then at hers, which was just as large. "You'll have them thinking I'm a pig."

"I'm more concerned with you having a good time." He speared toasted pecan and spring lettuce.

Sabra took a bite of both salads. "This was a good choice."

"I'm glad you like it."

Sabra leaned across the table and spoke over a low-burning candle surrounded by white rose petals. "How did the golfing appointment go this morning?"

"Not as well as I would have liked." He braced his arms on the table. "He's determined not to listen to my advice. He's chasing what's hot instead of holding steady in conservative funds."

Sabra recalled her father's own frustrations with his clients at times. Especially the ones who could ill afford to stand the loss. At the time, she hadn't realized how much in common he had with them. "Does he have time to recoup?"

"No," Pierce bit out. "And the worst of it is that he's spending as if he's still bringing in the high-six-figure salary. He's sixty-one. His wife has never worked. They're financially dependent on his retirement fund. If he doesn't stop, he'll be broke within three years."

"And you get blamed."

"I could take that. What I don't want to see happen is them going broke and having to sell the house they've lived in for thirty years, the house they raised their children in." He took a sip of his drink.

"Can their children talk to them?" she asked. If her father had talked to her, perhaps they could have found another way. Or at least he wouldn't have had to shoulder the burden alone.

Pierce's mouth tightened. "Even if our dealing wasn't confidential, his two children are both grown and still holding their hands out. The major reason I think he wants to make money is for them."

Sabra felt a catch in her throat. She'd been just as selfish.

"What is it?"

"They sound like me." She placed her fork on her plate. "I lost jobs going to casting calls, more jobs if I got the part. I never asked Daddy for money, but he always seemed to know when I was behind. I'd find the rent receipt in his letter." She swallowed. "He'd always write 'I love you' on the receipt. I still have them."

Pierce's hand covered hers. "There's no comparison. His children are leeches. The only time he and his wife see them is if they need something. As soon as the check is in their grasping hands, they're out the door until the next time." He squeezed. "I'm not a betting man, but I'd bet you paid your father back every cent and then some. But even if you hadn't repaid one penny, he did it out of love and you loved him back. He didn't expect anything in return but for you to achieve your dream."

She managed a shaky smile. "He always tried to give the money back or slip it into my purse."

"Parents stand behind their children no matter how old they are. That's what parents do."

"Ruth is a good role model."

"The best, although lately she has made me wonder."

The server arrived with their food. "Finished with your salads?"

"Not quite, but there's no room," Sabra said.

"Please make her a small salad of the two," Pierce suggested.

"Right away." One server took Sabra's two salads while the other served their entrées. By the time he'd finished, the other waiter had returned with her salad on a small plate.

"Thank you," Pierce and Sabra said.

"Our pleasure."

"I bet they won't want to see me again." Sierra picked up her wine.

"I doubt that. The owner is a client, yet I've never gotten this kind of service." He cut into the porterhouse that covered his plate. "One guess why."

Sabra slowly turned. A group of male employees congregating nearby scattered.

"Now the other diners might not feel so charitable." He chewed. "Since I hadn't eaten since breakfast, who am I to complain?"

"I missed lunch, too." She sent an apologetic smile to the diners on either side of her. The men returned the smile. The women did not.

"Eat up while it's hot. Nothing tastes worse than cold fish."

She picked up her fork but didn't move it toward her food. "This is one reason why I'm hesitant to make the movie. Once the studio puts the publicity wheels in motion, they plan to do a major push. I want to go out and just be like everybody else. No one pays any attention to me at home or at Brandon's restaurant."

"I don't know about New York, but the male waitstaff was scoping you out at Brandon's place, just doing it a bit more discreetly because you were with me."

"Territorial, huh?"

"Very." He waved his fork toward her food. "Get busy. Even if Antoine had takeaway containers I don't think Isabella would eat your fish."

She began to eat. "You should do something about that bossy attitude."

"Me?" He pretended innocence.

"You. But since the food is good and the company even better, I'll let you get by with it this time."

"Good, because the night has just begun. Next stop, the Rebel."

• • •

THE REBEL WAS A SWANK DANCE CLUB WITH LEATHER seats, two thirty-foot cherrywood bars on either side of the room, brass-plated fixtures, and a wooden dance floor. The music ranged from western to retro, thus the name. The live DJ in a Plexiglas booth over the dance floor played whatever the mood struck or the crowd demanded. Pierce and Sabra were greeted with the country-western tune "I Hope You Dance."

Pierce tucked Sabra's small jeweled bag in the shape of a butterfly into his jacket pocket and pulled her onto the floor. "I'm not taking a chance he'll play another slow song. I'm getting you in my arms."

Since that was where she'd been thinking she wanted to be since her confession at her apartment, she went easily. It was as amazing as she remembered. It didn't matter that they were surrounded by other couples, some singing off-key with Lee Ann Womack, some humming, the strobe lights dissecting the floor. The only thing that mattered was that she was in Pierce's arms and he was holding her as if he never wanted to let go.

Neither did she.

As luck would have it, the next song, "Private Dancer" by Tina Turner, was slow enough for them to stay on the floor and in each other's arms. "I hope I have her legs and her stamina when I'm sixty," Sabra murmured.

"That lady is phenomenal, but so are you." They swayed with the music. "You'll be even sexier."

"Sexy is overrated."

"Not from where I'm standing."

"Flatterer," she murmured, her fingers absently stroking the side of his neck.

The music changed to a pulsating salsa beat. Approving shrieks went through the club as people moved off the floor and others moved on. Reluctant, Pierce started off the floor. "I guess we'll sit this one out."

"That's what you think." Sabra stepped forward, then back, her hips moving as she kept a heart-stopping beat to the music. She danced around Pierce, her back against his, then moved away.

Not sure if he could take any more, Pierce circled her waist and just held her, which was a bad idea, since he was teetering on the brink. She smiled up at him, beads of perspiration on her forehead, her hair tumbling around her shoulders. He'd never wanted a woman more.

"Hey, man. Let the lady in red dance."

Whistles and applause sounded around them in response to the loudspeaker announcement. Pierce felt Sabra tense. He didn't have a doubt in the world that she had forgotten they were in a club the same as he had. No woman before had ever made the world disappear. Since he appeared to have the same effect on her, it wasn't quite so terrifying.

Pierce waved to the DJ in the booth. "Maybe next time. Good night."

"Night," called the DJ. "Some men were born lucky. For the rest of us, here's a song to ease the pain."

Hand in hand, Pierce and Sabra left to the unmistakable voice of Vanessa Williams singing "Save the Best for Last." Neither spoke as they waited for the valet to bring Pierce's SUV. Still trying to come to grips with her behavior, Sabra allowed Pierce to help her inside his vehicle. She didn't know what to say, so she didn't say anything on the way to the condo.

"Where did you learn to dance like that?" he asked as they stepped out of the elevator on their floor.

She thought she might escape his displeasure for embarrassing him. "In college a group of us would go out on weekends and dance."

"You're really something."

She bit her lip. What could she say?

"Brandon and Faith are terrific on the dance floor." Pierce stopped in front of Sabra's door. "Wait until they see you. Of course, I'll have to do more than stand there like a lump of coal."

"What?"

"I'm just glad I don't have heart problems." His hands settled on her small waist. "You were sensational."

Her head leaned against his chest. "I thought I embarrassed you."

His hands lifted her chin. He looked deep into her eyes. "For a while there were only the two of us on that dance floor. You didn't embarrass me; you mesmerized me."

Barking sounds erupted from the other side of the door. Pierce kissed Sabra softly on the lips. "Isabella and her timing." Holding his hand out for the key, Pierce unlocked the door and gave the key back to Sabra.

"Would you like to come in?" she asked.

"I'd like nothing more, but I don't think I should."

"I had a wonderful time," she said.

"Then how about brunch in the morning? We usually get together around eleven at the Mesa."

"You and Sierra?"

He played with a lock of her hair. "Brandon and Faith might join us if they can keep their hands off each other long enough."

"I would have loved to, but I'm going to church with your mother."

They all usually sat together at church. Was his mother being hospitable or trying to pull something? "I'll be there as well. Brunch is afterwards. You can ride with me back to the restaurant." He was taking a chance, but the pleased smile on Sabra's face was worth it even if his mother decided to join them, as she occasionally did.

"I'd like that. Good night." Sabra kissed him on the cheek, then went inside.

Pierce placed his hand on the closed door and wanted to beat his head against it, howl at the moon.

Drawing in one, then another breath, he slowly turned and went to his condo.

Inside, Pierce wondered again how Brandon had stood celibacy for so long. Sitting on the edge of the black-finished king poster bed, Pierce slipped off his loafers and the answer came to him.

When you want one woman, a substitute is impossible.

For Pierce it was Sabra or no one. He wasn't feeding her a line when he said he respected her right to say no. He just wasn't used to dating women who said no to him and meant it. He winced. He wasn't sure what that said about him. Unbuttoning his shirt, he stood, shucked his slacks, and continued to ponder his problem.

He dated one woman at a time. When he was ready to move on, he did. But he didn't jump from woman to woman, from bed to bed. He had more respect for the woman and for himself. Unfortunately, it had been a long dry spell between women.

As best man, he'd gotten caught up in Brandon and Faith's wedding plans. For a man who hadn't cared what he wore as long as it was clean, it had come as a shock to them all that Brandon was so fussy about the right tux. Since Brandon had no sense of style, Pierce had gone with him to shop. Then there were the bachelor parties to plan. Brandon's staff and loyal customers demanded Pierce throw one just for them. Pierce had, and it was a doozy.

Emptying his pockets onto the brass tray of the suit valet, Pierce neatly hung up his clothes, then went to the large walk-in shower, turned on the multiple jets, and let the cold water pummel him. Cold showers were another thing he wasn't used to. Yet, for the time being, he didn't have a choice.

Moving on wasn't an option. As much as he wanted Sabra, he also wanted to keep seeing that quick smile, hearing her full-throated laughter, holding her, kissing her. He also wanted to be there for her, to listen to her problems, her fears. He wanted the woman few others probably knew.

For that, he was willing to wait.

CHAPTER ELEVEN

SHE CAME TO HIM WITH OPEN ARMS, A SIREN'S SMILE on her tempting ruby lips. Even before the first touch, she made him want her, made the hunger he fought to keep under control strain to be free. Not yet. He wanted to enjoy every moment.

The tantalizing brush of her lush, naked body against his as he pulled her under him caused his blood to run hot, his arousal to harden almost painfully. He wanted to bury his face in her long black jasmine-scented hair spread on his pillow, bury himself in her velvet sheath.

He'd never wanted this fiercely. Hadn't known he could. He held it together by sheer force of will.

This was going to be explosive for both of them. His head lowered to let his lips slowly glide and feast their way down, then up her shivering body. His hands followed.

Her dusky nipple pebbled beneath his hot mouth. His tongue circled the hard peak, suckled. Her whimper of pleasure fueled his senses. She cupped his head to draw him closer. She was everything he had ever wanted. He couldn't wait any longer.

He brought them together with one sure thrust. She arched upward, her long legs wrapping around him, taking him deeper. Exquisite sensation rippled through him. The fit was perfect, just as she was. His eyes opened and met hers. In them he saw the same intense passion, the same driving need, that he knew she saw in his.

His hips moved downward; hers lifted. They moved in perfect harmony. He stroked her, loved her. Her legs around his waist tightened, drawing him closer, taking him deeper still. Her nails dug into his back, telling him how much he pleased her and urging him on. His deep moan of pleasure echoed hers.

He needed more. His hand moved to bring her hips— His ears rang. For a crazy moment her image wavered. Panicked, he gathered her closer. But the tighter he tried to hold her, the more she slipped away, and the louder the sound became . . . until she was gone.

Pierce jerked awake.

He blinked and discovered he was hugging himself. If he had been a lesser man he might have cried. Feeling the unfulfilled need of his body, he wasn't so sure he might not anyway.

The phone rang again. The clock dial on the nightstand read 8:13 A.M. His first thought was to disconnect the phone, but common sense prevailed. It was probably a client. Like a doctor, Pierce was on call 24/7. He plopped back in bed and groped for the phone. "Hello."

"Pierce."

He jerked upright. "Mama?"

"Are you all right? You sound strange."

"I'm fine, Mama." He threw his legs over the side of the bed and pulled a sheet over the lower half of his body. "I was asleep."

"Oh," she said.

Often, having a perceptive mother was a drawback. "Been working in your flower garden this morning before church?" His mother loved plants and had a beautiful year-round garden. She and Faith, who liked flowers as well, were always talking about this plant or that.

"Yes."

There was just a long enough pause for him to know Ruth wasn't fooled. There wasn't a woman in his bed, but there had definitely been one in his dreams. He shifted uncomfortably, fighting embarrassment. He'd sort his dream out later. Now he had his mother to deal with.

Certain things a man didn't want his mother to know about. His sex life was at the top of that list.

"How are rehearsals going?" he asked, hoping she'd stop thinking what she was probably thinking.

"Much better," she said, enthusiasm entering her voice. "Sabra is something to watch."

Pierce almost groaned. His unruly mind pictured Sabra in the wicked stop-a-man-in-his-tracks red dress, and his body reacted predictably. The duvet joined the sheet over his arousal. "The president and the others on the board of regents were suitably impressed." *As any man breathing would be.*

"Everything is going well. I hate to ask since you were asleep, but could you come out now? I need to talk with you."

Pierce came to his feet. His mother was as independent as they came. She'd taught her children to be the same way. "Are you all right?"

"Fine. If you could come over, we can have breakfast together."

By the time she finished speaking, Pierce was already moving to his closet. Since his three older brothers had married, their mother looked to Pierce if anything came up.

Although none of her daughters-in-law would have minded, in fact they would have been hurt if they found out, his mother didn't want to infringe on Luke's, Morgan's, or Brandon's time. She'd told Pierce a week after Brandon's marriage that there wasn't a problem in the world the two of them couldn't handle. Pierce didn't take the responsibility lightly. "Don't worry about breakfast for me. I'll be there in twenty minutes."

"I can always count on you, Pierce. Bye, and drive carefully."

"Bye, Mama." Disconnecting the phone, Pierce quickly showered, dressed, and was out the door in minutes. He shaved the drive time to his mother's house by six minutes. He jumped out of the SUV and rushed up the sidewalk to push open the unlocked black wrought-iron outer gate. He rang the doorbell, then rang again when she didn't answer, considered knocking on the recessed double doors.

"Come on, Mama."

The door opened. His gaze ran from her smiling face to her booted feet peeking out from beneath one of the long skirts she preferred. His heart stopped thumping in his chest. "Good morning."

"Good morning, Pierce. Come on in." His mother stepped aside for him to enter.

He was barely two steps into the living room when he came to a dead stop. Slowly his gaze went from the pretty young woman on the sofa to his mother. Her grin widened. She took Pierce by the arm and steered him across the room to stand in front of the woman.

"Pierce, I'd like for you to meet Raven Le Blanc, a new anthropology teacher at St. John's. My son Pierce."

A smile curving her lips, Raven extended her slim hand. "Pleased to meet you, Pierce. Ruth has told me so much about you."

Only his love for his mother kept the smile on his face. "Good morning, Raven." Ruth had tricked him. Again. And although he'd laughed about her matchmaking attempts in the past, this morning he wasn't in the mood.

"Raven is trying to figure out her investments. I told her you'd help her," Ruth said.

"I really do need your help." Raven picked up a thick manila folder from her lap, drawing his attention to her legs and the skirt that stopped five inches above her knees. "My last investor advised me to keep making 'pots' of ten thousand dollars. I didn't know until I read an article that he was getting a commission each time."

Some of the tension went out of Pierce. Perhaps he had jumped to conclusions. "Unfortunately, it's a common practice."

"Pierce, sit down." His mother nudged him toward the sofa. "I taught you better. Raven will get a crook in her neck."

Or perhaps he hadn't. He sat several inches away from Raven.

"I'll go get the coffee." His mother hurried away.

"I was hoping you could give me some advice. I'm single." Raven lightly touched his bare arm. Despite the temperature being cool in the morning, in his rush to get there he'd pulled on a short-sleeved polo and jeans. "If I don't get married, I'd like to make sure I have enough income to live comfortably when I retire."

Some people were natural "touchers." But the way Raven was looking at him was anything but natural. "A full financial analysis takes time."

"I can come by your office." She leaned closer. He smelled the floral-scented perfume she wore. "Or you can come to my place tonight."

Time to set the ground rules. "Ms. Le Blanc. You should know that I don't mix business with my social life."

She placed the folder on the oak coffee table in front of them. "You could always refer me."

"I think that would be best." He came to his feet. "Sam Elliott is one of the best in the business, and he specializes in working with educators. He's listed in the phone book."

Raven rested her arms on the sofa, causing the yellow knit top she wore to tighten over her high breasts. "Then you aren't interested?"

"No."

"Pity." Her arm lowered. "I'll call him next week."

Pierce's mother entered with three cups of coffee on a wooden tray. "Here's coffee. I'll go start breakfast."

Pierce took the tray and set it on the table. "Sorry, Mama. I have another appointment and can't stay. I've given Ms. Le Blanc the name of an investment agent who can help her."

"I wanted you," his mother said.

"Yeah, I know." He kissed her on the cheek. "Don't worry about Sabra; I'll pick her up for church. Good-bye." He turned to the other woman. "Good-bye."

Ruth walked him to the door, then closed it as he pulled off and went to the living room. "You were excellent."

Raven came gracefully to her feet. "I almost

wasn't acting. If I were looking for a man, I might have been tempted. You have one gorgeous son."

"But stubborn." Ruth picked up the tray again. "We'll take this into the kitchen. I took the quiche out of the oven when I went to get the coffee."

Raven followed Ruth and took a seat at the round breakfast table. "What do you think he'll do now?"

"Show me that I can't choose a woman for him and fall all the way in love."

"I CAN'T BELIEVE SHE SET ME UP," PIERCE GROWLED as he paced in front of Sierra, who sat cross-legged on her free-flowing arched-design sofa in her condo several blocks from his.

"Mama isn't the type to give up," Sierra reminded him.

"Tell me something I don't know." Pierce reached one end of the sofa, turned, and continued to pace. "That woman was practically in my lap once Mama left the room."

Sierra tucked her head to one side. "Most men would be flattered. Raven is quarter-blood Cherokee and French, has icepick cheekbones and the body and face of a pagan goddess. Her class on Native American history is filled to capacity. Mostly men."

"She's all right, I guess."

Frowning, Sierra uncurled her legs and stood patiently until Pierce turned and almost bumped into her. "Pierce, she has those long legs men go gaga over, not to mention that face."

"What has that to do with anything?" he asked, still annoyed at his mother.

"You, my selective brother, like tall, seductively built, exotic women. That describes Raven, and she's brilliant. She earned her Ph.D. by the time she was twenty-three."

"Should I ask why you know so much about her?"

Sierra stuck her tongue in her cheek and smiled. "Being aware of the going and coming of people is part of staying on top in the realtor game. When she first came here, Mama gave a reception at her house for her and I happened to drop by."

"You're her realtor, too?"

Sierra grinned and folded her arms. "Can I help it if I'm good at what I do?"

"Well, help me, and get Mama off my case."

Unfolding her arms, she studied him. "You laughed about the other women she threw at you."

"I'm not laughing this time."

"I see, and I'd have to wonder why if I didn't already know the answer."

His eyes narrowed. "Don't start."

"Don't you start falling," she countered.

"We're just enjoying each other's company." He rubbed the back of his neck. "I told Mama I'd pick up Sabra for church."

"Real smart, Pierce."

"It was a reflex action," he defended, then winced. He never made excuses for himself.

"Yeah, you wanted to show Mama she couldn't

pick a woman for you, but you forgot the implication of bringing Sabra to church with you, especially since you've never brought a woman before and our brothers will be sitting there with their wives."

Pierce dropped his head and muttered, "What have I done?"

Sierra nudged him with her elbow. "Don't worry; I'll come to your rescue, just as you'd hoped. I'll go with you and throw people off."

"You're as scary as ever, but thanks. I'll drop back by and pick you up." He went to the door. "I'd already invited Sabra to join us for brunch. And before you try to make something of it, she's Mama's guest and you brought her to the family table."

Sierra made a face. "I might regret that."

"She likes you," he said, aware of his sister's generous nature and good heart.

"Trouble is, I like her, too," Sierra said. "She offered me a five-hundred-dollar belt that I was drooling over. It wasn't to make points with you, either, but because she saw I wanted the darn thing."

"That doesn't surprise me. She cares about people." He looked thoughtful. "She's under a great deal of pressure and still dealing with her father's death. She needs time just to kick back and relax."

"You made your point." Sierra opened the door. "Get out of here so I can get dressed."

"You're pretty special yourself," he told her.

"Tell me something I don't know." The door closed.

Laughing, Pierce walked to the elevator.

SABRA WAS READY WHEN THE DOORBELL RANG. BIDding Isabella good-bye and instructing her to be good, Sabra opened the door. Surprise flickered across her face when she saw Sierra instead of Ruth.

"Good morning, Sabra. You're riding with us instead of Mama." Sierra bent down and petted Isabella's head.

"Is your mother all right?" Sabra asked as she stepped into the hallway and closed the door behind her.

"Fine." Sierra continued down the hallway. "Just a change of plans."

Sabra glanced at Sierra in a midnight black Yves Saint Laurent knit suit. "Love the outfit."

"Thanks." Sierra pushed the call button. The elevator door opened immediately and they stepped on. "Same here. I was never into swapping clothes growing up, but if you had been around that might have changed."

Sabra laughed at the compliment. "But neither of our parents would have let us spend as much on clothes."

Sierra ran her fingers up the hand-cut beads on the Yves Saint Laurent handbag outlined with black ostrich trim and gold chain that matched the suit.

The cost of the outfit didn't bear thinking about. "They gave us what we needed and, what was more important, love and unconditional support."

Sabra sobered. "We have more than love of fashion in common."

"I have to wonder, are we going to have more?" Sierra stepped off the elevator. "Pierce is waiting."

Sabra cut a glance at Sierra, but she had walked ahead. Was she talking about Pierce? If so, did she approve? Although nothing would come of it, Sabra wanted them all to part as friends.

Pierce came around the SUV and opened the back door and the passenger door. The charcoal gray suit fit his broad shoulders and lean body perfectly. Sabra's heart did a crazy little dance, reminding her of the restless night, her body yearning for the impossible, yet she hadn't been able to help herself.

"Good morning." Pierce greeted her with a heated smile that made her nerves dance and her skin warm. "I hope you slept well."

"Good morning." she managed, then made the mistake of glancing sideways and looked into the knowing eyes of Sierra. Quickly Sabra turned her heated face away to take her seat and fuss with her seat belt. *Get a grip, Sabra, you're going to church.*

Pierce climbed into his seat and flicked the key in the ignition. Sabra stared at his strong, long-fingered hand and recalled the way he'd touched her. Heat zipped through her.

"You're all right?" he asked.

"Fine." She looked out the window and hoped this time she was telling the truth.

RUTH GRAYSON'S CHILDREN HAD LEARNED BEFORE they reached their teens never to underestimate her. Pierce watched his mother and Raven Le Blanc, now dressed in a prim navy blue suit, walk toward them and wondered why he had forgotten.

"Good morning," Ruth greeted them, her face as innocent as an angel's. "Sabra, I'd like for you to meet a friend and associate of mine, Raven Le Blanc."

Pierce, standing beside Sierra, listened to the introductions, then glanced sideways at his sister. He wished he could ask her for her take on what was going on. Was Raven a smoke screen or his mother's choice? If so, she had miscalculated this time. But on the heels of that thought came another one: Brandon had thought the same thing, then fallen hopelessly, helplessly, in love with his mother's choice.

"Let's go in." Ruth started inside the church and the women fell into step beside her.

Pierce took Sierra's arm and hung back. "Well?"

"I think Mama is turning up the heat," Sabra said. "From all the attention the women with her are getting, I'd say a lot of men here wish they had your problem."

Grinning like hyenas, men were stopping them every few steps to speak and get introductions they knew Ruth was too polite not to give. "Enough of this."

"Pierce." Sierra caught his coattail before he had gone two steps. She ignored his narrowed look. "Which woman were you going to go caveman for in front of half the church?"

The answer leaped in his mind. He took a deep breath. "Thanks."

"Thank me by keeping it light and casual between you and Sabra." Sierra started up the stone steps of the one-hundred-year-old adobe church.

The trouble was, he didn't know if he could. Pierce slowly followed.

THANKFULLY, SABRA MADE IT THROUGH CHURCH without any more lustful thoughts about Pierce. Unwittingly Ruth had helped by seating Raven next to Pierce. Sierra sat next to Sabra. When church was over, Ruth insisted on taking Sabra home so they could discuss next week's rehearsals.

An odd look had come over Pierce's face when his mother had asked him to take Raven home. It didn't take much, though, for Sabra to realize Ruth was trying to push the two together. It was irrational to feel the tiniest hurt that Ruth had chosen Raven, but there was no way to get around it. Perhaps it was because Sabra admired Ruth so much and wanted her approval.

The doorbell rang exactly at eleven. Sabra started

across the room to answer, then stopped a few feet away, her hand over her wildly beating heart.

What was she doing?

The doorbell rang again. Already at the door, Isabella barked, impatient to let Pierce in. Then what? His mother wanted another woman for him.

He knocked on the door. If Sabra didn't answer soon he might call security. With Isabelle barking like crazy, he knew Sabra was inside. What he didn't, couldn't, know was that she was starting to care too much for him and that scared her.

The thought snapped her shoulders back, her head up. Impossible. Men didn't scare her; she scared them. Tossing her hair over her shoulder, she answered the door. And forgot her own name.

Pierce looked gorgeous and dangerous in a black polo shirt that defined the wide chest usually hidden by his suit jacket, and jeans that delineated strong, muscled legs. She trembled.

Temptation stared her in the face. His gaze swept over her in one bold, hungry sweep. He stepped inside. She backed up without thinking about it, her breath lodged in her throat. Closing the door behind him, he took her in his arms. His eyes seared her; then his mouth did the same.

Her body zipped into overdrive. She clutched his broad shoulders as her world tilted. Sensation rocketed through her. Her blood raced. The air around them seemed to crackle with sexual heat and desire.

She wanted this; she wanted him.

He lifted his head, then nipped her lower lip. "Hi, Beautiful."

She swallowed and swallowed again before she could get her mind to function and act as if it were a common occurrence for a kiss to scramble her brain. "Hi yourself, Handsome."

His lips brushed teasingly, gently, against hers. "Hungry?"

"Yes." She couldn't seem to stop looking at his mouth. What would it be like to feast on that sensual mouth, his sleek muscled body, at her leisure until this strange craving was sated?

"Yeah, me, too."

Her gaze snapped up to meet his. Her knees shook. His eyes were intense, dark and arousing. If he and Sabra didn't get moving out the door, they just might move toward the bedroom. The way her body hungered, she might beat him to the bed.

"If you keep looking at me that way—"

She briefly shut her eyes, then stepped away. "Sorry."

He raked a thumb across her lower lip, causing her to shiver. "I'm not. Is Isabella going?"

"Yes." Sabra took another breath, pleased it was almost normal and even. "If you don't mind?"

"Not at all." He opened the door. "How is the writing going?"

Thankful he was on a safe topic, she hooked on Isabella's leash and walked through the door.

"Slower than I like, but at least I'm getting something on paper."

"You'll get it done." As he took her hand, they walked to the elevator. He punched the call button.

His absolute faith in her was as warm and welcoming as his embrace. When they stepped into the elevator she unconsciously leaned her head against his shoulder. Raven would just have to get in line.

CHAPTER TWELVE

PIERCE WAS MOMENTARILY TAKEN ABACK WHEN HE arrived at the restaurant. Not only were Sierra, Brandon, and Faith seated near the fountain, but Luke and Morgan and their wives were there as well. They got together every Sunday afternoon at Brandon's restaurant or their mother's house, so they seldom saw one another Sunday morning unless they were in church as they had been this morning. There was only one reason: Sierra must have called them.

She was helping Pierce help Sabra forget her problems. His little sister had a lot of heart.

"We've already ordered," Sierra said by way of greeting.

"It figures. I bet it was your suggestion," he said, and pulled out the chair next to his sister for Sabra.

"Of course." Sierra propped her elbows on the table and placed her chin on her linked fingers. "I also ordered orange juice and coffee for both of you."

"Thanks, Sierra." Sabra accepted the menu from

the waiter but looked across the table at Brandon. "What do you suggest I order?"

Brandon winked at the waiting waiter and ignored his wife rolling her eyes. "The chef's huevos rancheros are fairly good, although not as good as mine."

"Matching your culinary talent is probably next to impossible." Sabra spoke to the waiter. "Huevos rancheros, home-fried potatoes, and whole wheat toast."

"Pierce, your taste in women is improving." Brandon curved his arm around his wife's shoulders. "Glad to see I'm a good influence."

Chuckles and groans sounded around the table. "Sabra, you don't know what you're creating," Morgan said. "His head is big enough."

"If a man doesn't know his own worth, he isn't much of a man," Brandon said mildly.

"And we all know that will never happen with you." Sierra turned to Sabra. "You getting homesick yet?"

"No," Sabra answered, unable to keep from glancing at Pierce. "Occasionally, a play opens out of town to get the kinks out. I've learned to enjoy myself wherever I am."

"I wish I could adopt that philosophy." Phoenix sent Morgan a warm smile. "I'm always anxious to get back home."

Three food runners stopped at the table, set up deck trays for all the food, and served everyone. "Is there anything else?" one of the men asked. When told no, he withdrew.

Luke blessed the food and picked up the conversation. "I feel the same way."

"You travel a lot?" Sabra spooned salsa on her eggs.

"No, but Cat does with her book tours and lectures." He sent her a warm smile. "Where she goes, I go."

"And I love you for it." Catherine leaned over and kissed Luke on the lips. "He even sits through my lectures on child psychology."

"Same here with Phoenix." Morgan cut into his breakfast T-bone steak. "She has a showing in Chicago at the DuSable Museum next month."

Sierra put her fork on her plate; a dreamy expression came over her face. "Chicago. Shopping on the Gold Coast. The Presidential Suite at the Palmer House. Sailing on Lake Michigan. Real pizza."

"Traffic. The biting-cold wind. The crazy airport," Phoenix ticked off. "I'd never leave home if it wasn't necessary."

"As long as Luke is with me, I don't mind." Catherine sipped her coffee. "I'm flying out next week to see my agent in New York."

Sierra slumped back in her chair. "A suite at the Palace Hotel with a view of Central Park. Bergdorf. Carriage rides. The view from the Empire State Building. Sandwiches so thick you have to eat from the sides."

"And overpriced at twenty-seven dollars with a ridiculous no-sharing rule," Brandon snorted.

"Which we always ignore," Sierra pointed out cheerfully.

Sabra looked at Faith, who answered the unspoken question. "We've only been married a short time, but we plan to follow the family and extended-family tradition of never sleeping apart. Of course, since we're all self-employed it makes that more manageable."

"You truly are an amazing family," Sabra said softly. "You've discovered the magic and plan to keep it."

"That we do," Morgan said, but he spoke for all of them.

For a moment Sabra felt incredibly sad. Pierce's brothers and their wives shared everything. She'd always thought her parents had a good marriage. What might have happened if her father had confided in her mother instead of taking it on himself to "borrow" funds? Sabra couldn't imagine any of the Grayson men keeping a secret from their wives that involved the welfare of the entire family.

"You all right?" Pierce asked.

She forced a smile. "Yes."

"Good, then maybe you'll want to join us." Catherine placed her napkin beside her plate.

"Thanks, but I can't afford to lose the rehearsal time to fly back to New York."

"Sorry, I wasn't clear. I meant horseback riding this afternoon."

Sabra couldn't keep the surprise from her face. "Horseback riding?"

"No offense, Sabra, but I hope you don't ride well," Faith said. "I'm still learning."

"And doing fabulous," Brandon said.

Sierra wrinkled her nose. "She'd do better if you'd pay more attention to teaching her than other things."

Faith blushed prettily. "Sierra rides like she was born in the saddle."

"I've never been on a horse in my life," Sabra confessed.

The men at the table looked horrified. "Never?" Pierce asked.

"Not even a wooden one," she confessed.

"Then I'd say you're overdue, if you're game," Pierce told her.

She hesitated. "If I fall and break something, your mother will have both our heads."

"You won't fall."

She stared into his eyes and believed. "All right."

PIERCE WANTED SABRA TO NEVER FORGET HER FIRST time on horseback. He wanted her to have memories that she hadn't shared with another man. He admitted it was selfish, then accepted it and moved on.

The sun-kissed day was certainly cooperating, with a gentle breeze and the bluest sky he'd seen in weeks. After leaving the restaurant, he took her back to the condo to change clothes. She dressed in a long-sleeved white cotton shirt and fitted black jeans that made his heart thump, and her black eel-skin boots.

By the time they arrived at the boarding and riding stable owned by Richard Youngblood, a close friend and the top veterinarian in the country, the others were already there. Entering the clean, well-lit stable, Pierce received his second surprise of the day.

Standing easily beside Richard, and a safe distance away from his brothers, was Naomi. Catherine, then Richard had befriended the wary young woman when she fled from her abusive husband. Holding Richard's hand was Kayla, Naomi's pretty and bubbly daughter. The young child was the exact opposite of her shy, wary mother.

"Hello, everyone," Pierce greeted them.

"Oh, Mama, look at the pretty dog." Kayla took off at a dead run, heedless of her mother's frantic call for her to come back.

"Kayla, no!" Richard said, two steps behind the running child.

Kayla stopped three feet from Isabella, almost quivering in anticipation. "I remember, Dr. Richard." She looked up at him with a gap-toothed smile. "Sometimes animals don't like to be touched unless they know they aren't being threatened."

Richard smiled and placed his hand on Kayla's shoulder. "Your mother wasn't so sure."

Kayla glanced over at her mother, a few feet behind Richard, her hands clenched. "I didn't forget,

Mama." She faced Pierce. "I'm going to be a veteri-na-rian, too."

Pierce hunkered down and tugged one of the thick plaits on either side of her amber-hued face. It was obvious she had practiced saying the word. "You'll make a good one, too." He looked at her mother. "Can I introduce Kayla to Isabella?"

"Isabella can be testy with adult strangers, but she loves children. She won't hurt Kayla," Sabra assured the obviously concerned mother.

Kayla's mother knelt beside her daughter and placed her hand on Kayla's shoulder. Pierce saw the emotions run across Naomi's pretty face. She'd been through a lot, remained wary of people, even frightened at times. He didn't know what to think when Richard casually swept his hand down her back, but it seemed to give her courage. She stopped clenching her hands.

"Yes," she finally said.

Pierce introduced Kayla to Isabella, then Sabra to Richard and Naomi. "Sabra is going to have her first riding lesson today."

Sabra knelt on the other side of Pierce. Kayla happily talked to Isabella. "Pierce promised not to let me fall. Do you ride, Naomi?"

She started to shake her head, then said, "No."

"Dr. Richard and I are going to teach her," Kayla said proudly, her arm around Isabella's neck.

"Not today, though," Naomi said.

"Whenever you're ready." Richard took Naomi's

arm and came to his feet, bringing her with him. Pierce and Sabra stood as well. "Yours and Sabra's horses are ready." He glanced down at Isabella. "What about her?"

"She's going with us. She doesn't like unfamiliar surroundings if Sabra isn't around," Pierce said. "We had our 'talk,' so she'll be all right. I'll see how she behaves before we leave. Then keep it slow and easy. Any problems, we'll come back."

"We'll let you get to it then." Richard reached out his hand to Kayla. Even with the strong lure of the animal, she immediately placed her hand in his. Together, he and Naomi walked while Kayla skipped to a single-level white ranch house with a red tile roof gleaming in the early-afternoon sun.

"Thank you for reassuring her," Catherine said, coming to stand by Sabra as she watched the trio enter the house.

"She was frightened and struggling not to let her child see that fear," Sabra said. "That's another kind of courage."

"And, hopefully, one day she'll see that," Catherine said softly.

"Richard will help her." Luke led two horses to them and curved his arm around his wife's shoulders.

Catherine looked up into Luke's strong, handsome face. "The right man can do that."

"I'll vouch for that," Phoenix said.

"There's nothing like it," Faith put in.

"Oh, brother." Sierra swung effortlessly into her

saddle. "Can we have less talk about love, and do some riding?"

"Scared it might be catching?" Brandon chuckled and gave Faith a boot into the saddle of a pretty roan mare.

Sierra snorted. "Why should I be? I'm not next on the list." As soon as the words left her mouth, she stiffened. Her contrite gaze bounced from Pierce's narrowed eyes to Sabra's puzzled ones.

"What kind of list?" Sabra asked, her brows knit.

"Nothing important." Pierce led Sabra to where their horses were saddled and waiting. "Now, let's talk about something important. Riding."

LATE THAT AFTERNOON SABRA RELAXED IN THE Jacuzzi tub, the jets on full blast. Her head rested on a foam pillow. She was a little stiff from riding, but not unduly so. In any case, it had been worth it to be with Pierce.

It had been after three when he dropped her off with a brief kiss and ordered her to take a long soak in the Jacuzzi. She'd wanted to ask him in, but he had walked away before she worked up the courage.

Once the horses were mounted, they'd set off together at a sedate pace and never gotten much faster. No one seemed to mind as they teased and laughed at each other. Isabella acted as though she had been around horses all her life. When Morgan's and Phoenix's horses wanted to go for a run, they'd taken off, with plans to meet up with the group later. Sabra didn't remember ever feeling so at peace and happy. It must have showed on her face, because Pierce had reached over and tucked her hair behind her ear.

"Having fun?"

"Yes, although my backside might regret it later."

"I give a great massage," he said so low only she could hear.

"Another talent?" she asked as her heart thumped crazily in her chest.

"Yes."

Her eyes shut as she remembered the searing look in his eyes. Pierce could definitely make a woman forget her good intentions. Cutting off the jets, she stood and stepped out of the tub to dry off. Instead of thinking about Pierce, she'd do better to strategize for tomorrow. Dry, she slipped on black lounging pj's and crawled up into the middle of her bed and reached for the laptop.

Several keystrokes later, she was looking at the list of investment counselors whom her father might have contacted eight years ago. There were eight on the list. She'd already made appointments to see them at their offices within the next two weeks. She wasn't going to take a chance that they'd run into Pierce in the building.

To get the appointments so fast, she'd had to risk using her own name. She wasn't sure of Pierce's reaction if he learned she was interviewing investment consultants. Heaven forbid he find out she had an ulterior motive for accepting his mother's invitation.

The laptop forgotten, Sabra stared out the window. She wished there had been another way. Pierce and his family were a wonderful, close-knit family. On second thought, Pierce wouldn't be the only one ticked if they thought for one moment she had used their mother.

When you mess with one Grayson, you mess with them all.

She shivered. The entire Grayson clan would come down on her like an avalanche. She just had to see that it didn't happen.

There was nothing she could do about it now. This was the last thing she could do for her father, and no matter how she felt personally about the deception, she was seeing it through.

She closed out the file and opened *Seasons,* a three-act one-woman play about a woman through the seasons in her life and the lessons she'd learned. Sierra worked on the play when *Anything for Love* was going slow. Millicent, the lead character, had loved and lost but had never given up on life, on hope that the next day would be better. The matriarch of the family, she'd buried two husbands and loved neither one of them. Life had given her some hard choices. She'd made them and not looked back.

The play opened the morning of Millicent Stewart's eightieth birthday with her wondering if her children and grandchildren would come for love or for her vast fortune, wondering if she had loved too well or not enough.

As Millicent stood on the balcony of the second-floor bedroom of her palatial estate in Virginia and waited, she thought back over her life. She'd been born the daughter of a poor farmer but dreamed of a better life. She'd gotten it but had paid a high price.

The antique clock on the Italian marble mantel over the fireplace struck quarter past the hour. Her hand shook on the walking stick she used when no one was around. They were fifteen minutes late. Would they come?

HOURS LATER, SABRA'S FINGERS PAUSED OVER THE keys and she felt the ache in her neck and shoulders. Darkness had come while she worked. She moved her shoulders, then read over what she'd written. Millicent had just married a spoiled rich young man who would make her life hell and give her the first of her three children. Satisfied, Sabra saved the material, then got out of bed and dressed.

"Thanks for letting me write," Sabra told Isabella as she pulled on undergarments and a soft gray velour jogging suit with a hood. Nights in Santa Fe were chilly. "What do you say we go for a walk and pick up takeout?"

Isabella immediately came to her feet, then picked up the leash from the lounge chair in the corner of the room.

"Glad you agree. Even if it won't be as good as Brandon's food or the Mesa." Ruffling the dog's fur, Sabra clipped on the leash, then shoved a coin purse with her keys and money into the zip pocket of her jacket.

"Which direction do you think we should walk?" she asked on the elevator.

Isabella barked.

"Would it be too obvious if we just walked by the Red Cactus?"

Isabella barked again.

"You're right. We'll walk over to the Plaza, then back." The elevator door opened and Sabra stepped out. In a matter of minutes, she was in the downtown area known as the Plaza, the very heart of the city.

Despite the obvious influx of tourists, the city kept its charm. As the capital of New Mexico, it was the oldest capital city in the United States.

She enjoyed the sights and sounds, the low-lying buildings and architectural marvels, adobe buildings, some of which were hundred of years old, covered with stucco to protect them. If not for the hustle of people around her she might have felt as if she had stepped back in time.

She strolled passed the Palace of the Governors, the oldest public building in the United States, past Burro Alley and the Federal Courthouse, one of the few Greek Revival buildings in the region. She could see why the Graysons loved coming back here. Even Sierra, who enjoyed the finer things and could probably live anywhere, appeared happy to be here. Sabra would hate to leave. She accepted that Pierce was a big part of the reason.

It wasn't until she was on her way back that she realized she was hungry and the Red Cactus was a short distance away. As usual, a line was out the double doors and the patio filled to capacity.

People were laughing, talking, and leaning or sitting on the three-foot-high iron railing enclosing the outdoor dining area. They didn't seem to mind that there was a chill in the air. The temperature had dropped twenty degrees since that afternoon.

Sabra slipped her hood over her head, thankful she had left her hair pinned up after she got out of the Jacuzzi. She considered crossing the street, then thought that would be silly. It wasn't likely she'd see Pierce. And if she did, she'd just say hi and keep going.

If he had wanted her to join him for the family dinner she'd heard Faith mention while they were riding, he would have asked her. Why she felt a certain sadness that he hadn't was beyond her. Or was it worry that he might have asked Raven?

Sabra blew out a breath. She wasn't the jealous type. Besides, she and Pierce hadn't made any commitment to each other. She had made sure of that. Sierra had had ulterior motives for asking Sabra to join them at a family celebration. There was no reason for Pierce to do so.

"Come on, Isabella." Continuing down the street, Sabra was aware that her grip had tightened, her body tenser with each step closer. She ignored the whistles and calls to join them from three young men about to enter the restaurant. A fourth man with the trio ducked his dark head. She recognized the lanky man as a St. John's student, an extra for the play.

"Honey, tonight is your lucky night," the tallest and brawniest of the three men said. "Ditch the mutt. We have a table waiting."

She ignored him and spoke to the student. "Hello, Paul."

The whistles and offers stopped abruptly. Their gaze bounced from Paul's unsure expression back to her. She could almost hear the wheels turning in their heads, wondering what the connection was and if it could get them in trouble.

Paul swallowed several times. He finally managed to get out, "Hi, Sabra."

Smiling, Sabra kept going. Perhaps they'd think twice before bothering another woman by herself. The incident had diverted her attention at least. But as she continued down the street, thoughts of Pierce came hurtling back.

"Mind some company?"

Sabra spun, her mouth gaped. Her grip loosened on the leash and Isabella bounded the few feet to rear up on Pierce, barking in delight. "I guess I have one vote."

"Where'd you come from?"

He motioned over his shoulder. "I was coming out and heard some college students talking about a woman walking her dog who was off the chart."

"I wish you had caught up with me earlier," she

confessed, feeling infinitely better. Raven hadn't been with him. Pierce wasn't the type to dump one woman for another.

"You hungry?" he correctly guessed.

She was suddenly ravenous. "I'd planned on getting takeout at the sandwich shop in our building, but after passing the Red Cactus, second or third best doesn't sound tempting anymore," she confessed. "I'd love a hamburger with steak fries."

Pierce took out his cell. "This is Pierce; please get Brandon."

She didn't say anything, simply waited. It was nice to have a man who wanted to feed you.

"Brandon, your new favorite customer is hungry, and doesn't want to settle for second or third choice. She wants a hamburger and steak fries."

"Please," she said, pressing her hands together in supplication.

"Medium well, red onions, applejack bacon, and American cheese all right?"

"Perfect."

"Perfect." His eyes watched Sabra. "Ten minutes sounds fine. We'll wait across the street. Thanks." He hung up. "Done."

"I should say it's too much trouble, but I won't."

Pierce curved his arm around her waist, and they started walking back. "Food is a serious business to Brandon. He likes taking care of people, and serving them the best food possible is his way of doing it."

"I can tell." She looked at Pierce in the streetlight.

"But I see the same quality in all of you. It's the best or not at all."

"Perhaps because you see that in yourself as well. That's why this new direction you're going in is a bit frightening."

She opened her mouth to deny it, then snapped it shut. "I can't make the wrong decision. Audiences aren't always forgiving."

He stopped and, in the light of the streetlight, stared down into her face. "Then do what pleases you. At least you'll have that satisfaction."

"That's what I'm trying to do, but the answer doesn't come easy."

"It shouldn't be. If it were easy it wouldn't mean as much to you." His hand swept a stray curl back beneath her hood. "Big decisions that impact our lives should make us sweat a little bit."

Seeing him, caring about him, was certainly doing that. "We better get moving or we won't make it in time."

"Wouldn't want that to happen." His hand slid down to hers, their fingers entwined.

PIERCE KEPT SABRA COMPANY AT THE KITCHEN TABLE while she ate her food, complimenting Brandon throughout the meal. Finished, they'd left Isabella gnawing on a bone Brandon had sent and gone to sit on the sofa in the great room. Sabra turned on the television, but neither paid much attention to the program.

"How about breakfast in the morning?"

Disappointment and guilt warred within her. "I'm sorry; I have an appointment," she told him.

"You have early practice?" he asked, his fingers playing with the hair falling over her shoulder.

She might have known an inquisitive man like Pierce wouldn't let it go at that. "No. A woman can't tell all her secrets," she teased.

His hand lifted her hair, wound it around his finger, his eyes meeting hers. "A waste of time and money."

Her eyebrow arched.

Still holding her hair, he gently touched her cheek. "Nothing any man can do will improve on how beautiful you look."

She hated misleading him, wished there was another way. "You should see me in the morning when I first wake up."

"It's one of my most recurring thoughts." His voice dropped to a soft rumble that Sabra felt all the way to her toes.

She flushed as she thought of them in her bed together. He wasn't the only one. "Pierce."

"Sorry, I forgot." His free hand took hers. "It's easy to forget when I'm this close to you."

Since she felt the same way, she believed him. "How about dinner?"

"There's a festival this week. We could take in the sights and have dinner afterwards," he countered.

"Wonderful."

"Good. Now I better get out of here and let you rest." Standing, he pulled her to her feet and went to the door. "I'll see you around seven."

"All right."

He leaned forward to brush his lips against hers, then drew her closer and deepened the kiss. Sabra let her mind empty and enjoyed letting Pierce fill it with sensations that caused her body to hum, her breasts to grow heavy with need.

His mouth lifted. "Night."

"Night." Sabra stared at the closed door, then leaned her head against it. Pierce could become a complication if she let him.

Or was it already too late?

CHAPTER THIRTEEN

SABRA ARRIVED AT SAM GARNER'S OFFICE TEN MINutes before her 9:00 A.M. appointment. The first thing that caught her eye when she opened the door was the elk head over what she assumed was the door to his office. At that moment she could have crossed him off her list. No one in her family believed in killing for sport.

"You must be Ms. Raineau."

Sabra switched her attention to the thin gray-haired woman in a dark conservative suit behind an L-shaped desk. Too late to leave, Sabra smiled charmingly. "Yes. Good morning."

"It's a pleasure, Ms. Raineau. Mr. Garner said to send you right in." Smiling, she opened the door beneath the elk head. "Ms. Raineau, sir."

A barrel-chested man rose from behind an oak desk. He appeared to be in his late fifties, balding and trying to hide it with a bad toupee. "Ms. Raineau, what a pleasure. Please have a seat."

Sabra took the chair and pulled out a copy of her

last bank statement. "I hope you don't mind, but I'm on a tight schedule."

"Of course not."

Sabra could tell the exact moment he saw the balance. She hoped the man never tried to play cards. He'd lose his shirt.

"You say you're looking to add a few investments?" He rounded the desk, the bank statement still in his hand.

"Yes. As I explained, I'll be here for three more weeks and I thought I'd see if a financial consultant and I clicked." She leaned forward in her chair. "Santa Fe is growing. When a city grows, there's always money to be made. I'd like some."

"How much of this are you willing to invest?" he asked, the paper shaking just the tiniest bit.

She couldn't help but compare him to Pierce. He'd never let anyone see him sweat, or let them see how much he wanted something. Unless—

"Ms. Raineau?"

Sabra chastised herself for letting her mind ramble. Garner wasn't the one, but if he broke his word and discussed her visit with anyone, she wanted him to be convinced of her sincerity. "Just thinking. Probably eighty percent." She leaned back as his thin eyebrows shot up. "I'm in negotiations to sign a contract that will make that one seem like pocket change."

He licked his lip. "You've come to the right place."

She thought of Pierce's lips, how they teased,

appeased. She twisted in her seat. *Concentrate.* "Prove it. Make me believe you can handle my money."

Garner set off on a long dialogue of his accomplishments in the past ten years. When asked if any of his advice had ever lost his clients money, he's been candid enough to say there were always risks with speculation. Her father had said the same.

Twenty minutes later, she decided she'd spent enough time not to arouse suspicion. "Thank you for your time, Mr. Garner. I'll be in touch." Picking up the statement, she placed it in her handbag.

He rounded the desk. "If you need any more information about me or the firm, just let me know."

"I will and, as we discussed, I'd like this to be confidential." Her eyes narrowed. "I wouldn't want anyone handling my finances who can't be trusted."

His barrel chest expanded. "Honesty and integrity are the cornerstone of our business."

"Glad to hear it. Good day." Sabra walked from the office and hailed a taxi. Her next appointment was in thirteen minutes.

SABRA WAS RUNNING LATE FOR REHEARSALS. THE appointment after Garner had taken longer than expected. She couldn't stop the man from talking after he'd seen her bank statement. His office had been ultramodern with glass and chrome, a bit more upscale than Garner's, but if she were really looking, she would have gone with Garner. Campbell talked so much, he'd never listen to what you wanted.

Rushing up the steps, she opened the door and almost bumped into Raven. The other woman had her slim arms wrapped around several books. This morning her long black hair flowed down her back. "Oh, Raven. Morning. Sorry."

"Morning. Going to rehearsals?"

Sabra glanced at her watch again. "Yes, and I'm late."

"Were you with Pierce?"

Sabra's head snapped up. She tried to remember that this woman was a friend of Ruth's. "I don't think that's any of your concern."

Raven casually shifted the heavy books in her arms. "It could be, if we're both interested."

So she'd been right. "But he's only interested in one of us."

"You know this how?" Raven asked with a tilt of her brow.

Sabra thought of the mind-altering kiss she and Pierce had shared, the tender way he held her, humored her. "You'll have to trust me on this one."

"I only trust what I can see or feel," Raven said, her gaze direct and challenging.

Sabra didn't doubt the woman for a moment, but she also didn't doubt that Pierce wasn't the kind of man who played with women's feelings. "Sounds like a personal problem to me. Good-bye."

Sabra continued down the hall, unable to believe she'd been challenged over Pierce. For good measure, she put a little something extra in her step, sure

Raven was still looking. Opening the auditorium's door, Sabra looked back, and sure enough, Raven remained unmoved. Then the other woman did something totally unexpected; she gave an exaggerated bow, as if admitting defeat.

Sabra laughed, then bowed her head in acknowledgment that she had a clear field with Pierce. The laughter abruptly died. She might not have any competition, but exactly what was she going to do with her prize?

Heaven help her. She had no idea. No, that was a lie. She had lots of ideas; she just wasn't going to act on them.

Pushing the wooden door open wider, she entered the auditorium, hoping she was right.

WORK CAME BEFORE PLEASURE.

It was an axiom that Pierce had grown up with. For the past three days he'd been neck high in paperwork. There had been times in his life that he hadn't been pleased that work interfered, but never had he regretted it as much as today. There was no way he would be able to finish up the report for Standext Oil Company and take Sabra out tonight, either.

He'd come to that unavoidable conclusion a little after one that afternoon and he'd left a message on her phone. He'd hated to cancel that way, but he didn't have her cell number and he certainly wasn't going to call his mother and ask her to have Sabra call him. Nor had he wanted to leave the message with Isabella's sitter.

Standext Oil Company was a lucrative account, running into the millions. The privately owned family business included vast amounts of property and had valuable oil and gas leases in Texas, New Mexico, Louisiana, and Arizona. Their investment portfolio was several inches thick. Toliver Yates, the patriarch and CEO, was one of the clients when James Robinson had conned him. At least that was what he'd called himself. He'd used forged identification and references, and he'd disappeared after leaving Santa Fe. Luke hadn't been able to track him. Yates, a referral from Pierce's cousin, Daniel Falcon, had lost a hundred thousand dollars in the con and could have bailed. He hadn't.

"Mistakes happen. It's how you react to them that counts. You won't be taken again."

Pierce hadn't. He checked and rechecked facts. No one was going to get one over on him or his clients ever again. Yates had kept Pierce as his investment counselor. He was one client whom Pierce never would disappoint.

Pierce clicked on the chart with Yates's foreign investments, noting they had inched up half a percent. Yates had enough money to take a hit and not flinch, but Pierce planned on keeping an eye on the volatile stock, although they had a stop order already in place.

The knock on the door brought his head up. His

brow bunched, then cleared. Sierra. She'd stop by at times to talk or to bring him food if he worked late. "Sierra, come in. I hope you have food."

Sabra came in instead, wearing a peach-colored camisole top that made her skin glow and a short white skirt that made his blood run hot. In her hand was a wooden picnic basket. "You're in luck."

Standing, he came around his desk, his gaze drinking her in, the long hours at the computer, the stiff neck and shoulders forgotten. "What are you doing here?"

Smiling, she held up her basket. "One guess."

He'd been a bit concerned that she might not understand. He should have known better. "I'm sorry I've had to keep leaving messages on the phone."

"Things happen," she said easily, smiling up at him.

His hand brushed the hair away from her exquisite face. "I'm not sure I'd be so forgiving."

Her beautiful eyes widened. She glanced at his computer. "How's it going?"

He would let her escape and change the subject . . . for now. "It's getting there." Taking the basket in one hand and her arm in the other, he seated her on the love seat near the window and placed the basket on the glass-topped table.

Sabra scooted forward and cleared a space on the coffee table. Opening the basket, she took out a large red napkin square and spread it on the table. "I thought you might be hungry."

"Starved." He moved the basket aside to give her more room and chuckled at the amount of food she placed on the napkin. "Although I don't think I can eat all this." There was a four-inch-thick po'boy, filled with grilled chicken, cheese, and veggies.

"We'll see." Sabra handed him another napkin and a plate with half of the foot-long sandwich and homemade potato chips. "Brandon said you love grilled chicken."

"You went by the restaurant?" Pierce bit into his food.

She looked unsure just for a moment. "I wanted to see if you'd ordered takeout and see if you'd mind if I interrupted you."

"Thank you, and you can interrupt me anytime."

"How much longer?"

Pierce looked at his desk. "Two hours, if I'm lucky."

She took out a clear plastic container with a large slice of carrot cake. "I hope your being with me didn't get you behind."

"Put that thought out of your head," he said, unwilling to have her worry. "A client is flying in tomorrow unexpectedly and wants an update on his account."

She unscrewed the top of a fizzy raspberry soda. "I don't guess it occurred to you to tell him you need more time."

"Even if he wasn't one of my wealthiest clients,

he's entitled to have an accounting update whenever he wants."

Sabra looked thoughtful. "Your clients come first, huh?"

"They trust me with more than their money. They trust me with their hopes and dreams. I can't, won't, let them down."

She nodded. "My father thought—" She stopped suddenly and looked away.

His hand covered hers. "It's all right to miss him."

Her gaze came back to his. "I think you would have liked him."

"I certainly like his daughter."

A slow smile took the shadows from her face. "Flatterer. Now finish so I can get out of your way."

He did just that. His meal over, he helped her pack things back into the basket, then walked her to the elevator and pushed the call button. "Thanks again."

"You're welcome."

His hand circled the back of her neck and pulled her to him. His mouth fused with hers; the kiss energized him and filled him with need. Dimly he heard the elevator door open behind them.

Reluctantly, he lifted his head. "Thanks. Tomorrow night. Eight sharp."

Her breath labored, her eyes slowly opened. "Tomorrow night."

Pierce watched her enter the elevator, the doors

slide closed. He wanted to go with her. One day. He turned back to his office.

I HAVE TO BE MORE CAREFUL.

The thought had drummed in Sabra's head the night before when she'd left Pierce and again now as they sat across from each other in a restaurant in Casa de Serenidad. She'd almost admitted her father had felt the same way about the clients he represented. The slip could have exposed her. She wasn't supposed to know anything about investments.

She hated having to censor every word with Pierce. Especially when he was so open with her.

"You're quiet this evening." Pierce sat across from her at a small table in a quiet corner.

"Just thinking." She sipped her wine. "I'm glad things went well with your client today." She'd asked as soon as Pierce had picked her up that evening.

"He wanted to meet you."

Surprise widened her eyes. "Me?"

Pierce leaned forward; the flicker of the candle made his skin even more golden. "He loves the theater and had read an article that said you were going to be here working with Ruth Grayson."

"Why do I get the impression you weren't pleased?"

Pierce stared down at his drink, then lifted his dark head. "Men fall all over themselves for you."

"But I don't fall back," she said, holding his dark gaze.

"I know." His hand covered hers.

"Sabra?"

She glanced up, then jumped out of her seat, hugging the slim man as tightly as he hugged her. "Chad, it's great seeing you! What are you doing here?"

He waved an expressive hand. "Don has a house here, and we flew in on his Gulfstream for a couple of weeks. What brings you here?"

"Special project with my foundation." She turned to Pierce. "Pierce Grayson. Chad Marshall, a good friend and fabulous fashion designer."

Pierce nodded. The man did the same, then turned his attention back to Sabra. Casually, he took her hand and twirled her in the sheer knee-length black chiffon dress. "I'd feel crushed that you're not wearing my design, but since you look so fab I can't."

"Good, because I had one on the other night." She smiled. "A week without wearing one of your designs is a week that isn't lived."

He touched his heart. "Music to my ears."

"And your bank account." She laughed.

"You were always sharp." The willowy man looked at Pierce. "Do you mind if she comes to our table and says hello?"

"No," Pierce lied.

"I'll bring her back." Chad placed his hand in the small of Sabra's naked back. Pierce didn't expect the rage that swept through him. He felt the imprint of the crystal stem in his hand and slowly uncurled his fingers.

The table wasn't that far away. There were three men and two women, all young, good-looking, and fashionably dressed. A broad-shouldered man stood, urging Sabra to sit. She glanced over her shoulder at him, gave a tiny wave, and then sat. Usually it was Pierce who could walk away with a smile and a wave.

A hard knot lodged in his gut. He recognized it for what it was, fear. There was a distinct possibility that this was one time, the first time, that he wouldn't be able to walk away with a smile and a wave.

A short while later, Sabra stood, hugged each one, then started back to him. The eyes of the men she'd left and most of the men in the restaurant followed. The sheer fabric fluttered with each step, making a man visualize sliding it off her exotic body.

Desire caused Pierce's body to clench, to throb with need. Her lazy strut tantalized, beckoned.

And he realized it would only get worse.

Last night he had done the impossible, the unheard of, and dreamed of her, hot and needy in his arms. Again. He'd awakened in a cold sweat, his body aching for release.

She was the kind of woman a man would beg on his hands and knees to come back. Well, not this man. He would walk away and not look back.

He stood when she reached the table. "If you're ready, we can leave." If she was surprised, she didn't show it.

"Of course." She picked up one of the small purses

she favored for evenings. On the way out, she waved to her friends and blew them air kisses.

Pierce saw the men whispering, their gaze following their every step. He thought he was used to the attention Sabra got from men. He was wrong. Neither spoke on the short walk back to the condo building.

"Now you're the one being quiet," Sabra said after he unlocked her door and handed her the key.

"Do you ever get used to it?" he asked.

Her brows bunched. "What?"

"Men falling all over themselves for you." He hadn't meant the words to come out so harsh and condemning.

"I wasn't aware that anyone was," she replied easily.

He searched her calm, beautiful eyes and decided she was telling the truth. She was probably used to it by now. Men fantasized about her, and she barely knew they existed. He wouldn't be one of them. He drew her into his arms, his mouth finding hers, kissing her deeply, wanting to block out everything except the two of them.

After a long time his head lifted. He stared into her dazed eyes, inhaled the subtle exotic jasmine scent that was so much a part of her.

No, she wouldn't forget him. But neither would he forget her. Reaching around her, he opened the door a few inches. Isabella barked. "Good night."

"Good night. How about breakfast around nine in the morning? My treat."

"All right," he answered, realizing that he could get in over his head if he wasn't careful.

"I'll knock on your door at a quarter till." Smiling, she went inside and closed the door. He just hoped he could shut away the growing feelings he had for her as easily.

SABRA WAS RUNNING OUT OF CANDIDATES. CLOSING the door to her apartment the next morning, she went to Pierce's door and rang the doorbell. There were only two names left and she was seeing them that afternoon. If they didn't pan out, she didn't know what she'd do next.

She'd tossed around the idea of asking Pierce in a roundabout way if he had heard any of his friends talk about an investment that went bad but decided that that was too risky. He was too inquisitive. Any answer she gave him had to be logical or he'd worry over it like Isabella did over a bone. Then, too, the investment broker might have been too embarrassed to tell anyone and had kept the entire incident a secret.

Pierce opened the door. This morning he wore a white shirt, herringbone jacket, and black slacks. In a word, yummy. Her pulse raced, her thoughts scattered.

"Good morning." He stepped into the hall and took her into his arms. He didn't ask permission. He just took her lips—and took her body on a wild, hot ride.

Her eyelids fluttered open when he lifted his head. She licked her lips. "That's some good morning."

"It makes up for the good nights." Catching her hand, Pierce started for the elevator.

"That it does. What are your plans for today?" she asked, enjoying the tingling sensation running up her arm. The elevator doors opened to let a resident out. They stepped on.

"Just the usual. More writing for you?"

"Yes." She thought again of asking him about the investors as the elevator door opened on the first floor and they stepped out. She wasn't sure how. Perhaps that was why she missed the two men approaching them.

"Sabra, darling."

She felt Pierce's hand clench on hers, then glanced around to see her agent, Dave, striding toward her. With him was Britt Powell, a renowned actor and one of *People* magazine's ten sexiest men. Britt was also her would-be leading man if she decided to do the movie.

In the next moment, Dave enveloped her in a hug as he always did when they had been apart for any period of time. Thin as a rail, with a long, boyish face, Dave was one of those people who lived life to the fullest. With Isabella's leash in one hand and Pierce holding the other, Sabra stood there until Dave stepped back.

"What are you doing here?" she asked.

"Tempting you, what else?" Always unflappable, he looked at Pierce and raised a brow. "A friend of yours?"

"I'm sorry. Pierce Grayson, Dave Hopper, my agent, and Britt Powell."

Pierce was as slow to release her hand as Britt was to extend his. Puzzled by their attitudes, she glanced between the two. Dave was the only one smiling.

"Sabra, Britt and I came down to talk about the movie." Dave said to Pierce, "You look as if you were on your way out, but it's important that we speak to Sabra in private."

"It's up to Sabra," Pierce said

Sabra had never seen Pierce's face so cold, heard his voice so devoid of emotion. Then she recalled last night and what he had said about men. "We were on our way to breakfast."

"I'm starved." Britt slipped his manicured hands into his well-worn denims that were topped by a black tailored jacket and white shirt. Scuffed cowboy boots peeked from beneath his pants. "We left in a hurry. They didn't have time to stock the jet."

"A pity," Pierce said.

Britt's green eyes narrowed in his starkly handsome face. He was broader in the shoulders than Pierce, more muscles, and he knew how to use them. He'd been a bad boy at one time and reverted back from time to time for the sheer hell of it, or so he'd told her when they first met six months ago.

"Why don't you join us for breakfast?" Sabra suggested before testosterone overruled good judgment.

"I had in mind something more . . . private," Britt said.

Sabra almost gasped at his suggestive tone. "Britt—"

"I'll make this easy." Pierce turned to Sabra. "You know where to find me. Good-bye."

Stunned, Sabra watched him walk away and couldn't decide who she wanted to give a swift kick in the pants to first, Pierce or Britt.

CHAPTER FOURTEEN

WHEN PIERCE TOOK HIS SEAT AT THE RESTAURANT HE was still steamed, but he was also angry at himself. What was wrong with him?

"What is it?" Sierra asked, taking a seat next to him. "Pierce?"

"I'm a fool."

"What happened between you and Sabra?" she asked, her hand on his arm.

His gaze cut to her. "How do you know it's about Sabra?"

"Look over my shoulder and you'll see."

Pierce turned and looked straight into Sabra's eyes. She didn't look happy. She was in line, waiting to be seated with the muscle-bound actor whom women went crazy over and her smiling agent.

She'd made her choice. Pierce signaled the waiter. "I'm having omelets this morning, Sierra. How about you?"

"The same."

Pierce gave their orders to Carlos, who'd brought

coffee, orange juice, and ice water with him. Sierra waited until the waiter withdrew. "Ignoring it won't make it go away."

"It's a start." Pierce picked up the cup of coffee only to immediately set it down when the coffee burned his tongue.

Sierra handed him a glass of water. "Do what you do best and think before acting."

The ice water cooled his tongue, but nothing could settle the churning in his gut. "I am. Whatever it was, it's over." He placed the glass on the table. "I don't stand in line."

Sierra placed her elbows on the table. "Could you be more specific?"

Pierce thought of not answering, but Sierra would just worry him until he told her. He'd rather get it out and over with so he could start forgetting Sabra. "Everywhere we go, men can't seem to take their eyes off her."

"So, her looks knocked you for a loop, but you expect all the other men on the planet to run in horror when they see her?"

"Of course not."

"Then what did you expect them to do?" Sierra asked, sitting up as the waiter placed their food on the table. She quickly said the blessing.

"I expect her not to look back," he said; then he clamped his teeth together.

Sabra stared at him a long time. So long, he stared back. "You're jealous."

He blew out a dismissive breath and cut viciously into his omelet. "That will be the day."

"And that day is now." She picked up her flatware. "Never thought I'd see it myself. It's a good thing she likes you."

Pierce stopped eating food he couldn't taste. "How do you know that?"

"Because they're seated in my line of vision and she keeps looking this way." Sierra forked in her ham and cheese omelet. "Any other woman wouldn't be able to keep her eyes off a hunky movie star like Britt Powell."

"You recognize him?"

"Yep." She sipped her juice. "He was rumored to be up for the lead in the movie version of the stage play Sabra starred in. I might as well tell you, there was a rumor they had a fling, but it was another tabloid lie."

"How do you know?" he asked, forgetting he shouldn't care.

Sierra propped her elbows on the table and placed her chin on her laced fingers. "For one thing, Sabra didn't strike me as the fling type, or you two wouldn't be still circling each other. For another, they might have on-screen chemistry, but I don't see any now. It could be because Britt is scoping out other women, including me."

"What?" Pierce jerked around to glare at the man. "Isn't Sabra enough?"

Sierra chuckled. "Thank you for being concerned about me."

Pierce faced her and tried to backpedal. "You can take care of yourself."

"So can Sabra." Sierra touched his arm again. "Just because men look doesn't mean she's looking back. Just like you're not paying any attention to the two women across from us who are scoping you out."

He didn't even glance in the women's direction. He knew in his brain what Sierra said was true, but he just couldn't process it. "Perhaps it's best this way. We'll part as friends."

"Your decision, but you're going to want to kick yourself if Britt decides to make the rumors a fact."

Pierce glared at Sierra. She glared right back.

SABRA HAD CALMED DOWN CONSIDERABLY BY THE time they reached the restaurant. Giving Britt a piece of her mind with both barrels and threatening not to do the movie if he didn't behave had done the trick. The role of Jeff Moore was a meaty one, and one that would show he could do more than just be an action hero. He wanted the part.

Sabra wanted Pierce to smile at her again. Didn't he realize that when he was with her, he was the only man she saw?

"Sabra, say the word and the deal is done," David said.

"What?" Sabra pulled her gaze from Sierra and Pierce, who were leaving the restaurant.

"I think she was paying more attention to the man she was with when we arrived." Britt sipped his espresso.

"And you to the woman he was with," Sabra countered.

Britt smiled good-naturedly. "She's a looker."

"And his baby sister and she has three more brothers who'd beat you to a pulp if you messed with her," Sabra said, somehow wishing that Pierce was as protective of her. He had blithely handed her over to Britt. If that was all she meant to him, so be it.

"Might be worth it."

"Please," Dave interjected. "Can we get back to the business at hand? Sabra, whatever you want, the studio is willing to listen to your terms. *Homeward* didn't do as well as expected on its opening Saturday, and they need a hit."

All business now, Britt leaned forward and pinned Sabra with his startling green eyes. "We could give it to them."

She wanted to believe. Her role as Jessica, a fallen woman searching for redemption and love, had been her father's favorite. "I'd give up a year of the theater. I might not be able to go back."

"Bull." Britt placed his hand over hers. "You're good. You're better than good. You're great. The screen test we did proved that. You won a Tony for that role; you'll grab the golden statue as well.

Producers of screen and stage will be beating down your door."

"I told her the same thing," Dave quickly interjected.

"You both told me. Now let me make my own decision." Pierce seemed to be the only one who understood her fears and didn't push her. She'd thought it was because he cared; now she wasn't sure. "Now, I have to get back and dress for rehearsals." The men came to their feet with her. "I appreciate your coming."

"We've been dismissed, Dave." Britt placed several bills on the table.

"Just think about it." Dave placed money on the table as well.

"I will. And I promise you'll be the first to know." Sabra started from the restaurant.

"But when will that be?" Dave asked after her.

"I wish I knew," was the only answer she could give.

PIERCE WAS DETERMINED TO FORGET THAT HE'D ever held Sabra in his arms, that she'd trembled from his touch, that she'd made his blood run hot. But his usually disciplined mind wasn't cooperating.

No matter what he did, he kept conjuring up images of her that, no matter how much he tried to bury himself in his work, kept reappearing.

It had been two long, excruciating days since he'd seen her. He left early and came home late to avoid the possibility. It didn't sit well that he hadn't been sure he wouldn't break down and try to win her back.

He tossed the pen on his desk. What was he thinking? He'd never had her. And it was eating him up inside that he never would. Pushing up from his desk, Pierce turned his back on the pile of client folders he was updating, something he had seldom done in the past, and stared out at the endless stretch of darkness.

At times he felt the same vast emptiness. He knew what would banish the feeling and fill his empty arms. Sabra. She'd gotten under his skin. Muttering, he whirled back around in his chair.

No woman was going to tie up his mind so badly that he couldn't work. Opening the folder, he swerved in his chair toward the computer and brought up the client's file on the twenty-one-inch flat-panel monitor. Besides having a backup on a flash drive, Pierce also kept hard copies of his clients' files. He was a cautious man.

Except when it came to Sabra. Pierce muttered an expletive, then jerked upright as a knock came on his office door. His heart raced. He wanted to deny the reason. When the door opened and he saw Sierra, he couldn't hide his disappointment.

"Sorry."

Denying it would have been impossible. "Did you bring me a sandwich?"

"You'd probably pick at it the same way you did breakfast." Sierra eased a hip onto the other side of his desk. "The same way Sabra does with her lunch, I'm told."

His hand poised on the key, then continued typing in data. "Oh."

"Brandon is practically beside himself with worry." Sierra picked up a bronzed letter opener. "You know how he is. I'm not sure he bought it that seasonal allergies had affected her appetite. Although her eyes did look a bit red and puffy when I saw her in the elevator just now."

Pierce knew when he was being baited—he just couldn't resist the bait. "She's all right, isn't she?"

Sierra shrugged and slipped off the desk. "I suppose. I better get moving if I want to squeak in under the wire and get takeout from Brandon. You want me to stop back by with something for you?"

"What? Er, no." He couldn't stand the thought of Sabra being ill and no one there for her. "Are you going to stop by Sabra's place?"

"Nope. She said she was going to bed, and I don't want to disturb her." Sierra went to the door. "I'm sure she's fine. Night."

"Night." The door closed, yet Pierce didn't move. Another thought raced through his mind. What if Sabra wasn't all right?

THE THINGS I DO FOR LOVE.

Sierra stood on the other side of Pierce's office door and smiled. She'd put things in motion. Now it was up to the two stubborn people to give in and admit they missed each other. She was definitely taking a chance that the attraction between Sabra and Pierce was only sexual and not the forever kind of love that would put her firmly in her mother's sights as the next one in line to get to the altar.

But Sierra didn't like seeing Pierce unhappy. She tried not to recall that she'd also interfered with Morgan and Phoenix, then indirectly with Brandon and Faith. And look where that had ended . . . at the altar.

Sierra snorted, then crossed to the door leading to the hallway and let herself out. She loved her mother and didn't look forward to being the one she was plotting against, but unlike her brothers, Sierra could handle it. Although her brothers were good, intelligent men, they'd tripped themselves up.

As Catherine had told Morgan, their mother could parade women in front of him all day long, but if none of them clicked, if he didn't fall in love, their mother's plan was useless. Of course, by that time, Morgan was already a goner.

Shaking her head, Sierra stepped onto the elevator. She liked men as friends but couldn't imagine that she'd get all weepy and miserable, and certainly she wouldn't stop eating if they were on the outs. A man who could mess with her emotions or get her all hot and bothered didn't exist.

SABRA WAS MISERABLE, AND IT WASN'T ALL DUE TO the seasonal allergies that had decided to pay her a visit. She didn't like being at odds with Pierce. Of course, it was his fault, but that didn't stop her from wanting things back the way they were.

That thought had brought her to his door. She'd called his office and hadn't gotten an answer. When she'd met Sierra in the elevator earlier, she had said Pierce was in his office and she was on her way to visit. She'd also said he hadn't been himself lately, then added that perhaps he had seasonal allergies as well.

Since there was the barest twinkle in Sierra's eyes and Sabra knew she was nobody's fool, she had to conclude—no, hope—that perhaps he was as miserable as she was about the riff between them.

She didn't run from her problems or unpleasant situations. Taking a deep breath, she rang the doorbell. She rang the doorbell again, hoping that Pierce didn't make her regret that long-standing record.

"Sabra?"

She whirled, her hand going to her chest. Pierce. He quickly closed the distance between them at a fast clip. She tried to search his face to determine how he felt about her being there and came up against a blank wall.

"Is everything all right?" Twin lines furrowed on his forehead. "What are you doing out here?"

She moistened her lips. Heat shot through her when his gaze followed. At least *that* hadn't changed. "Sierra said you weren't feeling well." So she *was* a coward where Pierce was concerned.

The furrows deepened. "She said the same thing about you."

"Allergies," Sabra said, hoping he'd see that as the only reason for her red eyes and puffy lids.

"You should be in bed."

Her face heated. It was too much to hope that he didn't see the flush that climbed her cheeks. She could stand there and embarrass herself further or get to the reason she was there. "I'm sor—"

"No." He cut her off. His hand tenderly cupped her cheek. "Not your fault. It was mine. Is Isabella's cartoon running?"

"Yes. I just put it in. I wasn't sure how long I would be here. . . ." Her voice trailed off as his eyes darkened and she realized the possible implication of her words.

"Please come in." Pierce unlocked the door, then took Sabra's arm and drew her inside. Five feet into the living area was a balloon and a note attached to the long string.

"Is today a special occasion?" Sabra asked as she stopped beside Pierce while he untied the string and opened the rolled note, then gave it to her. Sabra quickly scanned the note.

"Sierra."

"Sierra." Taking her arm again, he went into the kitchen. He had to smile. Sierra wasn't much of a homemaker, but she had an eye for detail and fashion.

The small breakfast table was set completely in white and gold. A cluster of three-inch-wide pillar candles of different lengths sat on a mirror tray waiting to be lit. Sterling silver gleamed. Napkins were shaped into swans. Soft, romantic music played on the intercom.

"She did this," Sabra said quietly.

"And according to the note, she and Brandon are not going to be pleased if we don't eat."

She glanced at the note again. "She set us up."

"How do you feel about it?" he asked, watching her closely.

"I don't suppose you'd tell me first?" she asked, hoping for levity, but her voice trembled just the tiniest bit.

His hands settled on her waist. "I wish she would have done it two days ago. I missed you."

"I missed you, too."

His hands tightened; then he released her and stepped back. "If I kiss you, I'm not sure I can stop, and you need to eat. One thing I do know is how to prepare a grilled Caesar chicken topped with honeyed glazed pecans. I'll have food on the table in no time."

"It will be faster if I help."

"I wouldn't have it any other way."

Five minutes later they were sitting down to dinner. Afterward, they cleaned up the kitchen together as they had the last time. It still got to him that she could be so down-to-earth yet take his breath away, make him act like a jealous fool.

She happened to turn from putting away the last dish in the cabinet and caught him staring at her. She stilled. "I guess we still need to talk."

"I guess we do."

Straightening, she leaned back against the black granite counter, her hands on either side of her. "I believe you have the floor."

"You want the honest truth?"

"Yes."

She'd said the word casually, but her knuckles blanched as she gripped the cabinet. *Thank goodness.* He wasn't in this alone.

"You scare me," he said, and saw her eyes widen in surprise. "No woman has ever done that before. I dream about you. A first. I want to lock you up so no man can look at you, want you, except me. I don't like feeling that way."

She pushed away from the counter and came to him. "You scare me. No man has ever done that before. I dream about you. A first. I don't like feeling that way." Her hands rested on his chest, felt his heart drum. "If you lock me up, will you be there with me?"

"Sabra," he cried; her name was a plea, surrender. He pulled her into his arms, his mouth finding hers, kissing her, devouring her. He wanted to wipe out all the men who had ever touched her. The selfish, illogical thought caused his hands to clench around her arm.

Her head lifted; her eyes opened. Wordlessly she stared up at him, patiently waiting. A woman like Sabra changed all the rules except one: trust had to be the cornerstone of whatever was going on between them. Despite everything, he trusted her. "I want to make love to you."

Her eyelashes fluttered downward, then lifted. "I sort of hoped you'd take that decision out of my hand."

He lifted his hand, not surprised to find that it was unsteady, and ran his fingers through her glorious hair. "I care about you too much for that. I don't want you to have any regrets, not ever."

Her gaze unwavering, she palmed his cheek. "Being in your arms is almost the perfect moment. It's wild, scary, thrilling. My body tingles. I've wondered what it would feel like to let myself go, to let you love me, for me to love you."

He trembled with emotions. "You make me weak."

"Not too weak, I hope," she quipped, but her voice wavered.

He grinned like a conquering warrior and picked her up in his arms. "Let's find out."

He quickly carried her to the bedroom and flicked on the recessed lights in the ceiling, casting a soft inviting glow on the wide bed. Briefly setting her on her feet, he tossed back the duvet, then took her into his arms and tumbled with her into bed. Her arms tightened around him as he expected. Her happy laugh was a pleasant surprise.

He grinned at her. She grinned back. They were content for the moment to just be in each other's arms. "I dreamed of you here, your hair spread out on my pillow."

Her hands released the clip at the base of his skull that secured his hair; then she ran her fingers through the thick, lustrous black strands. "I wondered what you'd look like with your hair unbound. Now, I know. A conquering warrior."

He certainly felt like one. He wanted to possess, but he also wanted to give. Sitting up, he sat on the side of the bed to remove his shoes, his shirt, and his slacks. Hearing the rustle of the sheets, he looked back over his shoulder. He'd been half-afraid that she was leaving. Brushing his hair aside, she ran her lips, then her hand over the muscled warmth of his back.

Her touch was heaven, torture. Just as in his dream. Air hissed through his teeth.

She quickly withdrew her hand and sat back on her knees. "I'm sorry."

The uncertainty in her eyes and her apology threw him for a split second. Then it hit him! It couldn't be. Yet, as he stared at her, he knew he was right. He didn't know if he wanted to whimper in pain or shout with joy, if he'd just been presented with a priceless gift or the means to drive him stark raving mad.

Aware that he was weak where she was concerned, he put another few inches between them. But he, a man who before this moment had never been at a loss for words with a woman, found himself unsure of how to broach the subject. He'd rather chew nails than hurt or embarrass her.

"Shouldn't you be getting closer instead of moving away?" she asked, a smile on her face as she watched him closely.

He decided to go for it. Prolonging the conversation certainly wasn't helping. "This is your first time, isn't it?"

"You have a problem with that?" she asked.

He swiped his unsteady hand across his face and scooted a couple more inches away. "I want you like I've never wanted another woman. But this changes things."

Her chin lifted. Hurt flickered in her eyes. "Because I'm not experienced?"

"Because you waited for a reason. I won't lie to you. I'm not the forever kind of man, but the thought of you with anyone else makes me crazy," Pierce said. "Why did you wait?"

Her hands flexed. "You always like things on the table, don't you?"

"This is too important not to have all the facts," he told her. "Why?"

She squared her shoulders. "As I told you, the man I thought I was in love with was just using me for another notch on his belt. I found out when I overheard him at a party. If I hadn't heard him, I wouldn't have believed it. That was a wake-up call that all the acting wasn't just on the stage." She shrugged. "I never wanted to be used again, so I put my time and energy into building my career. Does that answer your question?"

"He was a fool."

She stared straight at him. "We agree on that. Now what?"

"If we go through this, it will be a first for both of us."

"I guess I'm not your usual date," she said, her voice barely above a whisper.

"No," he said.

Pain flashed in her eyes. She started to scramble from the bed. Pierce caught her by the arms. "Sabra. Wait."

Shaking her head, she refused to look at him. "Let me go, please."

His heart clenched on hearing her shaky voice. "You didn't let me finish," he said gently. "Please look at me."

Her head lifted. He half-expected tears. Thank goodness there were none, but he knew this could get dicey. His hands flexed, then slid down her arms to lace his fingers with hers. If he messed this up, he'd never forgive himself. "There isn't another woman in the world like you. It's not just your incredible beauty; it's the strong, compassionate woman I've come to know and care about. You arouse my compassion as much as my passion. A first."

Her hands relaxed in his. "I never knew I could feel this intense ache, the hunger for you that builds each time I see you. A first."

His eyes blazed; his body stirred in response. The

right thing to do was to take her to her room. He didn't move.

Aware of his dilemma, she tilted her head beguilingly to one side. "So, Pierce, are you going to let me leave this bed without us making love?"

His hands flexed. "I should."

Smiling, she inched closer and put her arms around his neck, pressing against him, tempting him, testing his endurance. "But I don't want to go."

He drew in a shuddering breath. He had all that he desired in his arms, but he didn't think he could stand to see regret in her eyes afterwards. "Sabra, are you sure?"

"Yes," she breathed her answer, her lips brushing tantalizingly against his.

Air hissed over his teeth. "Heaven help me. I don't want you to go, either." With more courage than he thought he possessed, he sat her away from him. "Last chance."

Her gaze held complete trust. "I'm where I want to be."

"Heaven help both of us." His arms urgently drew her to him. "We're going to burn up the night," he whispered, his voice hoarse with need.

"Yes." The unsteady word quivered over her lips.

His mouth took possession of hers in a kiss that began tender and quickly built, heating the fire in his blood to a raging inferno. Feeling his control slipping, he lifted his head and stared into her eyes.

Hers glowed with the same hot passion he fought to keep in check. If she changed her mind, he prayed he could stop.

His hands lifted to slowly unbutton her blouse; then he watched in fascination as the opening revealed more and more of her silken flesh. With both hands, he swept the blouse over her shoulders and off her arms. Delicate pink lace cupped her beautifully shaped breasts. He wanted to replace the fabric with his hands, his mouth. He resisted the urge.

He unbuttoned her slacks but found his hands trembling as he shoved them past the tiny lace panties and off her long, shapely legs. Straightening, he stared at her incredible body—the swell of her breasts, the tiny waist, the flare of her hips—and found a dilemma he'd never experienced before.

"I don't know what I want to touch first."

Her hand brushed across his chest. "That's all right, because I want to feel you everywhere."

His heart and mind soared. Her bra and panties came away. His hand cupped one velvet-soft breast as his mouth suckled the other's taut nipple. She gasped in delight. Her body arched as her fingers tunneled through his hair to hold him closer. He pleasured her, relishing the way she restlessly moved beneath him, the arousing friction of her naked body, the long silky legs against him.

He stroked, kissed, and pleased her body, pleased his. He barely held it together as he left her to sheathe himself.

His body poised over her, he felt powerful and humbled. She trusted him. He'd do anything, everything, to make this right for her first time. Reaching between them, he found her hot, moist center and stroked.

With a low moan of pleasure, she lifted her hips. Her response caused his erection to harden even more. His mouth covered hers, his tongue imitating the tantalizing dance of his fingers.

"Pierce." His name was a ragged thread of sound, her hips rising to meet him again and again.

He began to slowly ease into her, stretching her, filling her. "Wrap your legs around me."

As soon as she did, his hand slipped beneath her hips. With gentle strokes, he allowed her body to become adjusted to his. When she relaxed again, he deepened the strokes by degrees until they were long and deep, taking them both to the point of no return. Pleasing her was paramount. His mouth went back to hers again as he set up a relentless pace, drawing cries of ecstasy from her. Pleasure built and rocked through them.

He felt her body tense. "Let go, Sabra. Let go and feel. Trust me."

He nipped her shoulder. She shivered beneath him, then caught the rhythm once again. She was with him all the way. Her nails dug into his shoulders. Her gathered her closer and took them over together.

When he could catch his breath, he rolled, drawing

her over him like a living blanket. With her in his arms he felt at peace for the first time in weeks.

"I never knew," she whispered, awe in her drowsy voice.

His arms tightened. He hadn't, either. He could be either pleased or worried. He kissed Sabra on the forehead, then followed her into a peaceful sleep.

CHAPTER FIFTEEN

DELICIOUSLY SATED, SABRA WOKE WITH A SMILE ON her face. Stretching languidly, she felt the slight soreness of her body, the muscled warmth of a man's thigh beneath hers. Her smile broadening, she lifted her head and stared into Pierce's lazy gaze.

"Good morning," she said.

"Good morning." He pulled her up in his arms, letting her naked body slide over his. "You'll never know how difficult it was to let you sleep."

Her skin prickled with heat and desire. She wished he had awakened her. "W-what time is it?"

He looked out the window instead of at the clock. "A little after eight in the morning."

Her fingertip brushed across his lower lip, as she enjoyed being able to freely touch him. "I haven't slept that well in a long time. Thank you."

He smiled, and she almost sighed. "Any time you need a sleep aid, I'm your man."

"I'll remem—" She suddenly jerked up and started to roll out of bed.

Pierce's hand on her arm stopped her. "What is it?"

"Isabella. When the DVD stopped and I wasn't there, she probably tore up Sierra's place."

Using both hands, he pulled Sabra flush against him. "After you fell asleep last night I went to get her. If I don't miss my guess, she's outside the bedroom door."

"You went to my apartment?" Alarm tripped down her spine. Had she left any incriminating information about her search lying around?

The easy smile slid from his face. "I only went as far as the DVD to cut it off. Isabella followed me back without the leash. I gave her some water and told her we'd see her in the morning. Just as Sierra has a key to my place, I have a key to hers. I'm sorry if I overstepped."

After last night, more than ever Sabra felt ashamed that she had to keep a secret from him. "You didn't. It was sweet and thoughtful to think of her. I certainly didn't."

His hand settled possessively on her bare butt. "You had other things on your mind."

"They are on my mind again," she said, surprising herself.

"Thank goodness." He pulled her up farther, then fastened his mouth on her nipple. The peak hardened instantly. She moaned, then moaned again as Pierce, already sheathed, slid into her. Her eyes widened as her breath shuddered out.

"Are you all right?"

She wasn't sure until he moved. Pleasure rippled through her.

"It's as easy as riding. And, just like riding, you can take control."

The idea appealed to her. From her position, she stared down into his handsome face and felt him hard inside her. She clenched around him. Air hissed through his teeth. She felt wicked and powerful that she could have that effect on him.

Just like he affected her.

His large hands settled on her waist, then slid up to cup her breasts. Even as she arched against his hands to increase the pressure, her hands splayed on his muscled chest. Eyes closed, she began to move, cautiously at first, then with more assurance as excitement replaced timidness. All coherent thought fled as she rode Pierce.

This was paradise; this was passion. The perfect moment. She let herself go and flew.

"WHAT IF SHE SEES ME AND KNOWS? I'LL JUST DIE."

Pierce caught Sabra's trembling hands. He'd followed her to her apartment to take a shower and get dressed. They'd ended up in the shower together, making love. Each time was more powerful than the last. He was tempted to strip the sweater and slacks away and bury himself deep into her satin heat again.

"Pierce?"

"It will be fine." She wanted his reassurance. He'd give her that and more if she asked. She had a glow about her. She looked like a woman thoroughly loved and satisfied, but to tell her that would make her even more nervous about seeing his mother this morning at rehearsals. "She'll just think you're feeling better."

"You think?"

"I think," he said, and pulled her into his arms, where she had been most of the time since last night. After they'd made love for the second time and Isabella became impatient at the door, they remembered the dog sitter and called to cancel. Thank goodness it was Saturday and they could be together soon.

After the shower, they'd taken Isabella for a walk and picked up takeout from a fast-food place, laughing and giggling like kids over the repercussions they'd face if Brandon found out. He thought fast food was a heart attack waiting.

"Do you want me to drive you?" Pierce finally asked.

"No." She stepped out of his arms. "She'd take one look at me looking at you and know."

"That would be the same way I'm looking at you." His hands settled on her waist again; he nipped her ear.

She sighed, then pushed against him. "Stop that."

"If I see you, I have to touch you," he said, meaning every word.

"Then don't come anywhere near me until after rehearsals." She went to his door. "You're sure about keeping Isabella?"

"She'll be fine. Have a good rehearsal."

She bit her lower lip. "You're sure she won't be able to tell?"

"I'm sure." The lie was for her.

SABRA WAS GOING TO STRANGLE PIERCE. IF ONE person had commented on the glow in her face, the sparkle in her eyes, ten had. That Ruth didn't comment made it worse, not better. At least Charles got through his lines without stumbling.

"You did great today," Sabra said when rehearsals were over.

He blushed with pleasure. "Thanks to Mrs. Grayson's son Pierce. He's cool."

Her interest was piqued as they walked from the stage for the next characters to take their marks. "How so?"

"He had a rep at St. John's as a Casanova, but he said . . ." Charles's voice trailed off, and he tucked his head for a moment. "I don't want to betray a confidence, but it was cool for him to help me not to be so intimidated by you. He was nice when he didn't have to be. It's no wonder half the women in town are hoping Mrs. Grayson picks one of them for him to marry."

The clipboard in Sabra's hand cluttered on the wooden floor. "What?"

Charles scooped up the clipboard and handed it back to her. Surreptitiously, he glanced around, then whispered, "Mrs. Grayson is marrying off her children, from the oldest to the youngest, one by one. Pierce is next."

• • •

PIERCE WAS NO STRANGER TO AN ANGRY WOMAN. His mother on a roll could make any of her adult children walk easy around her. But try as he might, he couldn't fathom why Sabra looked ready to tear into him. It certainly couldn't be that his mother had said anything. She only tried to run the lives of her grown children. The rest of the world she left to their own devices.

He slowly came to his feet but remained behind his desk in his office. Out of the corner of his eye, he saw Isabella come to her feet and trot over to stand by Sabra. He got the distinct impression that if Sabra gave the command, he'd have eighty pounds of trouble to contend with.

"Why didn't you tell me?"

"I did it for your own good," he told her, hating that she'd been embarrassed.

"My own good?" she hissed, coming closer. "Do you think I like being made a fool of?"

There was anger in her voice, mixed with hurt. The hurt drew him from behind the desk.

"I wouldn't advise it."

He heard a low, guttural growl. He kept his gaze on Sabra. "I'm sorry. It's not like Mama to comment on a person's personal life."

Her eyes shut, then opened. "Not that! Why didn't you tell me you were next to get married?"

He was taken aback for all of two seconds; then he was moving. Isabella's growl grew louder, more menacing. He speared the dog with a look. The noise stopped. The animal trotted over to her favorite spot and lay down. Sabra wouldn't be so easily subdued.

"Come back here, and bite him," she said.

He wanted to touch Sabra but didn't think it wise with her in her current state. "For now, how you heard doesn't matter. What does matter is that my mother might pick out a woman for me, but I make my own choices."

"Why didn't you tell me?"

"I didn't think it mattered then, and it matters less now." His hands closed gently around her arms. "Last night should have made it clear that I care about you, not some unknown woman."

"Does that include Raven?"

He had to work hard to keep the grin—all right, smirk—off his face. For once he could have kissed his mother for her meddling. "Especially Raven." He told Sabra about their first meeting at his mother's house. "She was never an issue."

"Then why did she try to warn me away from you Monday morning?"

"What!" His eyes rounded. "This has gone too far." He went behind his desk, then bent to get his keys out of the lowest drawer. When he straightened, Sabra blocked his path.

"I think I should tell you that she sort of relinquished her claim."

"She never had a claim," he snapped.

"You're pretty angry."

"I'm way past that. It took me a long time to get you to trust me, and now Mama and Raven want to mess things up."

Inexplicably, the angrier he became, the more hers evaporated. "I thought you were playing me."

His hard black eyes cut into her. "How could you think that?"

"I confused you with someone else."

Her mistrust hurt, but how much more had she been hurt? "If I could get my hands on him, I'd teach him a lesson. He should have treated you better."

"I survived."

"Yes, you did." He slowly drew her into his arms. "Are we finished fighting?"

Her arms circled his neck. "Maybe."

"Then why don't we go to my place, order in, and finish this discussion?"

"Lead the way."

THE MOMENT THE DOOR CLOSED, HE PULLED HER into his arms, kissing her, trying to get her clothes off and them to the bed. She laughed, then moaned, as he swept the black lacy nothing of a bra off, then the rest of her clothes.

By the time they tumbled into his bed, they were both naked. She evaded Pierce's reaching hands to straddle him and drop soft kisses on his chest, then went steadily lower.

"Sabra," he said, his voicc gritty.

She kissed his flat stomach, felt him tremble

beneath her lips. She wondered what would make him lose control completely and dipped her head lower. In the next instant she found herself on her back with Pierce towering over her.

"Playtime over." He brought them together. Her body welcomed him. The loving was slow, building in tempo until they could hold back no longer. He buried his face in the curve of her shoulder and took them both over.

He started to move, but her arms tightened. She relished his weight on her, the delicious heat of his body, the lingering aftermath of ecstasy.

He kissed the curve of her cheek. Then, despite her protests, he rolled to his side, taking her with him. "I'm too heavy."

She snuggled closer and ran her hand through his hair. "You feel good."

"So do you." He nuzzled her neck. "Are you hungry?"

"Ravenous."

"I guess I should feed you, but I don't want to move," he confessed.

Her head angled to look up at him, kiss his chin. "I don't suppose we could call Brandon for takeout?"

"We could, but I'd have to go pick it up." His hand swept down the elegant slope of her back.

She was already shaking her head. "If I have to give up being held by you, we'll skip food."

Pierce drew her up and stared in her eyes. "You mean I score higher than food?"

She kissed him on the lips. "Don't let it go to your head."

"Wouldn't think of it." Lifting her away, he rolled out of bed and looked around for his pants.

Sabra sat up. "You're not going out?"

He glanced up, felt his breath snag, his body harden, when he saw the hair tousled around her shoulders, her body flushed from their lovemaking. He wanted her again. Hurriedly, he grabbed his pants at the foot of the bed and pulled them on. He was turning into a sex maniac. "To the kitchen to see what's there," he finally answered.

"I'll help." Scrambling out of bed, she picked up his white T-shirt and pulled it over her head. "Hope you don't mind."

The T-shirt covered her to below the knees, but the softness of her breasts was evident. Plus he knew she was naked beneath. "You might be more of a distraction than a help."

Her gaze slowly tracked from his face down his bare chest, past his unmistakable arousal, to his bare feet. "I can say the same thing about you."

"I guess we'll just have to chance it." His hand reached out for hers.

LUCKILY PIERCE HAD THE INGREDIENTS TO MAKE AN omelet. Neither seemed to mind that it was overcooked and tough. They paid more attention to each other than the cooking and considered the burned food a small price for the long, hot kisses they'd shared, the intimate touches.

Pierce was sliding the omelet onto a plate when the phone rang. Planning to get rid of the caller as soon as possible, he reached for the receiver.

"Pierce."

"Hello, Pierce. You certainly sound happy."

"Mama." His gaze shot to Sabra, who was kneeling on the floor beside Isabella while the dog ate. Her eyes wide, Sabra slowly came to her feet.

"Could you do me a favor?" his mother asked. "I left a message on Sabra's machine, but I worry that when she comes home she might not listen."

"What kind of message?" he asked cautiously. With his mother, he could never be sure.

"Just that I won't be able to pick her up for church services in the morning. Raven and I are taking a little trip to the pueblos, but I'll be back in time for dinner."

Relief swept through him. "I'll tell her. Drive carefully."

"Why don't you come with us?" his mother invited. "Tomorrow will be a beautiful day for a drive."

He walked to Sabra and brushed her tumbled hair over her shoulder. "Thank you, but I'll pass."

"You don't know what you'll be missing."

He knew very well. "Drive carefully. I'll see you when you get back."

"Good-bye, Pierce."

"Bye, Mama." Pierce hung up the phone and curved his arms around Sabra's small waist. "Mama won't be able to pick you up for church services. She wanted me to let you know she's driving to the pueblos in the morning."

Sabra's hands lifted to rest on his bare chest. "Alone?"

A frown knit his brow before he could stop it. "Raven is going with her."

"She wanted you to go with them, didn't she?" Sabra asked.

He brushed his lips across her forehead. "She mentioned it."

Sabra nodded. She could worry about his mother's obvious choice or enjoy the time they had together. "The food is getting cold."

He picked up the plate. "In here or in bed?"

"You get one guess."

Pierce put the plate on a red lacquered tray while Sabra grabbed napkins and two glasses of raspberry juice. In bed, they fed each other, then feasted on each other.

SUNDAY MORNING, SABRA WOKE UP WITH HER UPPER body sprawled across Pierce's wide chest. His arms circled her. In the past thirty-six hours she'd spent more time in his bed than her own, and she couldn't be happier. "You're watching me again."

"I can't think of a more beautiful sight to wake up to."

Neither could she. Pleasure swept through her, and she lifted her head. He was magnificent. But time wasn't on their side.

His hand swept down the slope of her back. "What is it?"

She started to tell him but held back. Perhaps their interlude was all Pierce wanted or expected. "Nothing."

His fingertip gently brushed across her lower lip. "Are you worried about the decisions you have to make for your career or what happens between us when you leave?"

Her hand caught his. He read her so well. "I've seen people in the business try to make long-distance relationships work, and they seldom do, causing more heartache than happiness."

"I've never been one to follow the crowd."

She could believe that. "Let's just enjoy the time we have."

His mouth tightened into a thin line. "Is that all you want?"

"No, it's not, but I'm scared that this is all that it will be."

"Then I'll just have to show you differently, starting now." He kissed her and pulled her under him, joining them with an experienced thrust of his hips. She arched upward. A moan slipped past her lips as he began to move slowly, taking his time and letting the pleasure build.

Helplessly, she locked her arms around his neck,

her legs around his waist, and let his loving empty her mind and fill her body with erotic sensations. His warm mouth nuzzled her throat. His hand tenderly stroked her, worshipped her. As before, they found the perfect rhythm.

Coherent thought became impossible. If this was all there was, she was going to enjoy it to the fullest. She flexed her hips, took him deeper. Her hands clutched his shoulders, marveling at the restrained strength.

All too soon her body tightened. She felt his do the same. The strokes grew faster, longer, until they were clutching each other and racing toward completion. A wild exhilaration swept through her. She was made to be loved by this man.

He surged into her. She arched up to meet him. Their bodies strained to get closer. Their broken cries of release mingled as they found completion together.

PIERCE HAD NO ILLUSIONS ABOUT WHAT WOULD happen when Sierra saw him with Sabra. Unlike their mother, Sierra didn't mind getting in other people's business and speaking her mind about it. Nor would it have been lost on her that after she had pushed them together Friday night, neither he nor Sabra had been to breakfast or visited Brandon's place.

He and Sierra usually talked every day. They were the last two and thus had grown even closer as their brothers married.

"Sierra is already here. Wonderful."

Pierce didn't comment as Sabra rushed forward. She'd been excited since she'd gone to her place that morning to change clothes and heard on her voice mail that the concierge had a special delivery package for her.

He heard the shriek along with the rest of the breakfast diners, then saw Sierra tearing open a box with greedy haste.

By the time he reached them, Sierra was holding a long white silk strapless dress with a silver and jewel loop at the waist. "Valentino."

"I'm attending a charity dinner in Los Angeles the day after I leave at the Wilshire. I was hoping you'd be my guest. My assistant booked a three-bedroom suite in case my mother and sister were able to join me. They can't."

Sierra's hand reverently touched the gown. "I can't accept this."

Sabra leaned forward until they were eye to eye. "If there was something I wanted and you could give it to me, would you?"

Sierra's gaze flickered to Pierce. "That was purely selfish."

"Then see this the same way. I'm wearing black and we'll play well off each other."

"It's still too much," Sierra protested.

"If you insist." Sabra reached for the dress, but Sierra refused to let it go. "Change your mind?"

"You knew I would. I'm paying for the dress."

Sierra took one last look and closed the lid. "Thank you."

"Thank you and you're welcome." Sabra turned to Pierce. "Come on, Pierce. I'm starved."

No wonder. They'd existed on sex and burned food. He took his seat. "Morning, Sierra."

"Good morning." Sierra signaled the waiter.

Pierce looked at the two women as they ordered, listened to them chat about the theater and Sierra's plans to own her own brokerage firm. Not once did Sierra give the impression she knew what they had been doing. He breathed a little easier . . . until he saw Brandon and Faith heading in their direction.

After they were seated and had ordered, Pierce half-expected Brandon to tease him when Sabra wasn't looking. He got another surprise. Brandon simply commented that he was glad Sabra felt better and invited her to his restaurant for dinner Monday night.

Obviously pleased, Sabra, an impish smile on her beautiful face, turned to Pierce. "Can I bring a date?"

"Only if you must," Brandon replied with a smile.

Pierce looked at Brandon, Sierra, and Faith. They liked Sabra. He couldn't remember any of the other women he'd dated being teased and accepted so easily. But then, he'd never brought them around his family.

"How about it? You available tomorrow night?" Sabra asked.

"Always," he answered. Her smile faltered, then

firmed. She believed their time was limited. He didn't know how long this would last, but for the first time where a woman was concerned, he didn't want to think of when she would be gone.

And the thought unsettled him. He wasn't the possessive or long-term type.

He looked at Sabra laughing and talking with Faith and Sierra, who was showing her gown again. Something tightened in his chest. As if aware of him watching her, Sabra smiled over her shoulder and brushed her hand down his arm before turning her attention back to Faith and Sierra.

Her touch sent tiny flames licking over his skin. Some women changed the rules, and it was his good fortune to have found one.

CHAPTER SIXTEEN

"HE'S BEEN GONE FOR ONLY A FEW HOURS AND I miss him already."

Sitting on the sofa in her condo, Sabra blew out a breath and glanced at her watch. Six fifteen. After brunch, they'd all gone to church together; then afterward Pierce had taken her by Brandon's to eat before dropping her off at the condo.

"I'll be back as soon as I can," Pierce said, then, after a brief kiss, had left her at her door, lonely and staring after him. She understood and respected the Sunday afternoon get-together of the entire Grayson clan; she just wished it weren't today.

"What am I going to do when I go back, Isabella?"

The dog put her muzzle on Sabra's thigh and barked.

Sabra swept her hand across the dog's head and looked at the window. If the ache was this bad already, what was she going to do if she went to Canada? The thought made her realize that she was leaning toward doing the motion picture. She'd never been afraid of challenges. Except one.

Pierce.

The phone rang on the desk across the room. Setting the laptop aside, she went to answer it. "Hello."

"Hello, Sabra."

Happiness swept through her. "Hello, Mother. Did Laurel's final concert go well last night?" Laurel had been on a ten-week tour of Europe. Last night had been the final performance in London. Today they were scheduled to fly to Paris, then Rome. They weren't due back for another month.

"Magnificent," Sabra's mother said, excitement and pride in her voice. "Your sister's talent grows with each performance. She's brilliant."

"That she is," Sabra said, meaning it. She'd long ago gotten over the hurt that her mother thought *anyone* could act. Laurel had worked hard, giving up almost all of her free time to practice. She still did. If possible, Laurel dated less than Sabra. "How is she?"

There was a slight pause. "She misses your father. We both do."

Sabra's grip on the phone tightened. "He loved us."

Her mother sniffed. "He was a wonderful man, and he spoiled you."

There was no denying the truth, but he'd paid a high price. "He spoiled all of us."

"Yes. How is the play going?" her mother asked.

"Great. Mrs. Grayson, the chair of the music department, and the students are wonderful. We should have a hit on our hands," Sabra told her, wondering why she had told Ruth but not her mother that she had written the play or the songs. "I sing two songs."

"I always dreamed of you and Laurel onstage together."

The disappointment in her mother's voice hurt almost as much as if it had been critical. "My voice doesn't lend itself to classical music."

"It might if you had practiced instead of—" Her words abruptly ended.

"Mother!" Panic gripped Sabra. "Mother!" Sabra's father's sudden heart attack had been while he and her mother were out dining.

"I'm fine," her mother finally answered. "Laurel just came into the room and reminded me that you had practiced and succeeded. Lloyd never doubted that you would."

"Daddy always believed in me," Sabra said softly, and thought of Pierce. He had the same unshakable faith in her.

"He was proud of you, and so am I," her mother said. "You didn't choose the path I wanted, but you've made a success of your life. You're happy, and that's what counts."

Sabra almost looked at the phone. Her mother had always been against the theater. "Thank you, Mother."

"Here's your sister. I better check and see if the bags are packed. Good-bye."

"Good-bye, Mother."

"Hi, Sabra."

"Hi yourself." Smiling, Sabra walked to the sofa and sat down. She could visualize her petite, exotic sister. Men fell over themselves for her and she never seemed to notice. Music was her world. "I hear you wowed them."

"I love playing, but not the touring," Laurel confessed. "How are things there?"

"Fine." She tucked her feet under. "You and Mother all right? She sounded different. Your doing?"

"Life is too short to live with regrets," Laurel said slowly.

Sabra's feet slid from under her. There was something in her sister's voice that worried her. "What is it, Laurel?" Her sister could give lessons to a stone when it came to talking. "Is it about Daddy?"

"There were times I could have spent with him and didn't. I was too busy practicing. When you came home, you two were inseparable. I always thought there would be time. Now he's gone."

Sabra squeezed her eyes to keep the tears from falling. "Daddy loved you and was proud of you. He understood how important your music was to you. Your craft demanded a lot of practice; mine didn't. And no matter how much time we had with him, we'd still wish for more. It's hard letting go."

"I don't want to live with regrets ever again," Laurel said softly.

"Then don't," Sabra said, thinking of how afraid she had been to have a relationship with Pierce. "Live your life and be happy."

"You sound different, too."

Sabra debated only briefly. "I'm seeing someone."

"My goodness!" Laurel cried in excitement. "E-mail me a picture tonight. What does he look like? How did you meet?"

Sabra laughed at the enthusiasm in her sister's voice. "I don't have a picture, but he's gorgeous, brilliant, and the son of the sponsor for the play."

"To have caught your attention, he must be. The bellman is here for our luggage. Take care, and thanks for being such a great big sister," Laurel said.

"You make it easy. Travel safely. Good-bye."

"Good-bye."

Sabra hung up the phone. She didn't want to live with regrets, either. For as long as it lasted, she planned to be with Pierce.

The doorbell rang just as she picked up the laptop again. Isabella barked and ran to the door. *Pierce.* Sabra rushed after her and swung it open.

He stepped inside and closed the door. "I missed you."

She launched herself into his arms and just held on, feeling her body tremble. She lifted her head just to look at him. His mouth covered hers, his tongue moving with maddening slowness inside her mouth.

She made a small sound of pleasure and matched him stroke for stroke. Her lower body settled against the junction of his thighs. His hand pressed against her hips, holding her against his hardness.

Lifting his mouth, Pierce muttered, "I see you and I want you."

"That about sums up the way I feel about you."

His forehead touched hers. "You're irresistible. I'm not even sure what excuse I made to leave Luke and Catherine's house early."

"I tried to play the piano and that lasted about five minutes, then I turned on the laptop, but I never got around to opening the file."

"Can't have that." Lifting his head, he took her hand and went to the sofa. "Any objections to working at my place? I'd bring my things here if I didn't need my desktop computer."

Sabra picked up the laptop. "Do you think we'll get any work done?"

"We'll soon find out."

"WHAT'S BOTHERING YOU?"

Sabra lifted her gaze from the laptop. Pierce took off his half-glasses and laid them on a three-inch stack of papers on the desk in his home office. She'd ceased worrying or being surprised that Pierce could read her so well.

"I'm going to accept the movie role," she said. For some reason, her gut clenched.

Not a flicker of emotion crossed his face. Getting

up from his desk, he came to where she sat on the red leather settee, took the laptop from her, then hunkered down in front of her. "I bet your agent was happy."

"I haven't told him yet."

An awed, pleased expression crossed his face. He took her nervous hands in his. "Thank you, and don't worry. You'll wow the audience, and we'll find a way to be together."

She no longer worried about the audience. All she could do was her best. Her fear was in losing him. "I'll be there at least six months."

"Looks like I'll rack up a lot of frequent-flier miles." His hand lifted to cup her cheek. "That is, if you don't mind."

"Your business?" Her gaze went to the stack of papers on his desk. "You have a responsibility to your clients that I know you don't take lightly."

"I won't deprive myself of you or my clients from the attention their finances deserve," he told her.

She believed him. He wouldn't shirk his responsibility. He was a man of principle. Her hand covered his. "I wish you could have known my father."

His smile was gentle. "I would have thanked him for raising a beautiful unspoiled woman of compassion and strength."

"If—" Her head lowered.

His knuckled fingers lifted her chin. "What?"

She shook her head and tried to shake away the

bleakness that had crept over her. There was no sense thinking that if her father had met Pierce, he might have helped Lloyd so he wouldn't have had to resort to such desperate measures. But she couldn't discuss it with Pierce. She had a strong feeling that an ethical man like Pierce wouldn't understand her father's desperation.

"Sabra?"

She forced herself to smile. "Just thinking that life takes strange turns."

"You're right about that. I'll have to thank Mama for inviting you," he said with a grin. "And, of course, you for coming."

It hit her again that she was practicing just as big a deception as her father. She pushed the thought away. Pierce was too perceptive. "I think you've already thanked me."

His brow arched at the teasing smile on her face. He chuckled. "Sassy. Now, get to writing. I want to see pages before your surprise gets here."

She straightened. "What?"

His finger swept down her nose. "You'll see." Standing, he went back to sit behind his desk and swiveled to his computer.

"Not even a hint?"

"Pages." Although he wanted to look at Sabra again, Pierce kept his eyes on the monitor. He had "pages" he needed to produce himself. Sabra's presence gave him an edgy peace. He almost shook his head at such a dichotomy. If he could see her, smell her, he wanted her, but at the same time he enjoyed knowing she was near.

"I don't hear any keys."

"I'm working."

He heard the clatter of the keyboard and wondered what she would say when her surprise arrived.

SHE WAS SPEECHLESS. SHE LOOKED FROM PIERCE to the candles burning on the lip of the Roman tub, the red rose petals floating on top of the water inside, the flute of champagne, the tray of canapes on a small Chinese table nearby.

He hoped her stunned expression meant she was pleased. He'd had her stay in his office when the doorbell rang. The Garriety sisters had grinned when he asked about the bag of rose petals. Brandon had slapped him on the back when he ordered the tray and asked if he could include chocolate-covered strawberries.

"It occurred to me that this probably should have happened Friday night."

"You did this?"

He wished she'd look at him. "Jacuzzi is good for sore muscles. Earlier this evening I thought—" She threw herself into his arms. "You aren't upset?" His arms tightened around her.

Her head lifted. "No, but there's only one way I'm getting in there."

He glanced around to see if he had forgotten anything and couldn't. "Name it."

She reached for the snap of his jeans. "You join me."

"You only have to ask."

SABRA HAD JUMPED WITH BOTH FEET INTO THE AFFAIR with Pierce and she wasn't going to worry about it. She was happy and for now that was enough. Going to sleep in his arms and waking up cuddled against him was a pleasure she wasn't willing to go without. She couldn't remember a time she'd been happier. The world seemed better, the day brighter, life sweeter, and the reason was the man sitting next to her.

It was liberating to finally be able to show her emotions instead of hiding them. What made it even more special was that he felt the same way. The acceptance by his family . . . except Ruth . . . was an added bonus. Sabra had made good friends here. She'd miss them, but she'd be back; of that she was sure.

The only problem was that she hadn't been able to find the man her father had "borrowed" the money from. Since she had interviewed everyone on her list, learning the man's identity now wasn't likely. But at least she had one less worry since she'd decided to do the movie.

Her family, her agent, and Britt had been thrilled.

Aware that once the media knew she'd be swamped for interviews, she'd asked the movie studio not to make an announcement until she was back in New York. She didn't want anything to intrude on the time she had with Pierce.

"Help yourself to my salad."

Sabra speared a cucumber in Pierce's house salad. Her third. "Thanks."

"I can order you one."

"I just want a bite." She went back for a black olive. "Besides, it tastes better off your plate."

"You and Sierra are so much alike." He edged his salad closer to hers of field greens.

"You mean brilliant, hardworking, and diligent?" She speared his last olive.

"Food thieves," he said with humor in his voice.

She bumped him with her shoulder. "And you adore us." She tensed. Pierce wanted to keep this simple.

"Of course. I wouldn't let just anyone eat my food," he said easily.

She relaxed and sat back as the food runner arrived to take their salads and place their entrées on the table. "And we thank you."

"Sabra, what a wonderful surprise."

Sabra glanced up and froze on seeing the first financial adviser on her list, Sam Garner. For the life of her, she couldn't get a word out.

"Hello, Sam," Pierce greeted him.

She finally gathered her wits. "Hello, Sam."

The older man looked from one to the other, but as the silence grew, he shifted nervously. "Well, I better get back to the table with my wife. I thought I'd come over and speak. Good-bye."

"Good-bye," Sierra said, casting a glance at Pierce, wondering when the questions would begin.

"How does the chicken taste?"

Sabra stared at him in surprise. "You aren't going to ask me how I know him?"

"I assume it has something to do with investments." Pierce cut into his rare filet mignon. "Sam had that look."

"You aren't upset?"

He shrugged. "I admit I initially felt disappointment that you hadn't asked me; then I thought you probably considered the attraction between us and knew it would be unethical for me to date a client. You were smart to look to another agent."

She didn't feel smart; she felt like a fraud. Pierce didn't like subterfuge. What would happen if he learned the real reason she knew Garner? "I thought he was honest."

"He is. Two people you should always be able to trust are your minister and your financial adviser."

"Have you ever known a financial planner who wasn't?" she heard herself ask, her breath held.

Anger leaped into his dark eyes. "Unfortunately, more than one. They don't just steal money; they steal dreams. They should be prosecuted to the fullest extent of the law."

To Pierce, everything was cut-and-dried, black-and-white with no gray areas. Her heart sank.

"Was there something else?"

"No." She quickly shook her head and forced a smile. "I guess I'm still surprised that you took my seeing Garner so well."

"Me, too." He picked up her hand and rubbed his thumb across the top.

"Thank you."

"You're welcome. Now finish eating."

PIERCE SAW THEM IN FRONT OF THEIR CONDO BUILDing before Sabra did and halted. "What's going on?"

Sabra lifted her head from Pierce's shoulder and wanted to rail at the person responsible. More than a dozen men and women were gathered in front of the building. At least five had cameras. A cameraman with a TV station was taking footage of the area. "My guess would be that someone leaked word that I was going to do the movie."

Immediately, Pierce turned her around and started in the direction they had come. "Your agent or Powell?"

"Neither," Sabra said. "I trust both of them. Most likely it's someone from the studio. We'll probably never know for sure."

Pierce heard the anger in her voice, but there was something else. He stopped and drew her out of the busy flow of people on the sidewalk. "What is it?"

"I wanted this time for us." She glanced back in the direction of their condo. "You don't know how persistent they can be." She looked back at him. "Most of the media people are honest, but a few will print anything to sell a paper or magazine."

"You mean like the lies about you and Powell?"

Her eyes widened. "Yes."

His hand cupped her cheek. "They can print what they like. This is what I believe." His mouth brushed against hers, then settled. The kiss was long and thorough and drugging. When he lifted his head, they were both breathing heavily. "Now, what's to be done to get through this?"

Pierce's deferring to her banished her doubts and upped her confidence that they could get through this. "We need to take control and call a news conference. Your mother promised the media here an exclusive. If they can see me tonight, I'll give it to them. Then I'll schedule a news conference for the morning with the head of the studio and Britt."

"The media here is easy," he said. "Britt and the head of the studio might be difficult."

Sabra's chin lifted. "Leave that up to me. I just need a place to operate from."

"Leave that to me."

IN LESS THAN THIRTY MINUTES SABRA WAS BEING hooked up to a mic in Faith's office, while the cameramen and women from the local TV stations and newspapers jockeyed for position. Sabra only smiled when the nervous man kept dropping the mic that had to run under her sweater.

"I should have worn a different top. I'll do it." Taking the mic, she quickly clamped it in place on the scooped neck of her tangerine-colored knit top. "You'd probably rather be out on a date or home with your family."

The balding man blushed like a teenager. "Been married forty years."

"I'd say you were both lucky."

"Yes, ma'am," he said, and stepped back.

"Are we all about ready?" Sabra asked. She sat in a straight chair to the right of Faith's desk. Over her shoulder was *The Defender,* the bust of Morgan by Phoenix. Sabra had seen the piece in the lobby and asked if it could be a part of the backdrop for the taping.

Faith had quickly said yes, just as she had when Pierce asked if they could do the interview there. He wanted it in a neutral place they had control over. By the time the last media person arrived, Faith had picked out a spot, set the stage, and ordered coffee and light desserts for the media once they were finished. They all wanted the experience to be as successful as possible.

"She's good," Sierra said from beside him.

"What makes it better is that she means every word," Pierce said, his hand resting lightly on

Isabella's head. He'd sent Sierra to pick up the animal. She'd gone in and out the back entrance.

"We're ready when you are," said one of the local TV anchors. "Let me say for all of us that we appreciate you remembering." There was a round of nods and applause. All the local media were represented. Not one source had refused.

"Mrs. Grayson gave her word and mine. Neither of us takes that lightly." Sabra smiled into the glaring lights of the TV lens and flashing cameras. "Mrs. Grayson and I are both thankful that you were able to be here on such short notice. It shows a dedication to your profession. The entire city is one I won't forget. Now, who has the first question?"

Sabra in action was a joy to behold. Pierce marveled at the way she handled the reporters. Two minutes into the interview she had them eating out of her hand and forever grateful she'd allowed them the exclusive.

She didn't leave out his mother, who stood nearby with several of the students. "I can't tell you how excited I am about the production of *Silken Lies* and the talented students at St. John's who'll join me."

"Mrs. Grayson, how do you feel?"

His mother in one of her power suits, this one black with a white blouse and accessorized with silver jewelry, smiled. "Honored and pleased that Sabra accepted my request. Not only is she a brilliant actress but a caring one as well."

More questions were asked. Sabra answered each one, making sure the students were included and insisting that they join her in the many photographs. Thirty-seven minutes later, they were finished.

"Faith Grayson, executive manager of this marvelous five-star hotel, Casa de Serenidad, has refreshments waiting. She's also graciously lent us a room for the press conference in the morning at nine with the head of the movie studio and Britt Powell. You, ladies and gentlemen, will be allowed to enter first."

More applause and thanks. Unhooking the mic, Sabra came to her feet. "This way. I can promise the food is divine. Faith is married to a wonderful chef, Brandon Grayson, owner of the Red Cactus. You can't find better food than here or the Red Cactus."

"Brandon will be even more impossible once he hears she plugged his restaurant," Sierra said, following the crowd out the door.

"And the hotel and Phoenix's work." Pierce closed the office door. "She's something."

"I agree. I'll hate to see her go." Sierra stopped at the door. As expected, men surrounded Sabra instead of the food. "You all right with that?"

"She's a beautiful woman," Pierce answered, stopping just inside the door with Isabella by his side.

"You didn't answer my question," Sierra said.

There was a break in the crowd as Sabra urged them to the table where coffee and desserts waited. His and Sabra's gaze met, held for only a few seconds, but it was enough. They had her attention now, but later she was coming home with him. "It's part of her job. Part of who she is."

"Keep that thought when the media frenzy begins."

CHAPTER SEVENTEEN

"FRENZY" WAS THE RIGHT WORD.

From the second Sabra stepped out of the condo the next morning, cameras flashed; microphones were thrust in her face. For the most part, they ignored Pierce on her right. Dave, her agent, on the other side wasn't as fortunate.

"All of your questions will be answered at the news conference," Dave told them as they steadily moved toward Sierra's vehicle. He'd flown in that morning on the studio's jet with Britt Powell and the studio head, Marcus Nelson. Dave had come straight to Sabra's place while Britt and Nelson had gone to the hotel.

From his height of six two, Pierce saw Luke emerge from the passenger door of Sierra's ATV. He opened the back door. Last night, after Pierce and Sabra had entered the condo the same way Sierra had entered and left earlier, they had decided against walking the short distance to the hotel.

Now Pierce smiled. No one was going to push his oldest brother around.

"Why did you let the local media scoop us?" snarled one reporter.

"Because they were nice enough to ask," Sabra answered sweetly as she approached the vehicle. "Good morning, Luke. Thank you."

"Good morning. Anytime." Luke blocked the same persistent reporter. "You might want to watch where you're going."

The man's dark eyes narrowed. "You don't scare me."

"Remember those words later." Luke's voice was mild; his eyes were anything but.

The man backed up and let Pierce and Dave get inside. As soon as they did, Luke closed the door and got inside. "Drive."

Sierra chuckled. "You're scary."

Luke frowned at her. "Don't get any ideas."

"Wouldn't dream of it." Tires squealed in protest as Sierra shot out of the driveway.

THIS TIME THE NEWS MEDIA WEREN'T SO CORDIAL. They were obviously miffed that they had been shut out from an exclusive. They were only partially appeased by the interview being granted them now. Sabra and the three men were seated on a raised platform in front of several mics in one of the smaller conference rooms.

"What's the story on you and Britt? He came down here to see you. Is he the reason you're doing the movie? So you can be together?" the same annoying reporter from the hotel asked.

Pierce tensed. He'd like to ram the microphone down the man's scrawny throat.

Sabra smiled. "Do you want the truth or one that will sell more papers?"

The audience hooted. The man scowled.

"I take that as a request for the truth." Sabra glanced at Britt, leaning back negligently in his seat, looking dangerous and sexy. "I admire Britt, and while I can't imagine another actor in the part of Jeff, a man tormented by love and zeal for his country, we're just friends." She stared straight at the man. "I make my own decisions. That way, if it's the wrong one, I only have myself to blame."

"This is the right one," Marcus Nelson, the studio head, quickly said. "We actively pursued Sabra for the part even before the screenplay was written. Without her, we wouldn't have thought twice about doing *Sacred Passion*."

"What about you, Britt? You've only done action parts. The drama is a departure. Can you handle it?" asked a reporter.

Britt arched a brow, then came easily to his feet, his gaze on the man who had asked the question. The man scooted back in his seat. "Sabra."

She stood and went to Britt. His arm circled her waist, his hand tunneled in her hair. Her body sank heavily against his. "I don't want you to go." Her voice trembled with fear and love. "Please."

"Leaving you is ripping my guts out." His face was tortured, his hand clenched in her hair. "Loving you is the only right thing I've ever done."

"Then stay." Her voice quivered; tears rolled down her cheek.

His own eyes closed, then opened. "I can't."

"Then take this with you." Her mouth fastened to his, her body seemed to curl around his. He gathered her closer, closer still; then she was free as Britt strode away. The woman dropped to her knees and wept.

There was complete silence. "That, ladies and gentlemen, is why *Sacred Passion* is going to be next summer's blockbuster," Marcus said, standing to applaud. He was joined by those seated. Sabra came to her feet laughing, her hand reaching for Britt as he strode back to her. Instead his long arm went around her waist. He kissed her on the cheek.

"Any more questions about my ability?" Britt asked.

"One. Do you need someone to read lines with?" asked a female reporter.

Britt grinned devilishly. "You can never tell. Why don't you give me your number?"

The woman blushed, but anyone could see she was more than interested.

More questions were posed. The attention shifted back to the platform. "You can let go of me now," Pierce said.

Sierra released Pierce's hand. "She was just acting."

Luke's fingers slowly uncurled from Pierce's arm. "I understand, but Sierra is right."

Pierce ached from the tense way he'd held his body. He'd started for the platform the moment Britt touched Sabra. Sierra and Luke had grabbed him at the same time. For a wild, reckless moment he had wanted to turn on them to be free. That sobering thought kept him rooted to the spot, his gaze glued to the stage.

The kiss had caused a red haze to form in front of his eyes. The mist didn't begin to clear until Sabra stood, laughing. He didn't have to think long to recall the mindless passion that engulfed both of them when they kissed, touched.

"You're right. She was just acting." And he was glad his mother had class and hadn't been there to see his reaction to what had happened.

"WELL, PIERCE. WHAT DID YOU THINK?" SABRA ASKED.

From behind his desk in his office, Pierce watched her with unblinking eyes. She tried to relax and couldn't. Not with him so silent and unreadable.

She'd come directly from the last rehearsals. After the press conference, she had gone directly to the college. Dave, Britt, and Marcus, as well as some of the media, had followed. The students had been in awe of Britt, especially the female students. Ruth, as usual, was unflappable.

Taking the stage, Sabra hadn't been surprised to

experience the butterflies in her stomach; then she'd seen Pierce enter quietly through a side door. His presence had anchored her. She'd turned to the students. "This is a big chance for all of us. Give me the performance I know you're capable of."

They had. By the time rehearsals were over, Marcus wanted to meet the writer. Britt was asking for the part of Max. David wanted to represent the writer. *Silken Lies* had passed the test. Now if only Pierce could. He had to understand that what she did onstage had nothing to do with them.

On trembling legs, she pushed away from the door. "I saw you at rehearsals."

"I'm surprised, with all the people there," he said, his voice neutral.

Displaying more confidence than she felt, she rounded the desk. "You were the most important one."

His hand snaked out and pulled her into his lap. His voice was just short of a growl. "He kissed you."

"Technically, I kissed him," she said casually, her insides in knots.

"I guess you did." His hand swept up her rib cage, pausing beneath her breast. Her body tightened with anticipation. With slow deliberation, he lowered his head until his lips hovered above hers.

Her breath shortened. His mouth nipped her earlobe. She was powerless to prevent the shudder that rippled through her.

"Is this my punishment or my reward?" she said when she was able to speak.

His hands flexed. "I wanted to rip his face off for touching you. If Sierra and Luke hadn't stopped me, I would have. Then you laughed as if it meant nothing."

Tenderly her hands palmed his face. "It didn't."

"I know." He pulled her to him, his mouth fastening on hers, taking her, consuming her.

"If this chair didn't have arms we could go for a ride," she said with a seductive sigh.

Pierce hardened beneath her, telling her he was more than ready. "Don't tempt me."

She nipped his ear. "You mean like you tempt me?"

He leaned away and gazed into her eyes. Passion and unfulfilled need stared back at him. Without a smidgen of doubt, he knew there was no way in hell that she could laugh and carry on a normal conversation now as she'd done at the press conference. "There's a chair in my place."

"You read my mind."

MUCH LATER SABRA LAY NAKED AND HAPPY ON TOP of Pierce. "I'll always have fond memories of that dining room chair and table."

Pierce smiled and kissed her cheek. "So will I. What did Marcus think of *Silken Lies*?"

Her head lifted. She told him everything. "I didn't tell them I'd written the play. Too many media people around."

Pierce swept his hand over her shoulder. "Seems like you have another career, if you want it."

A small frown puckered her brow. "I still can't believe it."

"It hasn't sunk in yet," he told her.

"I suppose."

"Thinking about your father?"

She nodded and laid her head on his broad chest. "I started the play shortly before his heart attack. He said it gave me more options, and he never doubted I'd succeed."

"Parental approval and support means a lot." Pierce wrapped his arms around her. "Mama always told us there wasn't anything we couldn't do."

Sabra lifted her head. "Then why can't she let you choose who to marry?" She hadn't meant the words to come out so sharply.

For once, hearing the words didn't anger Pierce. He accepted the reason as Sabra's anger on his behalf. "She loves us, but I'm my own man. I choose my own woman."

"Me?"

"You." He sat up. Sabra automatically slid her legs around his waist, inadvertently opening herself to him. Pierce found her moist, welcoming center and entered. Their sighs of rightness mingled. With his arms wrapped around her, her lips pressed to the curve of his neck, he took them on another slow, lazy ride to paradise.

"PIERCE. SABRA."

In front of her door Friday night, Sabra jumped

out of Pierce's arms. She felt like a kindergartner getting caught misbehaving by the teacher she adored. A few feet away stood Ruth Grayson. Sabra didn't dare look at Pierce or check to see if all the buttons on her blouse remained fastened.

"Mama," Pierce said calmly, as if it were an everyday occurrence to get caught necking. On second thought, with Pierce's looks and charisma, perhaps it was, Sabra thought.

"Hello, Ruth," Sabra managed. "Would you like to come in?"

"No, thank you," Ruth said, her gaze bouncing between the two caught lovers. "I just wanted to thank you again for coming. We haven't had too much time to talk this past week. You'll leave as soon as rehearsals are over."

Sabra flushed.

"I'll say good night, and let you two talk." Pierce kissed Sabra on the cheek; then as he passed his unsmiling mother he did the same to her. "I'll be waiting for you," he whispered.

Sabra opened the door and invited Ruth inside. Isabella bounded to them, her tail wagging. She looked behind Sabra, as if expecting to see Pierce. "Please have a seat. If you'd like—"

"Please." Ruth caught Sabra's arm as she started for the kitchen. As soon as the younger woman turned, Ruth released her. "There's a happiness about you that wasn't there when you first came."

Sabra flushed again. "I—"

Ruth held up her hand. "You don't owe me an explanation. I'm sorry if I embarrassed you. That was not my intention. Obviously, you and Pierce are seeing each other."

"You wanted Raven instead," Sabra said, unable to keep the hurt from her voice.

For the first time Ruth smiled. "If you'll remember, I said Pierce was the most stubborn of my children. It's not what I want that counts. It's what his heart desires." She opened her purse and took out an elongated box. "Please have this as a small token of my thanks."

Sabra lifted the lid. Inside was a sterling silver charm bracelet with a single charm, a musical note. "It's beautiful."

"Music brought us together, and I believe there is always a reason for everything," Ruth said. "We were meant to know each other for a reason."

Pierce. Except that it wasn't Pierce who'd brought them together, but her father's crime. "Thank you."

"Tell Pierce I'll see him tomorrow night at the play." Ruth went to the door. "I'm not sure you're aware of it, but Santa Fe has movie studios that have produced some of the finest movies ever made. Good night."

Sabra's heart thumped in her chest. She waited until she thought Ruth was on the elevator, then peeped into the hall. When she saw it was empty, she hurried to Pierce's door. Rang the bell. It opened almost immediately.

Sabra smiled at Pierce. "Your mother thinks you're the most stubborn of her children. It's what you want that counts, and I'm to tell you good night." By the time she finished, she was inside with her arms around his neck.

He frowned. "Mama doesn't give up that easy."

Proudly, Sabra showed him the bracelet. "Isn't it beautiful? She really likes me."

The awe in her voice caused him to stop thinking about his mother's easy capitulation. "Of course she does. So do I. Let me put it on."

Once it was fastened on her wrist, she twisted her hand, obviously pleased. "I've never had a charm bracelet before."

Amazing. Sabra, who had diamonds, traveled the world, had a movie mogul at her beck and call, was giddy over a bracelet. But Pierce sensed it was more than that. It was what the bracelet represented. He pulled her to him. "I told you she likes you."

"Yes, you did." She gave him a quick kiss. "Thank you."

Pierce feigned insult. "You call that a kiss?"

She narrowed her eyes, then kissed him until his knees shook. "How was that?"

For an answer, Pierce picked her up and hurried to the bedroom. He fell onto the bed. "Now, let's try that again."

Sabra eagerly obliged, not stopping with his lips but moving to the smooth curve of his jaw, his flat nipple. Pierce's groan of pleasure pleased and excited her, urged her on. At his waist, she wrestled with the buckle of his belt.

Pierce helped, but instead of reclining again, he quickly undressed her; then it was his turn. Sabra clutched the sheets as Pierce took her taut nipple in his mouth, dipped his tongue in the indentation of her navel, then moved lower still. Sensations exploded inside her. Before she came down completely, he pushed into her, taking her back up again. She clutched him, her nails digging into his muscled shoulders.

Passion consumed her. She hadn't thought their lovemaking could get any better. She'd been wrong. The reason came to her the moment her body yielded to his in a firestorm of pleasure.

She loved him.

"Sabra!" Her name was a hoarse shout of ecstasy as Pierce gave one last thrust of his hips. Sabra's clamped and quivered around him. Shaken to the very core, he felt his body tremble in the aftermath. His head tucked between her head and shoulder, his breathing labored; he knew he'd never experienced anything more powerful or moving.

Even as he shied away from the reason, he gathered Sabra closer. He wanted to say something but didn't know the words.

"Pierce." Her voice sounded hesitant.

His head lifted. "Yes?"

Her fingertips traced his lower lip. "I . . . nothing."

Her hand was trembling. Something was worrying her, or perhaps she'd felt the same incredible emotions he had. He hoped he wasn't in this alone.

His arms tightened even as he hardened inside her. "I'll never stop wanting you." He frowned on hearing the words but accepted them as the truth. He didn't want to think of a time they wouldn't be together.

"Does that make you unhappy?" she asked.

Again he told the truth. "No. Surprised, yes."

"Good, because I feel the same way." She brushed her lips across his. "Now, where were we?"

He eagerly showed her.

THE SJC AUDITORIUM WAS FILLED TO CAPACITY. Seats were added on the aisle and they still had to turn people away. The numerous articles had increased interest in the play. Several people from Hollywood were there, including Britt Powell, Marcus Nelson, and the director hired for *Sacred Passion.*

Onstage, Sabra peeked around the curtain and didn't see the man she sought. Disappointment hit her.

"Looking for someone?"

She whirled around and almost threw herself into his arms. "Pierce."

His eyes said he wanted to hold her as well. "I wanted to give you this before you went onstage." He pulled a square jewelry box from his pocket. Her heart thudded before she realized it was too small for a ring. She was still getting used to the idea that she loved Pierce. She wished she could tell him, shout it to the world.

"Aren't you going to open it?"

With unsteady hands she took the black velvet box and lifted the lid. She gasped in surprise and pleasure. Inside was a small circle of diamonds on sterling silver.

"Wherever your path leads you'll always come back here."

To me was left unsaid but implicit in his eyes. "I'll treasure it always. Can you put it on?"

He unhooked the charm bracelet and slid the diamond circle on, then reclamped it around her wrist. "That will do until we can have it done properly."

"Ten minutes until curtain time. Ten minutes."

People scrambled. Pierce brushed his hand tenderly down her cheek. "Break a leg."

"Thanks." Sabra stared at him a few moments longer, then turned away. She had a play to put on.

SABRA TOOK THREE CURTAIN CALLS AND COULD have taken more. For the fourth one, she insisted every person who had anything to do with the production take their turn onstage for an introduction. It took her and Theo both to bring a reluctant Ruth on the stage. Her children and daughters-in-law whistled and stomped their feet, oblivious to her trying to shush them.

Onstage, Sabra laughed. "As you can tell, her family is well aware of her generous nature and loving spirit." She winked. "I'm told she speaks softly but carries a very big stick." Laughter erupted.

"Before I get into more trouble, will the president

of this great college, the teachers of these talented young people, and the board of regents please stand? Without them, this wouldn't have been possible." Sabra was the first to applaud. "Good night, everyone, and thank you again for coming tonight."

Pierce came onstage before the students completely dispersed. "In view of your hard work, my brothers, their wives, and my sister wanted to give you a little party. So grab your date or your best bud, and meet us at Casa de Serenidad in the Conquistador ballroom." He turned when he felt a tug on his coat.

"You said to grab your date," Sabra said with a smile.

He wanted to smile but couldn't quite manage. "You leave in the morning." The thought was never far from his mind lately.

"But I'm here now."

No longer caring who might see them, he curved his arms around her waist. "And you're going to be in my arms for the rest of the night."

"I wouldn't have it any other way." She leaned her head against his shoulder and they walked off the stage.

In the front row of the auditorium, Sierra stood alone and looked at Pierce and Sabra, then at her mother and her aunt Felicia on the other side of the stage. Sierra's aunt and her uncle, John Henry, Ruth's brother, had come down from their ranch in Oklahoma for the play. Now the two women were huddled in deep conversation. Grinning broadly, they watched Pierce and Sabra.

Their mother had struck again.

Raven had been a smoke screen. Sierra's mother was as crafty as ever. Sierra shook her head and followed the crowd out the door. Her family had already left for the party. She wasn't so sure she still felt like celebrating.

Depending on how long it took Pierce to realize he'd fallen in love, her time was drawing to a close. Of course, the way Pierce mulled things over, that could be weeks or months. But eventually he would, and when he did, she'd have to watch her step.

She was next on her mother's hit list.

CHAPTER EIGHTEEN

BEFORE DAWN ON SUNDAY MORNING, SABRA WOKE slowly. She frowned, sensing something wasn't right, then realized it was because she wasn't wrapped in Pierce's arms, his body cradling her.

Then it hit her. Today she was leaving. She almost cried out as she came fully awake and sat up. Pierce's broad back filled her vision. He sat on the side of her bed, his head bowed.

He hated the coming separation as much as she did. They'd stayed only a short while at the party before she'd used the excuse that she had to pack to leave. Ruth had quickly agreed, hugged her, and said that since Pierce was driving her to the airport they'd say good-bye now. Sabra had bid all the Graysons good-bye, except Sierra, who had already left.

Sabra and Pierce had gone to her condo and directly to her bed. He had undressed her, kissing her as he did, then made love to her. The sweetness of it made tears crest in her eyes. She didn't want to leave him, either.

She touched his back. He swung around. The coldness in his gaze struck her like a fist; then she noticed the photograph clutched in his hand. The family photograph was always the last thing she packed. Her stomach knotted. She couldn't tear her gaze away from his furious face.

"Who is this man?" he demanded.

"My father," she whispered.

Pierce's hand clenched on the sterling silver frame. He looked back at the picture as if trying to reconcile what she had just said. "I see." He came to his feet and picked up his pants. "There's something I need to take care of at my place."

She watched his agitated movements as he jerked on his pants. Her heart sank. Anger shimmered from him. If she let it go, it would come between them. She wanted forever with Pierce. "You knew my father?"

"Yeah." He shoved his arms into the sleeves of his shirt, jammed his feet into his loafers. "I'll call you later."

"Were you the one?"

He went still, then slowly turned. The look in his eyes made her shrink back on the bed. "You know what he did?"

"He intended to pay you back. He did it for his family, for me," she cried.

"The people he swindled from have families as well. He was a thief."

The word slapped her in the face. "He did what he felt he had to do," she defended. "He didn't think he had any choice. He'd lost heavily in the stock market. My mother wasn't very strong, and my sister and I were trying to get our careers off the ground."

"So was I," Pierce snapped. "I'd been in business less than a year. I'd done pretty well with the help of Daniel Falcon, my cousin. He warned me against your father's talk of buying oil leases, but I believed the smooth-talking man. He looked honest." Pierce snorted.

Sabra drew on the short robe she'd left on the bed. "He regretted that he had to borrow from you the most. He left a letter in his personal effects." She went to her dresser and came back with an envelope. "This is yours, compounded interest. A cashier's check."

He stepped back. "I don't want your money."

"Without my father's faith in me, I wouldn't have made it as an actress." She extended the envelope. "He planned all along to pay you back and would have if . . . if he hadn't had the heart attack. Please take the money."

"Is that why you came here?"

She had to be honest. "Initially, I accepted your mother's proposal so I could find out who Daddy had obtained the money from. But as I got to know Ruth, the students, and all of you, I was happy I was here."

"You used her just as your father used me."

"No. Never." She reached for him, but he stepped back.

"Your father almost ruined me."

"He was sorry. Please take the check."

He didn't even glance toward the envelope. "I need to think." He turned to go.

"Pierce, I'm sorry."

"Yeah."

She swallowed the painful lump in her throat. "I'll get a cab to the airport."

He nodded and left the bedroom. Hearing the front door close, she sank heavily on the bed. She had lost him.

"WHAT HAPPENED BETWEEN YOU AND SABRA?" Sierra asked, stalking inside the condo. "She called me on the way to the airport to say good-bye. She's not coming back."

Pierce didn't want to talk. "Sierra, please let it go."

She studied him. "You don't look so good. Have you had any sleep?"

He walked to the window and looked out. Instead of the mountains, he saw Sabra with tears on her cheeks. "You know I don't need much sleep."

"I also know when you're being evasive." She crossed the room, took a seat on the sofa, then placed her arms on the back. "She asked me not to think harshly of her."

That got his attention. "She tell you about her father?"

"Yes."

Pierce jammed his hands into the pockets of his slacks. "Mama and the students didn't mean anything to her." *He* meant nothing to her.

"You don't believe that."

"I can't believe you're on her side after she duped us."

"Exactly how did she do this?"

He was incredulous. "She came here under false pretenses."

"And honorable ones. To repay a debt by her father that she had no legal obligation to do."

"Her father defrauded me and my clients out of nearly two hundred and fifty thousand dollars. He could have ruined me."

"It made you stronger and more leery of the next man with a line that was too good to be true. In a roundabout way, he did you a favor."

"What!" Pierce spluttered.

"If you weren't so scared, you'd see that."

"Scared? That's ridiculous," he scoffed.

"Will you stop reacting and think this through?" Sierra came to her feet. "You liked her father. Maybe looked up to him a bit, and he let you down. You're scared Sabra will do the same thing."

"You're reaching."

"You're scared because you love her, and you want it to be for real."

"You're really reaching now, and I have work to do." He went to his desk in his office and took his seat.

Sierra slapped one hand on the folder he picked up. "You can't rationalize love. You can't plot a chart or project when it takes you."

"Like you're an expert," he chided, drawing his folder from under her hand.

"After watching four brothers take the fall, it's not so hard to figure out." Straightening, she folded her arms. "In a way, you should be grateful to her father. If he hadn't swindled you, Sabra wouldn't have accepted Mama's invitation."

"And I'd be better off."

"It's not like you to lie, especially to yourself."

His eyes narrowed. "Sierra, you're pushing it."

"All right, be stubborn. Just remember, we might belong to the wolf clan, but a trapped wolf will gnaw off its own paw to free itself from a trap. Don't make the same mistake."

She was headed for the door when the phone rang. They both turned toward it. "Tell me you don't want that to be Sabra."

He picked up the phone without answering. "Hello. . . . Brandon. What? . . . No! No!"

Sierra rushed to him. "What is it?"

"Turn on the TV. Hurry!" He quickly followed her into the living area.

Sierra ran to do as she was told. The thirty-two-inch screen filled with an aerial view of an airplane. "Is it—" Sierra couldn't make herself finish the question.

"We're not sure." Pierce's hand clenched and unclenched on the portable phone. His chest stung. He realized he was holding his breath. Air shuddered out of his lungs.

"If you're just joining us, that's Flight 341 out of Albuquerque International Sunport with a final destination of LAX in Los Angeles, circling the field trying to burn off fuel before attempting to make a landing after one of the rear wheels wouldn't retract. There are 176 passengers and crew aboard the crippled aircraft."

Sierra looked at Pierce with fear in her eyes. "Was that her flight number?"

His hand ran savagely through his hair. "I don't know, dammit. I wouldn't listen, and now it may be—"

"Don't say it." Sierra clamped down on his arm. "You didn't find her to lose her."

He tried not to think of his mother waiting for word about her husband, their father. It was useless. It had been a routine international flight. He was an experienced pilot and captain for ten years with the airline. He'd left home and never come back.

"Mama would know." Sierra pulled her cell phone from her purse.

Pierce stayed her hand. "What if it brings back too many memories?"

"Mama is stronger than that, and we both know it."

Pierce nodded and let his hand fall to his side.

The doorbell rang and both ignored it, waiting for his mother to pick up. He grew tenser with each ring. "She and Aunt Felicia might have gone to breakfast.

"She should have—" He broke off at the sound of

a familiar bark. He stared at Sierra as if to determine that he wasn't imagining things.

"Isabella."

They both lunged for the door at the same time. Sabra stood in the hallway.

"I know you don't want to listen. You believe the worst of me. But it occurred to me that if I left now you'd never believe that I love you." Her chin lifted. "I love you, and it has nothing to do with what my father did." She looked from one to the other. "One of you say something. Tell me I haven't made a fool out of myself."

Pierce pulled her into his arms and held her tightly, her face pressed against the hard wall of his chest. She couldn't breathe, then she felt him tremble, and that scared her. "Pierce."

Then his mouth was on hers, hot and avid. She welcomed the mindless rush of pleasure, the sweet homecoming.

He lifted his head and framed her face. "I love you, too."

Tears crested in her eyes. "I was so afraid you might never forgive me."

"I was a fool, but after watching the plane on television, I realized how much I loved you," he told her.

"What plane?"

His arms circling her waist, he drew her inside. Isabella trotted in behind them. "It's Flight 341."

"That was my flight." She looked up at Pierce. "I got all the way to the airport, but Isabella wouldn't go in. I realized I didn't want to go, either. I got a cab and came back here."

There was another knock on the door. "I'll get it." Sierra opened the door to Ruth, Luke, Catherine, Morgan, Phoenix, Brandon, Faith, and her aunt Felicia and uncle John Henry.

"Has Pierce heard—Sabra." Ruth rushed forward, hugging the woman. "You're safe!"

Sabra hugged her back, her gaze going to Pierce. "I couldn't leave."

"The pilot is about to make a landing," the TV announcer said.

"Master of Breath and God, guide him," Ruth murmured.

Pierce curved one arm around his mother and the other around Sabra. She was safe, but they all felt for the passengers, crew, and their families and friends who were going through the ordeal.

The jet hit the asphalt, dipped to one side, then skidded for fifty feet before there was a visible crack in the wing. Smoke billowed from the screeching tires, the wing scraping the asphalt. The wail of sirens and fire engines could be heard over the roar of the engine. Finally the plane stopped. Moments later, the emergency door opened and the chute unfurled.

By the time the first passengers hit the asphalt, emergency personnel were there to assist them. They were hurried to safety.

"Thank you," Ruth said softly, then looked at her children and the women they loved. "For everything."

Sierra folded her arms. "I love you, Mama, but it stops with Pierce."

Faith squealed. "Congratulations!"

Sabra kept her gaze on Pierce. "I think you might be premature."

Brandon slapped Pierce on the back. "My kid brother just takes his time. He wouldn't dare make my wife feel bad."

All eyes except Sabra's were on him. He opened his mouth just as her cell phone rang.

"Excuse me." Sabra pulled the phone out. "Hello. . . . No, I didn't catch the plane, Dave. I had my reasons. I'll call you back." She'd barely disconnected the call before the phone rang again. This time it was her assistant. The next call came from Britt, offering to send his jet to pick her up. Then the same offer came from the head of the movie studio.

When the phone rang again, Pierce blew out a breath. "How many more calls do you expect?"

"I'm not sure," she said, finally looking at him. She spoke to the producer of her last play, then hung up again.

"Then I better get this over." He took her hand. "I love you with all my heart. Before my family, the Master of Breath, and God, I'm asking you to be my wife."

The ringing phone dropped from Sabra's hand. Tears filled her eyes.

"Please let that be a yes."

"Yes!" She launched herself into his arms, kissing his face. Laughing, Pierce swung her around.

"This calls for a celebration!" Aunt Felicia leaned against her husband. "Faith, can you help us out?"

Smiling, Faith whipped out her own cell phone to call her executive chef. "Henri, we're celebrating the latest Grayson to find his heart's desire. We'll be there shortly." She disconnected the phone. "I better go and see to things." She hugged Sabra.

Brandon hugged his brother. "Welcome to the fraternity." Then he tugged his sister's hair and winked.

Sierra merely raised an eyebrow. Laughing, Brandon curved his arm around Faith's waist and left.

"Let's give them a few minutes alone," Ruth said, hustling everyone from the room. "Ten minutes and not a moment more."

Everyone congratulated the newly engaged couple. Sierra was the last to leave. Pierce smiled sheepishly. "If I said I was sorry I'd be lying." He pulled Sabra closer to him. "She's all that I wanted, even before I knew what that was."

Sierra started to tell him that he should have asked their mother, but changed her mind. He'd figure it out. Now he was too happy. "If you're over ten minutes I'm eating." She opened the door. "I'm happy for both of you."

"Tell me again," Sabra said when the door closed. "Tell me you love me."

"I love you. More than I thought it possible for a man to love a woman." His hands flexed on her arms. "We'll make it work. Our love will keep us strong, no matter that you have to be away."

Her arms circled his neck. "What would you think of me filming the movie here?"

He squeezed her to him. "You'd save my sanity."

"Marcus said he's give me anything I wanted. When I dangle *Silken Lies* and give him options on the other two plays I'm writing, I think he'll go for it," she told him.

He kissed her. "My brilliant fiancée."

She grinned up at him. "Your mother gave me the idea."

He sobered instantly. "What?"

"Your mother. Is something the matter?"

Pierce threw back his head and laughed. "No, everything is perfectly all right. And you are the most perfect thing of all, my beautiful irresistible you."

EPILOGUE

RUTH COULD HARDLY CONTAIN HER HAPPINESS AS they waited for Pierce and Sabra to arrive. Of course, it was past the ten minutes Ruth had allowed them, but that was understandable. When you were in love, time flew when you were together and stood still when you were apart.

Ruth looked down the elongated table Faith had placed on the patio to accommodate the family. Three beautiful bouquets of red and white roses in crystal vases served as centerpieces. The flatware was sterling, the plates trimmed in gold. Both had come from Faith's home. Ruth couldn't be happier about her choice for Brandon, the nurturer.

Then there was Phoenix, who might appear quiet but who burned with an inner fire. The ideal match for Morgan, the defender. Catherine possessed a quiet spirit except when it came to championing abused children or her husband, Luke, the protector.

Ruth's heart swelled with pride on seeing Pierce and Sabra. She had to smile at seeing Isabella with them. Things had gone exactly as planned. Pierce, the thinker, had learned there were no rules in love.

As those at the table got up to congratulate the beaming couple, Ruth caught Felicia's attention. They had done it again.

Ruth felt someone watching her and knew before she turned she'd see her youngest. Arms crossed, her thick black hair dancing in the morning breeze, with her high cheekbones and delicate features, Sierra was stunningly beautiful and gifted with a knack for discernment.

Ruth could almost hear Sierra vowing that she wouldn't fall as easily as her brothers. A moment of unease swept through Ruth. If this went badly— No, as she'd told Felicia, she'd go through with her plans. She couldn't stop them if she wanted to. Things were already in motion.

But she was a mother who loved her children intensely. The man chosen was as unpredictable as the wind. Some said ice water ran in his veins. He was feared as much as he was revered. A shiver raced down Ruth's spine. She said a prayer for all of them.

Sierra, the loyal one, would face a man who could deeply wound her, but he could also love her like no other man could.

For better or worse, Sierra was next.

Read on for an excerpt from Francis Ray's next book

ONLY YOU

Coming soon from St. Martin's Paperbacks

SIERRA GRAYSON WAS HAVING THE TIME OF HER LIFE in San Francisco. The city was breathtaking, the food fabulous, and the shopping superb. An added bonus was that she had left her matchmaking mother in Santa Fe. Ruth Grayson was determined that her youngest child and only daughter follow her four older brothers into matrimonial bliss—just as she had predicted and planned—whether Sierra wanted to get married or not.

What her children wanted hadn't mattered to their loving mother who had been sure they would be happier married. Sierra would give her credit for being right in choosing the perfect woman for each of her brothers, but Sierra had no intention of being next. She enjoyed life too much to be tied down to some man who'd want her to cater to his every whim.

When her sister-in-law, Sabra Raineau-Grayson, had invited Sierra to San Francisco with her and Pierce, Sierra jumped at the opportunity. Having her other brother, Brandon, and his wife, Faith, join them had made the trip a fun-filled romp. And, as of five minutes ago, it had just gotten better.

She had just been presented with the golden opportunity to meet the movers and shakers of the city's elite. Of course, when she did, she'd look for an opportunity to sell them a prime piece of Santa Fe real estate. She almost skipped with glee in her new Jimmy Choo sandals.

A winsome smile on her face, she sauntered through the spacious and opulent lobby of the St. Regis Hotel. She would have had to be blind not to notice the attention she garnered. Since nothing much ever got past Sierra, she dismissed the interested gazes of the men along with the curious stares of the women.

Without being conceited, Sierra knew she looked good. It helped that she wore a new purchase, an imported white Valentino embroidered-and-beaded couture cotton sheath that complemented her golden skin. As always she'd dressed with care, but especially this afternoon. Otherwise there was a distinct possibility that she wouldn't have charmed Ken Simpson, the chairman of the auction that night, into accepting her as a replacement for her latest sister-in-law, Sabra.

Not only was Sabra stunning, she was a two-time Tony-winning Broadway actress. But just as it was Sierra's brain that had taken her to the top of her profession in Santa Fe, that same sharp intelligence impressed Mr. Simpson.

As Sierra had explained to Mr. Simpson and the rest of his enthralled committee members over cocktails in a five-thousand-dollar suite, as much as Sabra wished to fulfill her obligations, it didn't seem the right thing to offer a bride on the auction block. What Sierra didn't say was that if they didn't agree, there would be a third person at the winner's dinner table—Sabra's love-smitten husband and Sierra's youngest brother, Pierce.

Stepping outside onto the terrazzo floor of the outdoor restaurant, Sierra searched the almost deserted area for Faith. She'd called just before Sierra had gone to meet Simpson and said to meet her on the patio when she finished. Brandon, Sierra's third brother and Faith's husband, had gone to visit a friend who, like Brandon, owned and operated his own restaurant near the Cannery. The lovebirds, Pierce and Sabra, had taken off with Isabella, Sabra's dog, for Fisherman's Wharf.

Continuing into the lush area overflowing with red bougainvillea, verdant ferns, and towering palms, Sierra searched for Faith. If Faith said she would be there, she'd be there. She was dependable to a fault.

Just as Sierra turned to search another area, a deep, masculine voice stopped her dead in her tracks. A hot shiver raced over her body. Disturbed by her reaction, a frown puckered her brow as she swung back and moved toward the engrossing sound.

Before that moment she would have bet she wasn't the type of woman to get all hot and bothered by a man's voice. Seemed she would have lost. Curious, led by instinct and an unexpected need, she sought the owner of the captivating voice.

She'd sensed something else in his tone, a tormented spirit.

Since Sierra was a direct descendant of an African high priestess and a Native-American shaman, she didn't question how she knew he was hurting or her own actions. Her breath held, her palms damp, she stepped around a ten-foot potted palm.

Less than fifteen feet away, Faith stood in profile with a broad-shouldered man. A gray tailored suit fit his powerful build perfectly. His muscular arms curved loosely around Faith's waist; her hands were splayed on his wide chest as she smiled up at him.

Since Sierra trusted Faith completely, she didn't jump to conclusions. Instead Sierra ignored the strange tingling in her body and openly studied the stranger. One of her unique abilities had always been to size people up quickly and accurately. She did so now. Wealthy, powerful, dangerous. This man would take what he wanted and damn the consequences.

As if sensing her, he slowly turned his head. Their gazes clashed. There was no other way to describe the shock of his onyx eyes boring into hers. Never one to back down, Sierra continued to stare boldly at him as his gaze assessed her in one slow smoldering sweep. The tingling spread like liquid fire over her body.

He was sensually beautiful, Native-American,

.nd magnificent with burnished copper skin. Thick et-black hair secured at the base of his neck with a ilver band hung past his wide shoulders. At least ix-foot-five, he had chiseled cheekbones, incredi- ly long lashes, and a mouth meant to make a sensi- le woman sin.

He was also one of the few men she had ever seen who was equal to her brothers, the Taggarts, or her ousin, Daniel Falcon. The sheer male beauty of the nan, the noble bearing gave her pause, but it was his yes, fierce and black, that sent another hot shiver acing down her spine.

Faith, apparently realizing the man's attention ad wandered, glanced around. Seeing Sierra, her mile broadened. The warm smile faltered when it vasn't returned. Quickly Faith stepped away from he man and moistened her lips in an uncharacteris- ically nervous gesture.

Sierra's sister-in-law ran a five-star hotel in Santa Fe with enviable ease. Nothing rattled her. She also oved Brandon to distraction.

"Sierra, I-I see you found me." Faith's smile lowly faded. "Sierra Grayson, Blade Navarone."

"Ms. Grayson," the man greeted, his voice troking her.

"Mr. Navarone," she returned just as formally, al- hough there was nothing formal about the midnight yes closely watching her or the heat searing her. So his was the infamous Blade Navarone, billionaire eal estate mogul.

Faith looked from Blade to Sierra, then wrung he hands when neither said anything further. "Sierra i Brandon's sister. Blade is a very good friend, Sierr He happened to be in town on business. We bumpe into each other in the lobby."

"You missed the wedding. It was beautiful, Sierra pointed out, but she already knew he attende few non-business social events. She'd done a thor ough study of the elusive man after he'd unrepen tantly shown up in Santa Fe at Faith's request. Hi mission was to make Brandon jealous.

Sierra hadn't seen Blade while he was there, bu he'd succeeded. Easygoing Brandon had becom possessive and territorial where Faith was con cerned. Only a fool wouldn't worry if a man lik Blade took an interest in a woman he wanted.

No Grayson could ever be called a fool.

"I was unavoidably detained elsewhere." Some thing flickered in Blade's eyes as he glanced back a Faith. "Faith understood."

Sierra's brow furrowed. There it was again, th pain just beneath the surface. There hadn't been an mention of problems, personal or professional, i the numerous news articles on Blade. There ha been a few out-of-focus photos and a lot to read an admire. Navarone Properties and Resorts, the play grounds of the rich and famous, were scattered lik priceless jewels around the world.

The titillating possibility of being his exclusiv broker for the next Navarone property in Dalla where fifty-five private estates were going for one to eleven million dollars would have been a dream job for Sierra. For that she would have put off opening her own brokerage firm. The commission would have been staggering, the prestige boundless.

She hadn't even received a response from her query. She'd shrugged it off and gone on. Now, what Sierra couldn't figure out was how Faith and Blade, complete opposites, were friends.

Faith was guileless, open, a nurturer like Brandon. Blade was known to be ruthless and relentless. He didn't give second chances. He'd come down on you like a hard rain if you crossed him.

Before her cousin Daniel had cut back drastically in his business to be with his newborn son, he and Blade had been friendly business rivals. They also had the same unforgiving personality. Marriage and a family had changed Daniel. From what Sierra had read, there was no special woman in Blade's life.

"He's just a friend," Faith explained as she moved toward Sierra and away from Blade.

"Just" was not a word you'd associate with Blade Navarone. He'd come seemingly out of nowhere almost twelve years ago with grit, nerve, and a razor-sharp intelligence to build a financial empire.

"Sierra?"

The unmistakable hurt in Faith's voice finally pulled Sierra away from her examination of Blade. Stepping forward, she extended her hand. The contact of his large calloused palm against hers sent more shivers skipping down her spine. His black gaze narrowed. He felt the unsettling sensation as well.

Pulling her hand back, Sierra resisted the urge to swipe it against her dress. She had a strong feeling it wouldn't do any good. Blade wasn't the type of man a woman could forget easily . . . if at all.

"Faith, I hate to interrupt, but we should be going before they give away our appointments at the spa," Sierra said, firmly turning her attention to her sister-in-law. "Because of the auction, we were lucky to be squeezed in."

"Did they let you switch with Sabra?" Faith asked.

Sierra smiled and almost relaxed. What was the matter with her? She hadn't met a man she couldn't charm. "Did you doubt?"

Faith laughed and hugged Sierra, then turned to Blade. "Sierra changed places with her sister-in-law, Sabra Raineau, so she could be one of the prizes for a dinner tonight at the auction."

"And to keep my brother from being an uninvited guest at their dinner," Sierra explained with a chuckle.

"I won't detain you further then. Goodbye, Faith. Ms. Grayson."

Still trying to figure out why she'd reacted so strongly to him, Sierra watched Blade walk away. No, not walk. Saunter like a big lazy cat.

"You had me worried for a moment there." Faith hooked her arm through Sierra's and started back to the hotel's lobby.

Sierra bumped her shoulder against Faith's.

"You're smitten with my brother. The same over-the-moon way he is about you." She tilted her head to one side. "I guess I was just caught off guard by seeing Blade Navarone in the flesh."

The words had no more left her mouth than her mind tried to conjure up a picture of a naked Blade—strong wide shoulders, bare chest delineated with muscles, rock-hard abdomen. She shook away the unnerving image before her mind ventured further down his incredible body. "Or that you two were such close friends."

Faith tucked her head before answering. "I hope one day he finds the happiness he helped me find with Brandon."

Sierra caught the sadness in Faith's voice. Instinctively Sierra knew Faith could tell her the reason behind Blade's unhappiness, but she was just as sure that she wouldn't. Faith would never betray a confidence. And Blade Navarone was definitely a very private man.

"Come on, we better hurry." Arm in arm they entered the lobby and headed for the elevator.

In the spacious room Sierra was unable to keep from searching for Blade. With his towering height, she quickly located him heading toward the revolving front doors. Two men, both tall and athletically built, flanked him. Suddenly he stopped, turned.

She felt the rush, the punch of his gaze. Without taking his gaze from her, he said something to the man on his right. Then as abruptly as he had stopped, he spun and continued. The man he had spoken to watched her for a second longer, then he followed.

She'd see him again. She was sure of it. She just wished she knew how she felt about finally meeting a man who made her glad she was a woman.